E.R. PUNSHON
MYSTERY VILLA

Ernest Robertson Punshon was born in London in 1872.

At the age of fourteen he started life in an office. His employers soon informed him that he would never make a really satisfactory clerk, and he, agreeing, spent the next few years wandering about Canada and the United States, endeavouring without great success to earn a living in any occupation that offered. Returning home by way of working a passage on a cattle boat, he began to write. He contributed to many magazines and periodicals, wrote plays, and published nearly fifty novels, among which his detective stories proved the most popular and enduring.

He died in 1956.

Also by E.R. Punshon

E.R. PUNSHON

MYSTERY VILLA

With an introduction
by Curtis Evans

DEAN STREET PRESS

INTRODUCTION

By the time of Bobby Owen's fourth murder case, recorded in the atmospheric *Mystery Villa* (1934), E.R. Punshon's police detective had been promoted, owing to his performance in the extraordinary affair of the *Crossword Mystery* (1934), from Constable to Sergeant. Bobby Owen eventually would serve as series sleuth in 35 Punshon detective novels, published between 1933 and the year of the author's death in 1956, having taken a highly visible place of honor in the pantheon of fictional British police detectives. Today, it must be admitted, the historical significance of Bobby Owen, and the novels in which he appears, are less known to the mystery reading public. This unmerited neglect of a one-time Golden Age critical and fan favorite should be remedied with the ongoing reissuing by Dean Street Press of the entire series of Bobby Owen detective novels.

The period between First and Second World Wars is known as the Golden Age of detective fiction. It is, for many, the great era of the amateur sleuth, when gentlemen geniuses like Lord Peter Wimsey and Philo Vance gamboled over the bloody plains of murder, nonchalantly dropping their g's and screwing in their monocles while collaring not-quite-clever-enough crooks. However quite a number of professional policemen acted as lead detectives in long-running and extremely popular mystery series during the Golden Age. Some of the better-known ones, such as Freeman Wills Crofts's Inspector Joseph French and GDH and Margaret Cole's Superintendent Henry Wilson, "came of respectable, but impecunious, middle-class parents," as Margaret Cole put it with reference to Superintendent Wilson; but others, like Ngaio Marsh's Roderick Alleyn as well as Henry Wade's Inspector John Poole and Punshon's Bobby Owen, sprang from altogether more privileged circumstances. Alleyn was the last of this high-end trio to appear in print, in Ngaio Marsh's debut detective novel, *A Man Lay Dead*, in 1934. Inspector Poole preceded Alleyn into fictional life by five years, in *The Duke of York's Steps*, while Bobby Owen just beat Alleyn to the presses, featuring first in 1933's *Information Received*.

Bobby Owen differed from both Alleyn and Poole, however, in that devoted readers of Punshon's detective series, which ran for nearly a quarter-century, were able to witness Bobby's rise through the ranks, from a lowly Police Constable to a lofty Commander of Scotland Yard (the word "bobby," it should be mentioned for non-British readers, is British slang for a police officer). In this respect the fictional police detective whom Bobby Owen most resembles is a cop created by Sir Basil Thomson named Richardson, who appeared in a short-lived though well-received series of eight detective novels that debuted, like the Bobby Owen series, in 1933, and ended in 1937, upon Thomson's death. Like Bobby Owen, Richardson commenced his fictional career as a stalwart Police Constable and rose through the ranks over the course of the series, ending up a Chief Constable in the last two books (no doubt even greater glory lay in store for Richardson, had Sir Basil not passed away in 1937). Yet there is a fellowship that the reader feels with Bobby Owen—no doubt encouraged by the author's tendency to call him "Bobby" rather than "Owen" in the novels—which is

lacking with the rather stolid series policeman created by
Thomson (who was, it should be noted, former head of both
Scotland Yard's Criminal Investigation Department *and* the
Special Branch). The reader grows to like Bobby and to follow
his developing career and life with a sympathetic interest—surely
a sterling testament, as Dorothy L. Sayers noted in her crime
fiction reviews in the *Sunday Times*, to the unique humanity and
charm in E. R. Punshon's fiction writing.

It is Bobby's sympathetic interest in others, particularly the
decade's downtrodden and dispossessed, which leads to his
uncovering of the horrific deeds done in *Mystery Villa*. Now
Sergeant Bobby Owen, B.A. (Oxon. pass degree only), he becomes
intensely concerned with the fate of a reclusive elderly woman
names Miss Barton, who lives alone in squalor in her old house,
Tudor Lodge, located in "the sedate, desperately decorous, highly
respectable, slowly decaying suburb of Brush Hill, once a favorite
home of prosperous City merchants, but now so derelict it had
not one single block of up-to-date miniature luxury flats to boast
of, nor even so much, in all its borders, as a county council estate
of dolls' houses for workers." Bobby's pity is piqued when he
hears about Miss Barton, causing him to reflect, in words
resonating today, that "here and there in London, as in almost all
big towns indeed, are strange old people, living strange, aloof,
solitary lives, hermits amidst crowds, lone islands in the midst of
the vast flowing tides of modern city populations."

Having become curious about the sudden influx of visitors to
Tudor Lodge (including, it appears, a notorious cat burglar
named Con Conway), Bobby proceeds to make inquiries that
ultimately propel him and his mentor Superintendent Mitchell

into an exceptionally lurid murder case, one with distinct literary echoes of Charles Dickens, Robert Louis Stevenson and William Faulkner. In her rave review of *Mystery Villa* in the *Sunday Times*, Dorothy L. Sayers conceded that inevitably readers would discern similarity between Punshon's Miss Barton and Dickens's Miss Havisham, but she declared that in her view "the honours are with Mr. Punshon." Sayers pronounced that in *Mystery Villa*, in contrast with *Great Expectations*, "we have the real thing—real solitude, real filth, real starvation of mind and body, with a real and ghastly necessity underlying the whole horrible superstructure of unreason." She concluded that with *Mystery Villa* Punshon had found a "superb subject for a mystery," and that he "handled it superbly."

Unaccountably, Punshon's impressive *Mystery Villa* was passed over by American publishers, although in Britain the novel was published by Gollancz, Punshon having earlier in the year jumped ship from Ernest Benn to this highly-reputed firm, along with two other notable British detective novelists, J.J. Connington and Dorothy L. Sayers herself. Punshon would remain with Gollancz for the rest of his life, although his American publishing record would be spottier. *Mystery Villa* itself was reprinted just once, in paperback by Penguin in 1950. Its reappearance after sixty-five years is a welcome event indeed.

Curtis Evans

Chapter 1

CON CONWAY'S TERROR

SERGEANT BOBBY OWEN, B.A. (Oxon. pass degree only), recently promoted as a reward for what his superiors considered good work accomplished, realised abruptly that he had missed his way, and, simultaneously, that it was beginning to rain.

Both facts annoyed him; the first, because it would probably mean missing the last train from Brush Hill station to Baker Street; the second, because it might necessitate unrolling the beautifully neat, gold-mounted, brand-new, silk umbrella he had treated himself to that very day, for he knew that a plain-clothes C.I.D. man should always make a good impression, and he understood well how universally a man is judged by the umbrella he carries.

However, this last necessity was not upon him yet, for the warning rain-drops ceased as suddenly as they had begun. But there remained his doubt concerning the best way to take whereby to reach the railway station.

At Brush Hill police-station, which he had been visiting in connection with some not very important bit of routine business and had left only a few minutes ago, he had been given clear enough directions for finding his way to the railway, since the buses whereby he had journeyed down from the Yard would at this hour have ceased running for the night. But somehow he had gone astray.

By the light of a street lamp near, he made out that he was in Windsor Crescent, and was none the wiser for the knowledge, since he had no idea how Windsor Crescent stood in relation to the railway station, nor at this late hour did there seem a single soul abroad in all the sedate, desperately decorous, highly respectable, slowly decaying suburb of Brush Hill, once a favourite home of prosperous City merchants, but now so derelict it had not one single block of up-to-date miniature luxury flats to boast of, nor even so much, in all its borders, as a county council estate of dolls' houses for workers.

Perplexed, Bobby stood at the corner of Windsor Crescent where Balmoral Grove cuts it at right angles on the way to join Osborne Terrace, and watched two cats prowl, sinister and swift and silent, across the road – but silent not for long, since, a moment later, there came from one of them a long, ear-splitting, nerve-piercing, sleep-destroying howl, a little like the product of a circular saw undergoing thumb-screw treatment in some machinist inquisition. Instinctively Bobby's eyes went searching for the stone we have the warrant of the poet for believing it is a proper man's first impulse to heave at any cat in sight, and then upon the silence following that fierce feline howl broke the sound of running footsteps, as there fled the length of the Crescent one who seemed driven by some dreadful fear.

Bobby stiffened to attention. It seemed to him there was a quality of terror needing investigation in those uneven, rushing, running steps whereof the sound troubled so suddenly and strangely the quiet of the suburban night. No man, he told himself, ran like that, save for bitter need.

He stood back a little into the shadow cast by the house near which he had paused. He could see now, by the dim light of the street lamps, the dim figure of the approaching runner. None pursued, it seemed, and somehow that gave an added terror and a keener poignancy to this unfollowed flight through the indifferent darkness. Nearer the fugitive came, and nearer still, still running in the same wild, panic-driven manner, and, when he was so near he was about to pass, Bobby shot out a long arm and caught him by the collar.

'What's up?' he began; and then, with extreme surprise, 'Good Lord, why it's Con Conway.'

The startled scream the fugitive had been about to utter died away. He was a wizened shrimp of a man, undersized, pale faced, and now he hung limp in Bobby's grasp, rather like a captured rabbit held out at arm's length by a gypsy trapper. He was trembling violently, either with fear or from the extreme physical exertion he had been making; the perspiration was running down his cheeks, whether from terror or from effort; his breath came in great, wheezing gasps, till at last he managed to pant out:

'Lor' blimey, guv'nor ... s'elp me, if ever I thought to be glad to meet a ruddy dick.'

'Meaning me?' asked Bobby.

'Meaning you, Mr Owen, sir,' Con Conway agreed; 'and no offence meant, so hoping none took neither.'

'Oh, none,' agreed Bobby pleasantly. 'Only I'm wondering, Conway, if you're really so very glad to meet me, for you know you seemed in the dickens of a hurry, and I'm rather wondering why.'

'Mr Owen, sir,' Conway assured Bobby earnestly, 'I was gladder to see you than ever I was to see the bookie still there after I had backed the winner at long odds.'

'That so?' said Bobby, with some doubt, and yet impressed by the strength and fervour of this declaration.

As he spoke he leaned his umbrella against the garden railing by which they were standing, and, still holding Con Conway with one hand, ran the other lightly over him. Conway, who knew the significance of this gesture well enough, submitted meekly, merely remarking:

'You won't find no tools on me, guv'nor.'

'I didn't much expect to,' retorted Bobby, for Mr Conway was an expert of that species of the genus burglar known as the 'cat' variety, and had no need of any aid but his natural talents and his painfully acquired technique for swarming up the gutter-pipe that seemed to pass near some conveniently open window. From his own pocket Bobby produced a small electric torch, and flashed its light on the other's knees and elbows. 'Doing a bit of climbing lately?' he asked, for both knees and elbows showed certain suspicious signs of dust and dirt.

'Oh, them,' said Conway, interested. 'Oh, them's where I slipped on a bit of bananna-skin some bloke had thrown away, and went right down on my hands and knees. The mercy of providence,' added Conway piously, 'I wasn't worse hurt; and a fair scandal, if you ask me, the way them bananna-skins is throwed about. If I 'ad my way, that's what you Yard blokes would be looking after, instead o' persecuting poor hard-working chaps what only wants a chance to earn their living quiet and peaceful like.'

'We know all about the honest, hard-working side of it,' retorted Bobby. 'Any objection to turning your pockets out?'

'As one gentleman to another,' answered Conway frankly, 'none whatever, seeing as there's nothing in 'em.'

This statement at least proved to be true enough, for in fact they contained only a dirty handkerchief, an empty cigarette carton, an equally empty matchbox, some bits of string, and one solitary and somewhat battered penny.

'O.K.,' commented Bobby. 'Any objection now to telling me what you were in such a hurry about? Old Harry himself might have been after you. What was it all about?'

'As one gentleman to another,' said Conway slowly, 'it was just this – I was running to catch the train at Brush Hill station. And now,' he added reproachfully, 'you've gone and been and made me lose it.'

'How were you going to pay your fare?' Bobby asked.

'Well, now, do you know, guv'nor,' declared Conway, with a great air of surprise, 'I hadn't never thought of that – me being always used to my money in my pocket when I wanted it.'

'Other people's money, you mean,' retorted Bobby. 'What made you so glad to see me, then?'

'Why, that was just it, guv'nor. I just remembered like as I had no money to buy my ticket, and then there was you; and all in a flash I thought: "Why, there's Mr Owen, always generous, free-handed as the day. He'll lend me my fare all right, he will." '

'Confound your impudence,' Bobby exclaimed, half laughing in spite of himself. 'Why not tell me what was really making you run like that?'

'Guv'nor, I will,' declared Conway earnestly. 'It was all along o' me not having only the one brown in my pocket, same as you saw, and not knowing where to get the price of a doss nowhere, and so I says to myself: "Con, my boy, run; run, my lad, that'll keep you warm anyways." So I run, guv'nor; and then, guv'nor, you collared me.'

'Cheese it,' Bobby exclaimed. 'I suppose the fact is, you had been paying someone a visit, and got greeted with – with a cold bath, eh?'

This was a reference to a painful incident in Mr Conway's past career when, having been discovered by two stalwart undergraduates in a bedroom where he had no obvious business, he had been obliged to submit to a sound and thorough ducking in a cold-water tank before being kicked off the premises. The last part of the proceedings he had taken in good part, and glad to get off like that, but the ducking, he still felt, had been carrying the thing too far – he might easily have died of it, pneumonia or something, and where would his thoughtless assailants have been then? Why, he had swallowed pints of the stuff as they held him down in it with brooms, and altogether it was not an experience he cared to think about or be reminded of. His tone was more than a little reproachful as he answered:

'Now, guv'nor, Mr Owen, sir. If it had been like that, wouldn't there be the whole lot of 'em piling after me, like, like' – he said pathetically – 'a 'orde of 'ungry dawgs persooing of the 'unted fawn? Now, wouldn't there?'

That this observation was as true as it was picturesque, Bobby was obliged to admit to himself. And though he remained convinced it was something very strange indeed that had driven Conway on at such desperate speed, that had made even the meeting with one of his natural enemies, a C.I.D. man, a blessed relief, yet there was no means of making him tell. A quarrel with some colleague in roguery on whose preserve he had been trespassing, perhaps. An offer of a bribe might possibly be effective, but would be more likely to produce only some new impudent invention.

'Cut along, then, if you won't tell the truth,' Bobby said. 'Only, remember, I've seen you here, and, if any report comes in, it'll be all the worse for you. We shall know, whatever happened, you were in it – and had your own reasons for keeping quiet, and then we shall know what to think.'

'Guv'nor,' declared Conway earnestly, 'if you do, you'll do me wrong. If any job was worked round this part tonight, I wasn't in it. I won't deny I had a turn, but there won't be nothing said; because for why? There wasn't nothing done; and for that I'll take my dying oath, straight I will, guv'nor.'

There was a certain accent of sincerity in this that did impress Bobby. But he made no comment, and then, in a different tone, Conway said again:

'Guv'nor.'

'Well?'

'Luck's been dead out with me, gov'nor, ever since I come out of the big house. There's times I almost wish as I was back. I ain't got no more nor that one brown you seed, guv'nor. It was the Waterloo Bridge hotel for me last night, and crool cold them arches is, and hard as you never would believe if you hadn't never tried, and as for luck – why, the night afore I did 'ave the price of a doss, and, if you'll believe me, that was the very night the Mad Millionaire, what the papers call him and no one's ever seen, had been along that way plastering every bench almost with his one-pound notes.'

'Is that yarn really true?' Bobby asked, for he had heard before of how some unknown, mysterious individual no one had ever seen would, at long, irregular intervals, deposit on the Embankment benches sealed envelopes, containing each a one-pound or ten-shilling note, and marked on the outside of the envelope: 'For the finder.'

A similar story told how a shower of such notes had once

descended on the heads of a queue of unemployed and homeless waiting for admission to a casual ward, thrown to them by some person no one had seen. Another variety was a tale of how, once or twice, in East-end streets the residents had wakened in the morning to find that during the night pound or ten-shilling notes had been thrust through the letter-boxes – unexpected but welcome manna from heaven. Bobby had been a little sceptical of the truth of these stories, but Conway assured him they were accurate enough, though he himself, such was the weight of the malignant forces for ever pressing him down, had never had the luck to be the recipient of this mysterious bounty.

'Some say it's a millionaire what's being sorry for all he's done in the past,' Conway explained. 'And some think it's a parson of some kind, doing good according to his lights, what no man can't 'elp, but what I say is, if it was that way, he would be along quick enough to rake in the souls what he'd been laying down the bait for. But some says it's a sportsman what's brought off something good, wanting to share his luck so as he shan't lose it.'

'It's a queer yarn,' Bobby observed. 'What do you think yourself?'

'It's a looney what' – began Conway, and then stopped so abruptly that Bobby had the idea he had intended to say more and then had changed his mind – 'a looney what his keepers don't look after proper,' Conway completed his sentence, differently, as Bobby felt more certain still, from the manner first intended. 'Guv'nor,' he added, 'what about the price of a doss, guv'nor, so as in your own bed to-night you won't have to think of no poor bloke keeping them stones warm under Waterloo Bridge?'

Bobby sighed, and produced a couple of shillings, but, before handing them over, felt himself called upon – it must be remembered he was still quite young – to improve the occasion by a short but earnest homily on the advantages of hard work and honesty, and the extreme ruggedness of the path chosen by the transgressor. Conway listened with an air of meek yet absorbed attention that Bobby found distinctly pleasing, so that he really did not mind very much the loss of his two shillings as he handed them over.

'That'll do you bed and breakfast,' he said. 'Though I believe you men think we are at the Yard only for you to touch between one job and the next.'

'Well, guv'nor,' observed Conway thoughtfully, as he accepted the two shillings, 'if it wasn't for the likes of us, where would the likes of you be? Unemployed, that's what,' declared Conway darkly, as he melted away into the night, and not until he had vanished did Bobby discover that his smart, brand-new, gold-mounted, silk umbrella he had been so proud of had vanished, too.

At the same moment the long-threatening rain began to fall – heavily.

Chapter 2

TUDOR LODGE

THOUGH it did not keep Bobby awake, nor trouble his slumbers with vexing dreams – for he was still of an age that knows little of sleeplessness or vexing dreams – nevertheless the memory of that strange flight of Con Conway's through the silent and unheeding streets remained teasingly in his mind.

Something, it was certain, must have happened to drive the little man in such headlong panic, something so strange and terrifying it had actually come to him as a relief to find himself collared by a C.I.D. man. After he woke, before he got up, while he was dressing, Bobby worried himself with endless conjectures; while he was shaving he cut himself, because he was thinking about it instead of about what he was doing; so absorbed, indeed, was he that he actually forgot all about his second rasher of bacon, and allowed it to

be taken away untasted – much to the alarm of his good
landlady who, startled by so unprecedented an occurrence,
was inclined to fear that he must be either ill or in love.

Later, Bobby made an excuse to ring up Brush Hill and
inquire if any report of any unusual happening in the district had come in, explaining, as he did so, that he had seen
Con Conway there the night before, and wondered if he
had been up to mischief. The facetious reply came back
that all was quiet on the Brush Hill front, but when, partly
by chance, partly through a little manoeuvring on his own
part, Bobby found himself, next afternoon, in the same district again, he took the opportunity of having a look round
the scene of his odd encounter with Conway – perhaps not
without a lingering hope that, with luck, he might run a-
cross Conway himself again, and so get that opportunity for
which his soul yearned of a quiet little heart-to-heart chat
with him about brand-new, gold-mounted, silk umbrellas.

He found Windsor Crescent easily enough, and strolled
down it, and then by Osborne Terrace into Balmoral Grove.
The houses all seemed much the same; large, roomy, comfortable but neglected-looking dwellings, generally de-
tached or semi-detached, with good gardens, and nearly
all with those basements that prove so conclusively by their
very existence the truth of the theological doctrine of ori-
ginal sin and the natural perversity of man. The whole district appeared to have everywhere much the same shabby,
neglected air, the same appearance of a prosperity that had
passed and a poverty that had replaced it. A small propor-
tion of the houses were vacant, many of the others showed
those contrasting curtains at the different windows of the
different floors that suggest occupation by different families
of different tastes, and, indeed, there were a good many bills
displayed proclaiming that there were to let flats described
according to the fancy of agent or landlord as 'self-con-
tained', 'convenient', 'eligible', 'desirable', 'mansion', or
'family'. Gardens and fences, too, had all the same neglected air, for this was, in fact, a neighbourhood that, fifty or

sixty years ago, had been a favourite with well-to-do City
men, but that since then the flow of the high tide towards
the flat in Town, and the ebb of the low tide towards the
villa on the Surrey Downs, had left desolate. For the tubes
had passed it by, the trams knew it not, the motor-buses
ignored it, and this lack of convenience of access to the City
and the West-end had resulted generally in tenants to whom
the consequently lower rent was of importance. Agents and
landlords had found themselves finally driven to recom-
mend it as 'quiet' - desperate device indeed to suggest 'quiet',
as an inducement, to a generation that adores in equal mea-
sure jazz, the motor-cycle, and the loud-speaker, and that
has invented the pneumatic drill.

It was with a distinctly puzzled air that Bobby peram-
bulated this little decaying backwater of London life.

'Now what on earth can Con Conway have been after
round here?' he asked himself, as he hesitated whether to
turn down Teck Gardens into Battenberg Prospect or to
retrace his steps up Windsor Crescent, which, by the way,
was no more a Crescent than Battenberg Prospect was a
prospect or Balmoral Grove a grove - though probably
their builder was a loyalist. 'But I'll bet,' Bobby added to
himself, 'there must be something that brought Conway
here - something he was after, just as something certainly
happened that scared him like the devil.'

For Con Conway - no one knew for certain whether the
'Con' represented his first name or was merely a pleasant
allusion to the numerous occasions on which he had been a
convict in one or other of His Majesty's gaols - was a man
of some standing in his profession, and, as a self-respecting
practitioner, was not likely to have been attracted save by
the prospect of a job really worthy of his attention, such a
job, and such loot, as in fact none of these 'converted' resi-
dences seemed very likely to offer. Several of the empty
houses would no doubt yield a visitor a certain amount of
plunder in the shape of brass taps and lead piping and so on,
but such vulgarities were not likely to tempt a man like

Conway, who dealt only in jewels or cash. Indeed, so highly specialised a business is that of crime, so water-tight are its different compartments, that Conway would most likely have had no more idea than the average honest citizen how best to dispose of such stuff as brass taps and their like, though for a diamond ring or a gold brooch he would have known at once the best available market.

Turning back, Bobby retraced his steps along Windsor Crescent, and, about half-way, paused to look again at a house that he had noticed before. With the careful, quick attention he had taught himself to give, overlooking no detail, for he knew well that strange realities may lurk behind the most ordinary appearances, he let his gaze travel over this residence that showed no notice that it was to let or to be sold, but that yet had about it an even more strongly marked air of desolation and neglect than had any of those displaying house-agents' bills.

On the gate, secured by a rusty chain and padlock that seemed to have been in position for years, was just visible, in faded paint, the name, Tudor Lodge; and as Bobby had recently read two novels about Henry VIII, and two violently contradictory lives of the same monarch, as he had also quite recently seen one film that specialised in depicting the table manners of the same historic personage, one play about him, and another about his daughter, Elizabeth, he found himself wondering vaguely if the Tudor cult was older than he had supposed. Beyond the gate was a gravel path, overgrown with weeds and grass, and the front garden had evidently not been touched for a very long time. The windows on the ground floor of the house were closely shuttered, and from the front door most of the paint had long peeled off. At most of the upper windows the blinds were drawn, and all seemed thick with the dust and dirt of years. But a gap by the side of the padlocked gate admitting to the drive showed signs of use, and the path leading to the back of the house seemed less grass-grown than the drive.

'Perhaps there's a caretaker,' he thought idly, and he

noticed that a small window at the side of the house, on the first floor, was open, and that a gutter-pipe passed close by so that, to a man like Conway, access and entry would be perfectly easy. 'Only there wouldn't be likely to be anything there Conway would think worth taking,' Bobby told himself, as he walked away.

His watch informed him he had half an hour to spare, so he went on to the Brush Hill police-station, where he looked in, ostensibly to make a purchase at the canteen, but really for a chance of getting a talk with someone. In the billiard-room he was lucky enough to find one of the sergeants attached to that division, a man named Wild, with whom Bobby had chanced to be associated in some small case shortly before, and who now was watching a game of pool then in progress.

Sergeant Wild, a portly, dignified person, not far from retiring age, greeted Bobby with a nicely calculated mixture of the condescending patronage a veteran may justifiably show the young recruit, and of the deferential amiability due to a rising C.I.D. man whose name was already becoming known. But he did not seem very interested when he found that it was still Con Conway of whom Bobby wished to talk.

'Most likely he was only doing a prowl round, on the lookout for any likely prospect,' declared Wild. 'Nothing's been reported, that I know of, and I've asked some of the boys, but none of them seem to have seen him, or anyone answering to the description. Besides, there's not much in his line round about this part; it's the big stuff he goes after, as a rule.'

'Something had scared him; scared him pretty bad, too,' Bobby insisted. 'I can't help wondering what.'

'Perhaps he saw one of our chaps, and thought he had better clear while the going was good,' suggested Wild, with a chuckle.

'Maybe he's one of the football gang,' remarked one of the pool players, who had been listening while waiting for his turn, and who wanted to join in what seemed like a little gentle chaff of one of those smart Yard chaps.

'Football? How's that?' Bobby asked.

'Richards only means,' explained Wild, a little coldly – for he remembered that he and Bobby were both sergeants; and, while it is one thing for a sergeant of many years' experience to smile away the fancies of a sergeant of junior standing, mere constables should be more discreet – 'that there's been complaints from the residents in Windsor Crescent, and round that neighbourhood, of boys playing football in the streets. We're badly off for open spaces in this part, and Windsor Crescent is a good, wide, open street without much traffic – only, the trouble is, soon as our backs are turned, there they are at it again. Richards – he was on the beat last week – says it's nothing to make a song about, but he's a football fan himself, and I wouldn't put it past him to join in if he thought no one was looking. I shall have to go round myself, and see what it's really like – don't want to detail a plain-clothes man unless we have to.'

'Know anything of a deserted, neglected-looking house in Windsor Crescent – Tudor Lodge it's called, I think?' Bobby asked.

Wild nodded, and his plumb good-humoured features took on a serious expression.

'We shall have to break in there one of these days, most likely,' he said.

Chapter 3

THE BROKEN WINDOW

A LITTLE startled by this remark, Bobby looked up sharply.

'In what way? How do you mean?' he asked.

'Old party lives there all alone,' Wild explained. 'Some

of these days one of the neighbours will come along and say she hasn't been seen for a week or two, and then we'll break in, and we'll find her dead in the kitchen or somewhere, and the verdict will be, "Natural death, accelerated by neglect and exposure." I've known similar cases before, and that's the way they always end.'

'There wouldn't be any need to break in just now,' Bobby observed. 'I noticed one of the windows on the first floor was open, and there's a gutter-pipe runs quite close. Anyone could get in with a ladder easy enough. Conway could swarm up the gutter-pipe and be inside in less than no time.'

He spoke with a certain troubled uneasiness, for there was still a vivid picture in his mind of Conway fleeing through the streets as though driven on by some dreadful memory, and there still teased him, with the fascination an unsolved problem always possessed for him, the question of what it was had caused such extreme, strange terror. But Wild guessed what was in Bobby's thoughts, and his grave expression gave way to a slightly superior smile.

'Nothing there worth picking up,' he pronounced. 'Rates haven't been paid for donkey's years. Gas cut off ever since I came to this division. Water turned off by the board, and turned on again by the sanitary people, quite as a regular thing. Besides, as it happens, Turner was on that beat last night, and he's always taken a bit of interest in her, and been sorry for the old party, along of having a mother-in-law himself what's half balmy, too. And, when he came off duty this morning, he told me he had seen the old lady of Windsor Crescent and said good night to her, and she said 'Good night, officer,' and scuttled off fast as she could. He didn't say what time it was, but it must have been after he went on duty at 2 a.m., and that was later than you saw Conway, I take it?'

'Oh, yes,' agreed Bobby. 'It was before midnight when I saw him.'

'Well, then,' Wild pointed out, 'can't have been anything to do with her that was upsetting him, or she would have said something about it to Turner – she's not too balmy for that.'

'I was thinking, just for the moment,' Bobby confessed, 'that Con Conway might have been up to mischief there – but, then, anyhow he's not the violent type; for one thing he wouldn't have the pluck to face an angry mouse even. How does the old lady live, do you know? She must get food and coal, and so on, somehow, mustn't she?'

'I think I've heard she leaves an order for a small general shop round the corner by Battenberg Prospect – Humphreys, I think the name is. But I don't think they ever see her. She leaves the money with the order, and they leave the stuff at the back door, and she takes it in after they've gone.'

'Poor old soul. It sounds rather an awful existence,' Bobby remarked, with pity in his voice, though, indeed, he knew the case was by no means rare, and that here and there in London, as in almost all big towns indeed, are strange old people, living strange, aloof, solitary lives, hermits amidst crowds, lone islands in the midst of the vast flowing tides of modern city populations. 'Has she no friends or relations?' he asked.

'Don't look like it,' Wild answered. 'No one who calls ever gets an answer. You can spend all day knocking, and no notice taken. She's never seen out, except sometimes after dark, and then, if anyone speaks to her, she runs like she did from Turner. They tried to get in touch with her from the church once, but it wasn't any good – nothing to be done, if you ask me.'

Bobby did not answer. He was musing vaguely, a little confusedly, on life that might be so rich and splendid rolling on like a great river carrying with it limitless cargoes of joy and wisdom, but, instead, so often runs to waste, like the stream losing itself in the desert sands that choke it up. Was it the fault, he wondered, of life, or of the life bearer? But Bobby was too young and too healthy minded to burden his mind for long with such useless and morbid speculations, and he got to his feet.

'I must be pushing on,' he remarked.

'Half a tick, and I'll come with you,' Wild said. 'I'm going your way. I've to see if there's anything in this foot-ball complaint, and turn in a report. In writing,' he added moodily, for, though he could talk as well and as long as anyone, when he sat down before a sheet of blank paper his mind was apt to go as blank as the paper.

Bobby waited accordingly till Wild was ready, and then walked with him towards Windsor Crescent where, when they turned into it, about half-way down from Battenberg Prospect, they found a busy, animated, and extremely noisy game of football in full swing, the players taking no more notice of the protests of one or two indignant residents than cup players at Wembley would of the yapping of a small dog in a neighbouring street.

'Well, I'm blessed,' exclaimed Wild, and at the same moment the hefty youngster who was just kicking off, after a goal won and lost, caught sight of him.

'Look out. P'leece,' he yelled.

He could not quite stop the kick he was in the act of delivering – a good kick, too, it would have been, bestowed with skill and zeal and force, that most excellent of trinities – but its aim and impulse were deflected. and, instead of sailing straight down the Crescent to where two piles of hats and coats marked the opposing goal, the ball flew to one side, over the Tudor Lodge front garden, till a crash of broken glass announced that it had found its predestined billet.

Thereon, all in a moment, as in the twinkling of an eye, as dissolves the baseless fabric of a dream, those football players had vanished as though they had never been, only a little rising dust at each end of the street left to tell that they had passed that way. After them pounded the sixteen-stone sergeant, in gallant but ineffective pursuit, much as a prize bull might chase a fleeing hare, and after him followed Bobby, running with a great appearance of zeal and a great stamping of feet, but somehow managing to get over less ground than legs so long might have been expected to cover.

At the corner where Windsor Crescent meets Osborne Terrace, Wild paused and wiped a perspiring forehead.

'Little devils; too quick for me,' he confessed.

'Like quicksilver, they are,' agreed Bobby; 'here one second and gone the next.'

'Anyway, I can run a bit still, if they hadn't had such a start,' observed Wild, with a touch of satisfaction. 'I didn't notice you got ahead of me much, though you can give me years and weight.'

'Took me all my time to keep up with you,' confessed Bobby, little disposed to lament, however, that now he would not be called upon to appear in court to sustain a charge of football playing in the street before a sarcastic magistrate, probably secretly sympathetic with the culprits, and inclined to regard the police as officious spoil-sports. 'It was their start did it,' he agreed gravely.

'That's right; a good start they had,' Wild repeated. 'Didn't I hear broken glass?'

'At Tudor Lodge, I think it was,' Bobby answered.

They walked back towards it, escaped, as soon as they could, two or three housewives anxious to tell their stories of disturbed rests, wakened babies, trampled gardens; promised that 'steps would be taken' – a satisfying phrase – and then turned into Tudor Lodge, through that gap at the side of the padlocked gate by which, apparently, entrance was effected generally.

To Bobby it seemed that there strengthened, as they approached the house, the general air of dreariness and neglect that brooded upon it. Hard, indeed, to imagine such desolation giving shelter to any living creature. The rotting woodwork, the discoloured bricks, the gravel drive so overgrown with weed and grass it could hardly be distinguished from the stretch of garden – now a tangled wilderness of shrubs and trees and grass and rubbish – that it skirted, all served to heighten that impression. The windows, closed inside by wooden shutters, were broken in one or two places, and covered everywhere with the grime and dirt of years. A huge spider's web spun across the front door proved no one recently had opened it, and no sign of life showed anywhere. Only Bobby remarked, as they turned by the side of the house in search of the damage done by the erring football, that the small window above he had noticed open the time before was now closed.

'What's the landlord thinking about, anyhow?' Bobby asked.

'No one seems to know who the place belongs to,' Wild answered. 'Someone told me once it was a freehold belonging to the old party herself, but I don't think that's right. Mr Howard, that's the rate collector, told me they couldn't find out, and had given up trying to get any rates paid – they didn't know who to summons, and the summononses they've issued no one's ever taken notice of. You can bang the door as long as you like, but there's never any answer.'

They came to a standstill by the window through which the football had smashed. It was that of the scullery, apparently, and it seemed that no inmate of the house, if indeed inmate there were, had taken any notice of the crash. Bobby climbed on the sill of the window, and peered within. It was an interior matching the desolation that reigned without. Ceiling, walls, furniture, everything, all thick with the accumulated dust of many years, and the door of the room sagging upon one hinge, as if in the decrepitude of extreme old age. He shouted once or twice, but got no answer. He could not see the football itself, and supposed it had rolled into a corner. He got down to the ground again, and said:

'I don't think there can be anyone there.'

'Oh, the old party's never out in the day; only she'll never show,' Wild answered, and strolled on to where a rotting fence and some tumbledown trellis-work had once screened off the garden. 'Lummy! Come and look here. Ever seen such a sight?'

Indeed, it was a garden that seemed now more like a bit of the primeval chaos than anything else. For nearly half a century the vegetation had grown, or not grown, at its own will, and mingled with it was a confusion of empty tins, of old rags, of ashes and cinders – for dustmen had long ceased to call – of piles of rotting paper blown here by the wind and then trapped.

'Even a dead cat,' Wild said, pointing to one. 'I suppose when anybody round about wants to get rid of anything, they chuck it over the fence.'

'I am wondering about this,' Bobby said. 'She must have food, and so on, at times, and she must pay for what she has. That means she must get money somehow, unless she has a hoard in the house, which doesn't seem very likely. I should like to see the money she pays her bills with. If it's of current date, that would prove someone must be sending or giving it to her.'

'Yes, I daresay,' agreed Wild. 'Only it's not police business. She's doing no harm. No Act of Parliament against living alone – at least, not yet; though very like there will be soon, when some of them up there happen to think of it.'

They went to the back of the house, and Bobby said: 'Shall we knock?'

'What for?' asked Wild. 'You'll get no answer; no one ever does. If it's about the football, serve those kids right if they lose it. Teach 'em not to play in the streets any more, perhaps.'

'Might as well try,' Bobby said, always an obstinate and persistent young man.

He went up to the front door. The bell, one of the old-fashioned wire bells, hung, in evident uselessness, on a length of broken wire. The heavy knocker, red with rust, Bobby lifted, and beat a rat-tat upon the door, and, even as he did so, it opened and swung back.

Chapter 4

THE GIRL

SURPRISED indeed was Bobby that this door, so evidently so long unused, should thus swing open instantly in response to his summons, but still more surprised was he – surprised, indeed, to the very limit of astonishment – by what he now saw. For there, upon the threshold, stood no such ancient withered, half-crazed crone as he had expected, but, instead, a young, fresh, dainty girl, smartly and fashionably dressed, her youthful elegance most strange against that dreary background of neglect and desolation.

In figure she was small and slight, very fair, with fair hair that had a tint of gold, and very clear eyes of the deepest blue. Her features were small: a tiny mouth, a small though well-shaped chin, a delicately chiselled nose – all so dainty that the big, wide-opened blue eyes above seemed enormous by comparison. Her complexion, all cream and roses, was as Heaven had given it and her own good sense had left it; and her small, gloved hands clasped to her body a crystal-handled umbrella as though she loved it.

But yet there was something strained and rigid in the attitude of, this small person of an almost Dresden-china-shepherdess beauty; and while Bobby still gaped at her in his frank bewilderment – while, behind, good Sergeant Wild gasped out almost audibly: 'Bless my soul' – he grew aware that in her great eyes of clearest blue there showed an unimaginable terror; that through those red lips, curved like Cupid's bow, there might break at any moment a wail of terror and despair; that those small hands clasping the umbrella so closely to her were held like that in a desperate attempt to still the wild beating of her heart.

How long they would have stayed like this, watching each

other – Bobby in blank and complete bewilderment; the girl paralysed, as it seemed, by the sheer extremity of the terror that held her in its grip - none can tell, but, from behind, the comfortable, untroubled voice of Sergeant Wild broke the tension.

'Ain't the old lady in, miss?' he asked, and the commonplace, ordinary question, and the everyday tone in which it was asked, seemed alike incredible to Bobby; and yet, at the same time, served, as it were, to bring him back into touch with ordinary life.

Wild, in fact, was feeling a little pleased at Bobby's silence. He took it as indicating that this smart young Yard chap realised the lead ought to be left to the senior and more experienced man, even if that senior had happened to spend all his service in the uniform branch, and none the worse for that, either. Of course, such an attitude was only right, but some of those C.I.D. chaps were a bit pushing, and thought no one counted but themselves, so it was quite gratifying, Wild felt, to find one who understood the uniform branch mattered, too. Moreover, from where Wild stood, a little to one side and a trifle behind Bobby, he could not see the girl so plainly, nor recognise as plainly as could Bobby those signs and tokens of an awful terror that she displayed so clearly.

'No ... No.' She answered his question now. 'There's no one here but me ... no one at all ... no one. ...'

She shuddered as she spoke, and somehow Bobby was on the instant quite certain that what she said was not true, as instinctively as he knew, also, that only most dire necessity had induced her so to lie. 'You mean ... Miss Barton?' she asked, her voice controlled by an effort so intense and violent, Bobby wondered so small and slight and frail a body could produce it.

'Is that the party's name, miss?' Wild asked, in his most benevolent, fatherly voice, for all he saw was a pretty young girl naturally a little startled by the abrupt appearance of two strange men. 'It's about the football, miss,' he went on, 'some of those boys have been and kicked through your window, and a good hiding's what they want, if you ask me. Though I'm not saying liking a bit of fun isn't natural enough when you're young, as you'll know yourself, miss,' he added, in polite recognition of his listener's youth. 'But, all the same, there's limits, and I'll see if I can't get a plain-clothes man put on here for a while, to stop the annoyance.'

He paused then, a faintly puzzled look on his broad, good-humoured face suggesting that he was beginning to be vaguely aware of something somehow out of tune some-where in his amiable chatter, and, indeed, to Bobby it had sounded as grotesquely, almost as indecently incongruous, as jest and song would have seemed by a deathbed, so that he had wished to stop it by some word or gesture of protest. But on the girl this flow of everyday commonplace had evidently a reassuring effect, and though the terror was still in her eyes, the deathly pallor in her cheeks, her voice was better under control as she said:

'Oh, yes ... the football ... yes. I'll get it for you, shall I?'

Without waiting for an answer, she turned and dis-appeared into the house, leaving Bobby and Wild standing there.

'Rum start,' commented Wild. 'Fancy a smart girl like that being here! Wonder if she's a relative or what?'

Bobby did not answer. He was staring into the dreary interior of the house, noting the dust that lay so thickly everywhere, the cobwebs that hung like a black tapestry on the walls, the hat- and umbrella-stand where busy spiders had spun great webs between hats unworn for half a century, and sticks and umbrellas untouched for as long, and asking himself how, into that drear, bizarre picture of neglect, there had come to fit itself such a picture of bright youth and beauty. He noticed that, on the right, a door was open, and that just within was piled an inconceivable confusion of bills, letters, circulars, papers of all sorts and kinds, none opened, all apparently thrown in there out of the way when their accumulation threatened to block up the hall.

'Ever see such a sight?' Wild asked. 'You get into some queer places sometimes in our job, but none so queer as this, as ever I've known.'

The girl came running back, flitting light and swift through the gloom. She had the football in her hands, and she held it out to them.

'Here it is,' she said.

'Thanky, miss,' Wild said, taking it. 'Miss Barton all right, miss?'

'Oh, yes,' she answered.

'You'll excuse our asking, miss,' Wild went on, 'but we feel a bit uneasy at times, knowing she is all alone here and anything might happen like, but that'll be all right now you're here, miss, I take it – and so much the better, too.'

She did not answer. She stood very still and silent, and Bobby had the thought that her first extremity of fear was beginning to return to her.

'If there's anything we can do, miss,' Wild went on, without appearing to notice her silence, 'and you'll let us know, we're always handy. Or would you like someone from the church to call round?'

'Oh, no, no, no; not that,' she breathed, and for once Wild looked a little disconcerted, as if he did not quite know what to make of so prompt and decided a refusal of his well-meant suggestion.

'Well, there's some as don't hold with churches,' he conceded, 'though I've nothing against them myself. You any relation, miss?'

'Oh, no ... no. ... Once my father knew her,' she breathed, and shuddered as she spoke, as if with a kind of vision of what the past once was, of what might be the future.

But Wild noticed nothing, and beamed approval on her.

'Glad to know the old lady's got friends, miss,' he continued, with the same bland amiability Bobby could hardly believe he did not see was torture to the girl. 'Didn't seem

right for her to be living all alone, same as she seemed, without a soul knowing nothing about her, and anything we can
do, miss, as I said before, you've only to let us know; and
very glad I am there's a young lady like yourself to look in at
times, for our chaps often said it was a shame the way the
poor old soul lived all alone, and I'll do my best to see
there's no further annoyance from the football. I suppose
Miss Barton doesn't want to lodge any complaint, does she?
There's her window broke, and, if we could find out what
boy it was did that, she could come down on his father and
make him pay up, though whether worth the trouble or
not is another thing.'

'Oh, no. Please don't,' the girl breathed. 'She wouldn't
want, I'm sure she wouldn't ... You won't, will you ...?'

'Not if not wished,' Wild assured her. 'And there's no
denying accidents will happen, and losing their football
will be a bit of a lesson to them to be more careful another
time. We'll take it with us, shall we, miss?'

'Oh, yes ... yes, please do,' she answered, and Bobby was
quite sure he heard a slow, shuffling step going up and down
somewhere in the dim background.

'Did you say Miss Barton was out?' he asked.

She threw him a quick and startled glance, as if terrified
afresh that now he, too, had spoken.

'Yes ... yes ... yes; she's out,' she whispered, but the
shuffling, hesitating footstep was now still more plainly
audible – at least to Bobby. Wild did not seem to hear or
notice. 'Oh, I must go,' she said, with a little cry. 'Please,
I must go, if you'll let me, please.'

'That's right, miss,' Wild rambled on. 'Much obliged,
miss, and sorry to have troubled you, and if you would like
a doctor or a nurse sent in, miss, just you let us know; and
a very good thing, too, miss, if I may say so, the old lady's
got someone –'

But this time the door shut to, and Bobby knew, as well
as though his eyes could penetrate the solid wood, that
on the other side the girl clung, half fainting, half uncon-

scious, able only by leaning against it to hold herself upright. In another moment, he knew for certain, the strain would have been too much for her, and she would have broken under it.

'Bit quick that was,' Wild commented, a trifle disconcerted again, as he surveyed the closed door. 'Nice young lady she seemed, too; and as pretty as they make 'em – reminded me of my own old woman when we was walking out before we had our nine kids. But quick in her ways, too, with it, don't you think?'

'A little that way,' Bobby acknowledged. 'Did you hear anything? I thought I heard footsteps, somewhere inside, just before the door shut.'

'Now you mention it,' agreed Wild, 'there was a sort of sound – perhaps there's someone there with her, mother or someone. Or it might be just mice scuttling. I'll lay there's plenty in there.'

'There is something that is frightening her to death,' Bobby said, staring at the closed door as though by sheer force of vision he could penetrate to the secret that it hid.

'Oh, most like she was just a bit scared with us turning up so unexpected like,' Wild suggested. 'There's some as is always scared when they see our uniform – think it's handcuffs and penal servitude, and what not, right away,' he said chuckling, for he was so kindly and soft-hearted he loved, above all things, believing that all the world shivered with terror at the mere sight of his round, smiling, good-humoured, friendly countenance.

'It was more than that,' Bobby insisted. 'She looked the way Con Conway did the other night. She had the same look in her eyes there was in his.'

Wild only stared; he simply could not conceive how this smart, pretty, well-dressed girl could possibly ever at any time share even a look or an expression with such a little rat as the ex-convict Con Conway. He was trying to formulate some kind of expostulation to express this feeling, as they walked down the overgrown drive towards the

padlocked gate, when, through the gap at its side that everyone seemed to use, there came towards them a small, thin,
elderly man in shirt-sleeves, carrying a tradesman's
basket on his arm with, in it, various parcels.

Chapter 5

THE SHOPKEEPER

THE little tradesman, with his basket of groceries on his
arm, stood still as he caught sight of them, and even looked
a little startled. Wild said to Bobby:

'It's Humphreys, I think – keeps the shop near the bottom
of Battenberg Prospect, I told you about, where the old
party here gets what she wants.'

'For anyone living all alone and solitary,' Bobby remarked, 'Miss Barton seems to have a good many callers.'

Humphreys was now walking on towards them after
his momentary pause. Wild said to him:

'Afternoon – bringing the old lady her week's groceries?'

'Nothing wrong, is there?' Humphreys asked.

'What should be? Why do you ask?' Bobby interposed,
slightly surprising Wild by slipping in this unexpected and
abrupt question.

'Boys kicked a football through one of the windows, that's
all,' Wild said, subconsciously intending this as a kind of
implied rebuke to Bobby for asking unnecessary questions.

But Bobby seemed to expect a reply, and was looking
keenly at Humphreys, who, with the merest tinge of
discomfort in his manner, answered:

'When an old woman's living all alone, the way she does,
you don't never know what mightn't happen – many's the
time I've said to my missus: "Mark my words, some day
she'll be found dead along of not looking after herself

proper." Besides which, it's tempting Providence living all alone in a big house, with thieves and burglars and smash-and-grab brigands going on the way they are, and the police never stopping 'em – though doing their best, of course, as we all know,' he added, with a deprecating glance at the sergeant, as if doubtful whether he had been prudent in permitting himself to repeat the criticism lately appearing in that special national paper from which he secured every morning, new and fresh, his opinions, his beliefs, and his creeds.

'Not as many as there were,' said the sergeant firmly. 'We've got the situation well in hand,' he pronounced, repeating, on his side, what the Home Secretary had remarked in a speech a day or two before. He added, glancing back over his shoulder at the shuttered, deserted, neglected-looking habitation they had just left, 'Nothing much there for anyone, either; gas cut off; rates never paid – don't look like any money there.'

'Stories get about sometimes, with very little foundation,' Bobby observed. 'Are there any about Miss Barton, do you know?' he asked Humphreys.

'None that I've ever heard tell,' Humphreys replied, with emphasis. 'Anyways, none that come from me, I'll swear to that,' he added, with still greater emphasis – rather unnecessary emphasis, indeed – and with a somewhat oddly obstinate expression that Bobby noted, remembered, but could not understand.

'There's no stories of that sort about,' confirmed Wild, with equal emphasis. 'If there were, we should be the first to hear them. Everyone knows the poor way she lives.'

'That's right,' agreed Humphreys. 'Nothing there except spiders and mess and dirt.' He added, as if anxious to change the conversation, 'Those boys did ought to be stopped, so they ought – smashing people's windows and everything.'

Bobby was looking into the little man's basket. It contained bread, a packet of tea, a tin of condensed milk, and some candles and matches.

'Doesn't she get more than that?' he asked.

'Never more; sometimes less,' Humphreys answered. 'Sometimes no matches wanted, and sometimes no candles; and sometimes neither of them, but only bread and tea and tinned milk – that's reg'lar, and has been for thirty years and more.'

'But she must get more than that! From someone else, perhaps?' Bobby insisted.

'Not that I knows of,' Humphreys replied. 'And never any more from me. One Christmas after the war, when business was better, and a living to be made at it, which it isn't now, my missus, being soft-hearted like, put in a quarter of butter what was a bit too gone to sell, and a quarter of our best slab cake. Believe me or not, they wasn't touched – just left in the basket; and the missus says, well, if that's the way she takes it, we won't try no more; so we never did. As for her going anywhere else,' he went on, 'why should she? me having served her, and give full satisfaction, for years and years, and then I've asked the neighbours, and they all say they never see anyone but me once a week reg'lar. If she went anywhere for personal shopping, most like we should hear of it; and then, too, she don't hardly ever go out, and if she does it's mostly after closing time. Of course, there's no saying for certain.'

While listening to this, Wild had been looking into the basket with an air of almost comical dismay and disapproval.

'What a way to live,' he said. 'I couldn't stand it – drive me dotty, it would. She must have been like anyone else at one time. How did she get the way she is now?'

Neither of the other two seemed disposed to offer any answer, and, indeed, Wild seemed a little surprised himself that it had come into his mind to ask the question.

'Well, that's the way I feel about it,' he said, with an air of finality.

'Strange to think,' agreed Bobby, 'of anyone like that now as once a jolly little child or a happy young girl, and then growing into such a life. I suppose it comes about gradually. There may have been some reason at first; something happened perhaps, or perhaps it was just a gradual dying away of every interest.'

He turned and stared at the gloomy, deserted house behind as if in challenge; as if daring it to hold any longer its secret from him; as if, once again, he felt that odd, indefinable demand upon his mind that every unsolved problem seemed to make.

'Do you never see her? Does she never come to the door?' he asked Humphreys.

'Never set eyes on her since I don't know when,' Humphreys declared. 'There's an outhouse near the back door – sort of tool-shed or something. She hangs a basket on a nail in it, with the money and a bit of paper to say what she wants, and next time I leave the order and the change, if any.'

'About the money?' Bobby asked. 'What is it, paper or silver, or gold?'

'Gold?' repeated Humphreys, astonished. 'Why, I ain't seen gold since – why, not since a gent came in to buy some cheese, and paid for it with a half sovereign the boy I had then didn't want to take, never having seen nothing like it; thought it was a counter or something. Luckily I came in in time, only, of course, I got rid of it again before the price went up the way it has now – which was sure to be the way of it,' he added, with a kind of early-Christian-martyr sigh. 'Once in a while,' he went on, 'she puts in a pound note, and I bring back the change; and then it always seems like I get the change again till it's all done, and then there's another pound note, and it's like that all the time.

'First there were sovereigns,' Bobby remarked, 'then Treasury notes came in, and now we've Bank of England notes – if she's used them all in turn, she must have some regular source of income, some way of getting money somewhere to carry on with.'

'Looks like it,' agreed Wild. 'Gets it sent, perhaps –

anyhow, it's not a police matter. How's business?' he added to Humphreys.

Humphreys hesitated, looked round, swelled perceptibly, and said, in a voice of mysterious importance:

'Working it up.'

'Are you, though?' said Wild, evidently astonished at the idea. 'Getting on all right?'

'Not so dusty,' admitted Humphreys. 'Working it up,' he said again, as though he repeated some magic formula. 'When we have, we'll sell out; and then, maybe, we'll buy another in Bournemouth, just for something to do and keep going on. In Bournemouth,' he repeated, and it was almost as though he sang the word, so that his little, worn, worried face lit up, while for an instant he stood in a glow of ecstasy, as the drab London scene faded from his sight, and he walked in a dream of Paradise, amidst perpetual sunshine and soft sea air and the scent of pines. 'Bournemouth,' he said once more, very softly. 'Me and the missus went there August Bank Holiday after we were married – before the war, that was – and, ever since, we've said, that's where we would go if we ever got the chance.'

He was so lost in this dream that had haunted all the days of his poor meagre little life, and that it seemed he thought might soon become a fact, as happens to so few, so very few, of the dreams of men, that Wild had to speak to him twice over before he realised he was being addressed again.

'Glad to hear it,' Wild was saying. 'I had an idea things down your way weren't so bright now they've changed the bus route.'

'And a dirty trick that was, too; and quite uncalled for,' exclaimed Humphreys, jerked back to present-day surroundings by the memory of this outrage. 'And something ought to have been done about it, but we're working it up all right. Working it up, we are,' he repeated, his tongue lingering lovingly over this phrase that was to him the key to open the earthly Paradise he knew as

Bournemouth of the sea and the sun and the pine-scented air. 'Going in for gardening stuff, we are now; one window full of it – tools and seeds and manures, and lawn sand and lime, and what not. Doing well, too; big profits in them lines.'

He nodded, and went on towards the house, and as they, too, continued on their way, Wild remarked:

'About the first time I've heard anyone say business was doing well, and I shouldn't have thought there was much of a demand for garden-stuff down where he is, or so much profit in it, either. If you ask me, they've as much chance of selling out for anything worth while as they have of winning the Irish Sweepstake. They'll never see Bournemouth on what they get for their little one-horse show.'

'It's a queer affair altogether,' Bobby said, and he and Wild were still standing talking when Humphreys came back with an empty basket, Miss Barton's purchases having been deposited in the accustomed place. He made some vague remark as he passed, and Bobby was thinking, with gentle amusement, that the light in the little man's eyes and the smile lingering at the corners of his mouth were both due to his dear dream of Bournemouth, when there appeared from across the road an indignant housewife, who had evidently been watching for him.

She was in a state of high indignation. It seemed that the previous Saturday night an order of hers had been delivered all wrong – nothing that she wanted, and everything she didn't want, and too late for any correction to be made. There had been nothing for Sunday-morning breakfast, and she had had to leave her washing on Monday morning to go out and buy things. Her opinion of Mr Humphreys was emphatic and little flattering, and she was very scornful of his efforts to put the blame on his new man – 'well-meaning and 'ard-working', Humphreys declared, but with no experience. The indignant lady denounced the new assistant in question as a great, tall, stupid thing, fit for nothing but standing outside the pictures and a way of talking as if he didn't think you good enough for his lordship's notice; and Humphreys protested that his new assistant was doing his best, but not used to the grocery business, having only come into it as a result of the general economic crisis, and glad of the chance, too.

But the indignant lady, memory of that meagre Sunday breakfast rankling in her mind, refused to accept this as an excuse, and leaving her still venting her wrath, and Humphreys still proffering meek excuse, Wild and Bobby walked away, the sergeant evidently very much impressed by so unexpected a revelation of a prosperity in the Humphreys' establishment sufficiently pronounced to permit of the employment of a full-time, grown-up assistant.

'Though him doing well, and working it up on garden-stuff and suchlike,' said Wild, shaking his head in a mystified manner as he bade farewell to Bobby, 'beats me clean, so it does; especially now the buses have changed their route.'

Chapter 6

THE SHOPKEEPER'S ASSISTANT

AGAIN a day or two passsed, and Bobby, busy with un-interesting routine work, found often breaking in upon his thoughts as he drew up statements, filled in forms, went here and there on one dull errand or another, the teasing, troubling memory of the shuttered house in Windsor Crescent, of the old woman he had never seen dragging out there her strange and drear existence, of the mystery of fear that seemed to hang about the place.

Nor, try as he might, could he imagine any reasonable cause for the extremity of terror that had seemed to be holding in its grip the girl whom he and Wild had seen there.

'If there was anything or anyone scaring her,' he reflected, 'she knew we were police, and she only had to say a word;

and, if it was because we were police she was upset, she had only to keep the door shut. But it's not even reasonable to suppose there can be anything criminal happening in a house where an old woman has been living alone for half a century or so, when all the neighbourhood knows about her, and would spot it at once if there was anything unusual going on.'

Yet, in spite of himself, he could not help thinking that there must be some connection between the terror that had sent Con Conway flying in blind panic through the night and that other fear which so evidently the unknown girl was experiencing. Not that he could imagine how any such connection could exist, but it was in vain he tried to persuade himself that only coincidence linked together those two terrors. It was as though an intuition told him differently.

In a quiet, unofficial way he tried, too, to get in touch again with Con Conway. Having no desire to experience the riot of leg-pulling that he knew very well would ensue, he had made no report of the umbrella incident, and so could not explain why he was so anxious to find Conway. But that enterprising gentleman was evidently taking very good care to keep out of his way, realising, no doubt, how ardently Bobby longed for a quiet little private talk with him on the subject of umbrellas, and, indeed, he seemed to have vanished altogether from all his accustomed haunts. Sometimes Bobby wondered if this disappearance could have any connection with whatever it was had caused his panic on the night of their meeting, but that did not seem to him very likely. Sometimes, also, he wondered if the unknown girl, too, had vanished in the same way from her usual circle.

Then, opportunity serving, he found himself once again, very shortly afterwards, within a brief bus-ride of the Windsor Crescent district, and with an hour or two to spare before he was actually due back to report at the Yard before going off duty. For Bobby an unsolved problem had always an attraction – it would go on teasing his mind till he was able to satisfy it with an adequate explanation; it was for him much what some unusual play of light is to the artist, or some rush of image and emotion to the poet. A bus, going in the required direction, came up; he jumped on, and got down again at the Osborne Terrace end of Windsor Crescent.

Walking along it, he came soon to Tudor Lodge. No change was apparent. Deserted-looking and lonely, blinds down and shutters closed, rotting wood and crumbling brick, there it stood with its padlocked gate and its front garden where all the rubbish of the world seemed gathered.

With his own strong, vivid young life throbbing through his veins, Bobby tried to imagine what existence must be like, dragged out in that dreary place, solitary, unknown, forgotten. A hermit in a desert or a wilderness had some kind of natural background and tradition, and could, at least to some degree, be understood. But to live like this all alone, in the midst of the roar and bustle of a great town's throbbing life, seemed to Bobby the most unnatural thing conceivable.

He wondered again how it could have come about, how anyone at all could drift into such a condition, and he supposed that would never be known. But how had it happened there had been no friend or relation to rescue this lone, unhappy creature from her own perversity?

For some time he stood there, looking and wondering, and finding no answer to his questions. It was growing late – Scotland Yard, of course, knows nothing of regular hours – and the falling shades of the evening added to the gloom and depression of the scene. At last he turned away. There was nothing he could do, he supposed, certainly no ground on which any official action could be taken. He had not even an excuse for knocking and making any enquiry. He gave a final glance before departing, and noticed, suddenly, that the scullery window at the side of the house had not been mended. Entrance by it could be easily effected. One had only to lift the sash and step inside.

'Not quite safe to leave it like that,' Bobby reflected, and then it struck him that here was an excuse to knock at ьhe door.

He could even suggest nailing a bit of boarding over the broken pane for her for the time – if, that is, the old lady answered his knock. Anyhow he would try. The window really ought not to be left like that, for any passing tramp or vagabond who chose to enter by, and possibly, if she were really hard up and hadn't the money to pay for repairs, she would be glad of his suggestion, and he would, for his part, get a chance to see what she was like and exchange a word or two with her – always, that is, if she answered his knock, since that, he understood from Wild's story, was seldom her habit.

He passed through that gap between the padlocked gate and the crumbling rusting garden railings every visitor seemed to use, and walked up the drive. It was growing darker each moment, for heavy clouds were coming up with a threat of storm about to break, and the trees in the front garden cut off what light there was and threw their heavy shadows across the weed-covered drive right up to the walls of the house.

In this growing darkness of the declining day, something more even than usual of its air of gloom and depression and old, unforgotten griefs appeared to brood upon the place; and to Bobby it seemed that a kind of warning lay implicit in the totality of the scene, as though there were an evil lurking there it was best to beware of. He made an effort to throw this impression off; he told himself, crossly, that he was growing nervous and imaginative, and that too much imagination is as bad in a police officer as too little. It is only facts that he must pay heed to, not vain fancies, and what could there be wrong or harmful about a house where a poor old woman had dragged out her solitary, half-crazed existence for so many years, since before Bobby himself was born even, for that matter?

He was half-way along the drive to the front door now,

and he paused, almost inclined to walk away and trouble his head no more about what was neither business of his nor police business. Why, the old lady herself, Miss Barton, if that was her name, had been spoken to by one of the constables on the beat the very evening Bobby had seen Con Conway, and everything had apparently been all right. Besides, if he knocked, most likely he would get no reply, and his excuse for calling was pretty thin. Until recently, at any rate, few callers had got any reply at all – of that there was the evidence not only of Wild's story, but also of the spider's web Bobby himself had noticed spun across the front door to prove how long must have elapsed since it had been opened. Of course, that might be different now the girl was there he and Wild had seen. It was to be hoped she was looking after things, and had perhaps already been able to persuade the old lady to come away with her and live somewhere else in a more normal and natural manner. Apparently there was some money somewhere, though, for that matter, even a workhouse infirmary would be better than such an existence as had been led so long in Tudor Lodge.

Bobby was, in fact, turning away, having made up his mind there was nothing he could do, when round the corner of the house there came quickly, almost running indeed, the figure of a tall man in shirt-sleeves, carrying a basket on one arm. He did not see Bobby at first, for the young sergeant was hidden in the dark shadows the trees before the house cast now that night was falling, and when Bobby stepped forward to speak to him he gave a low, strangled cry of fear, and leaped wildly backward as though he meant to take to instant flight.

'What's the matter?' Bobby demanded.

Flight was, in fact, not possible, for Bobby blocked the only way, save that back to the closed house and the impenetrable wilderness that once had been a garden. As though he recognised this, the stranger paused, and turned, facing Bobby.

'I didn't see you; you gave me a start,' he said, in a voice oddly high-pitched and none too steady. 'I was leaving Miss Bartons' groceries – this place always gives me the creeps, scares me somehow, and then, when you jumped out on me like that –'

He left the sentence unfinished, and taking out a very dirty handkerchief began to mop his forehead. What with the gathering darkness of the night, the heavy clouds that were coming up, the shadows cast by house and tree, Bobby could not see him very plainly, but could make out that he was tall – quite as tall as Bobby himself, or even taller for that matter – with strongly marked features, and a specially prominent nose, on which he now blew a resounding peal. Beneath it he wore a heavy, dark moustache, a noticeable feature in this clean-shaven age, and his height and his nose, and a trick he appeared to have of actually looking down it at the person he was speaking to, reminded Bobby of the indignant housewife's complaint about the 'airs' Mr Humphreys' new assistant gave himself. Rather an unfortunate trick of manner in a small suburban grocer's assistant, Bobby thought, and one that possibly accounted for the difficulty he must have had in finding employment before accepting the terms, conditions, and wages Humphreys most likely offered. Bobby said aloud:

'Are you from Mr Humphreys?'

'Yes, Battenberg Prospect – where you turn into the road,' the other answered; and then, as if beginning to resent these questions, 'You live here? We always thought the old girl was all alone.'

'No, I don't live here,' Bobby answered. He put a hand on the other's basket and looked inside. It was empty, except for a pair of new leather gardening gloves, bright yellow in hue. 'Have you been leaving her things for Miss Barton?' he asked.

'Same as usual,' the other answered. 'Them gloves is for another customer. Only, what's it got to do with you?'

'What made you so startled when I spoke to you?' Bobby asked, ignoring this.

'Why, the way you jumped out at me; what do you think? And this house, too, gets on your nerves; you never know what mayn't be going on. Like an old witch, she is.' He paused, and gave an uneasy unnatural laugh. 'Nerves,' he repeated, 'that's all – and then you jumping out of the shadows there ... what were you doing, anyhow, if it comes to that?'

'I'm a police officer,' Bobby explained, 'and we aren't easy about the way Miss Barton lives – an accident might easily happen.'

'Well, it's her affair, isn't it?' the other retorted. 'She's all right, isn't she? Nothing for anyone to worry about; she's doing no one any harm – except giving you the creeps. Scares me, I know, every time I go near the blessed place.' He turned and looked up at the house. 'There she is now, watching us,' he said. 'You can talk to her about it, if you like – that is, if she'll come to the door. Mr Humphreys says she never answers anyone.'

'Where is she?' Bobby asked. 'I don't see her.'

'She's gone now,' the other answered. 'She was at that window, up there, that's half open, peeping out – at least, I thought I saw her there; perhaps it was only a shadow or something. I don't see it's any business of anyone else's how she chooses to live. She troubles nobody, and nobody is likely to trouble her – an old woman like her hardly able to keep body and soul together, and everything in the house gone to wrack and ruin through neglect.'

'Have you ever seen her?' Bobby asked.

'Only a glimpse, once or twice, dodging behind the windows. I always knock when I leave her order, but she never answers. Perhaps she will now, if you try; but it isn't likely – not a bit likely.'

He nodded and walked on, swinging his nearly empty basket on his arm, and from a loud-speaker, posted at an open window near so that all the street might hear, burst suddenly the first strains of a new opera, by a well-known woman composer, that the B.B.C. was broadcasting, and

that Bobby now remembered he had intended to listen
to himself.

Sounded jolly good, he thought, as he walked on towards
the house. He looked into the outbuilding by the side door,
and found there the meagre provision of a loaf of bread, a
little tea, and a tin of condensed milk that composed,
apparently, Miss Barton's customary order. For a little
time he waited, half hoping Miss Barton would appear to
take in her supplies. It would be an opportunity so see
her, he thought, and perhaps to talk to her and gain her
confidence. But she did not seem inclined to show herself,
and after a time Bobby walked away to the strains of the
new opera the loud-speaker at the open window was re-
producing to all the neighbourhood.

Chapter 7

OBSESSION

WHEN Bobby woke next morning he was much annoyed to
find he had been dreaming of Tudor Lodge and of that
strange miasma of terror that seemed to hang about it,
so that therefrom the ex-convict, Con Conway, had fled
in panic, therein the young, unknown girl had seemed on
the verge of swooning in horror, where even the grocer's
assistant pursuing his homely task of delivering bread and
tea and tinned milk had not escaped the general fear.

That there must be some cause and reason for it Bobby
was well persuaded, and yet what that cause could be he
entirely failed even to imagine, or why none of those
experiencing it seemed to wish to speak of it or to ask for
help; or, indeed, why a house so seldom visited that spiders
span webs across its door should seem now to have become
the centre of so much animation.

Bobby had at the moment fully enough office work to keep him busy, for the present job was reading anonymous letters. A sensational child murder had been committed in the Notting Hill district, and, though Bobby had not been employed in the actual investigation, he had been detailed for the task of examining anonymous letters about the case, of which so many had been sent to Scotland Yard that an old sugar crate had been brought up from the canteen for their reception.

The task was one which was at the same time extraordinarily tedious, extraordinarily dull, and extraordinarily important, for while many of the letters were from obvious lunatics, and most of the rest from mere busybodies, still, each one had to be read over with extreme attention and care, since there was always the possibility that, amidst all these bushels of chaff, a really valuable grain of information might lie concealed, while, if any such piece of information were missed, the whole, not only of the success of the investigation, but also of the reputation of all Scotland Yard, might be compromised. Little mercy Press or public would show if it ever became known that some information had been sent to Scotland Yard and had been overlooked or neglected. Small allowance would be made for all the thousands of useless letters sent in, small thought for the difficulty of distinguishing the true in the midst of such a welter of rubbish. Bobby realised well enough how much hung upon his missing nothing, and to every fresh ill-spelt, ill-written, often almost illegible, communication he knew he had to come with fresh and keen attention. Even those letters chiefly concerned with expressing the writer's firm belief that the police were certainly incompetent, and probably corrupt, had to be read with the same concentrated care, since there was always the chance that in the midst of the spate of more or less ignorant and ill-informed criticism some useful hint might show itself.

Before Bobby were two trays in which he put any letters he thought worthy of further attention. The first tray, as yet empty, was for those he considered deserved the direct and immediate attention of Superintendent Mitchell himself. The second tray was for letters containing suggestions that seemed worth acting on, or facts worth following up. So far this tray held five letters.

Behind Bobby was another old capacious sugar crate, also requisitioned from the canteen. Into this he dropped in bundles, neatly tied and docketed, those letters that seemed to him purely incoherent, trivial, malicious, or frankly insane. This was nearly full now, and there were times when Bobby, strong man as he was, nearly broke down and wept aloud with sheer boredom of the job.

When lunch-time came, with its promise of happy release for a while, he begged permission to take an extra hour or two, so that he might get a little exercise and fresh air.

'A ten-mile walk is what I want,' he confided to one of the other men. 'Those letters will give me a nervous breakdown if I go on with them much longer without a change and the chance to walk 'em off a bit in the open air.'

He would make up for it, he explained, when he got back, and he thought he could promise that, even if he did extend his lunch hour, he would be able to finish not only with the letters in hand, but also with the further shoals to be expected by the later posts, before midnight, and have his report ready, together with those letters he thought worth further consideration, for submission first thing next morning, which was all that was necessary. On this understanding, therefore, he was given permission to take as much time as he liked for his lunch; and like a dog let loose from its chain, or a schoolboy released from lessons, he shot off – at a good six miles an hour, honest toe-to-heel walking.

' 'Ere's a bloke what's after the Brighton record,' one cheeky youngster called after him, and indeed, but for the fear of attracting attention, Bobby would have been not walking at all, but running at top speed, so glad was he to be out in the open, exerting his muscles cramped by so long sitting at his desk, so glad to be able to relieve his eyes from the strain of poring over so many half-illegible scripts.

Almost unconsciously his legs bore him away towards the Brush Hill district that had been so long in his thoughts, and when, presently, he woke up to the direction he had been taking, he put on a little extra speed till finally he arrived once more in Windsor Crescent, his body in a pleasant glow with the exercise, his muscles satisfactorily stretched, his mind blown clear of all the cobwebs his morning's work had spun therein.

Opposite Tudor Lodge he came to a halt, and, leaning on the gate, he lighted a cigarette and began to smoke it. Everything seemed just the same – a few more scraps of paper blown in by the wind perhaps, another empty tin or two lying about, but nothing more than that. He noticed that the window the football had smashed had not yet been mended. When he had finished his cigarette he decided it was time to get back to that awful treadmill of the anonymous letters, but first, he thought, he would stroll up the drive and back, keeping the while a cautious eye on the front door he more than half expected to see suddenly open to allow egress to some entirely new and still more panic-stricken personage. He noticed that the persevering spider whose work these recent comings and goings had destroyed had now respun its web across the door.

'Might be misleading, in some cases,' Bobby told himself. 'Easy to think a web like that has been in position much longer than it has in reality.'

In spite of his expectation the door remained closed, no fresh terror-stricken fugitive made any new appearance, and Bobby was in the act of turning away when some impulse he hardly understood, but that was, in fact, a proof of the extraordinary fascination the place exercised upon him, made him go to the door and knock.

There was no answer. He knocked again, and yet once more, and still there came no reply.

It might have been a house of the dead for all the answer that he got.

He could not help feeling a little disappointed. What he had expected he hardly knew, but certainly some development of some kind or another, not this blank unbroken silence.

'A house of the dead, it might be,' he muttered half aloud, as he turned away after a final, and again unanswered, hammering with the knocker.

Then he reflected that perhaps it was just as well no one had answered his summons, as he would have a difficulty in explaining what he wanted. He supposed he would have had to say he was selling vacuum cleaners or something of the sort. And then, after all, for many years past apparently, every knock upon that closed door had been ignored, just as his had been.

But he felt the thing was getting an obsession with him and he must stop thinking about it, and in this wise resolution he was confirmed when he observed a neighbour at a window of the house next door watching him with great interest and attention. Very likely she had seen him before in the company of Sergeant Wild, and would guess, therefore, that he was connected with the police. Only the good Lord knew what trail of gossip might now be started.

The last time, Bobby told himself with emphasis, Tudor Lodge was going to see him, or very likely some complaint would be coming in about police interference and spying.

So far as he was concerned the thing was done with. People might go running in and out of the house in all the stages of panic and terror they liked. It was no affair of his, Bobby repeated in his thoughts, and he wasn't going to run the risk of being asked by his superiors why he had been poking in his nose where it had no official business, and if there wasn't trouble enough in the world already for a harassed C.I.D. without going looking for more? So,

turning his back resolutely on Tudor Lodge and its unsolved problems, off he went at his best pace, without
once looking back, but well aware all the time of the neighbour's eyes following him with intense and eager interest
till he was out of sight.

As he had been rather longer away than he had intended,
he took a bus back to the Yard. He was entering the building when he saw his chief, Superintendent Mitchell,
approaching, and stood aside to allow him to enter first.

'Ah, Owen,' Mitchell said pleasantly. 'Nice weather
we're having ... I thought it looked a bit like rain though,
so I brought my new umbrella along.'

As he spoke he swung forward, carelessly, an umbrella
he was carrying; an expensive, brand-new, gold-mounted,
silk umbrella that, with eyes fairly popping out of his head,
Bobby recognised as his own – the one he had last seen
when he had also last seen Con Conway.

'Ah,' said Mitchell, 'admiring my new umbrella, I see –
not bad, is it?'

Bobby, quite unable to speak, gurgled some inarticulate
response.

'You're wondering,' observed Mitchell, in his most
thoughtful tones, 'how, in these days of cuts and income-
tax and breakfast bacon costing the eyes out of your head,
a poor devil of an overworked underpaid super can afford
a swell umbrella like this?'

'Yes, sir,' said Bobby faintly.

'Of course, really,' explained Mitchell, 'it's to impress
the Home Secretary next time there's a conference. Gold-
mounted, best silk cover,' Mitchell pointed out apprecia-
tively. 'Why, I haven't felt such a swell since I went court-
ing ... gives a man a leg up to be seen in the company of
an umbrella like that.'

'Yes, sir,' said Bobby, eyeing longingly his lost treasure,
as Mitchell, with a friendly nod, passed on.

But then the Superintendent turned back.

'After all,' he said, 'I don't much think it'll rain to-day, so you can keep it for me for the present, will you? I'll let you know when I want it again; next time I'm going to Buckingham Palace probably – and,' added Mitchell, 'take a tip from me. Next time a chap like Con Conway tries to touch you, watch out. Walking pensions some of his sort would make us, if we let them. I should like to see,' Mitchell went on, with a grim smile, 'any of them trying to get anything out of me, or Con Conway trying to touch me for two bob for bed and breakfast with a yarn about sleeping on the Embankment when he has a comfortable room of his own down Brixton way, and as likely as not something still left in the bank from the last job he did. There, take your umbrella, my lad; and remember, in our work it doesn't do to be soft with men like Con Conway. Let you down, they do, nine times out of ten, or a lot oftener than that.'

Chapter 8

THE YOUNG MAN

FORTUNATELY the spate of letters, anonymous and other, in the Notting Hill case had begun to abate, the later posts that day brought in a bare score of them, and Bobby, in spite of his lunch-time excursion, was able to get finished in quite reasonable time.

Next morning when he reached the Yard he was told there was a phone call for him, and when he answered it he found it was from Brush Hill – from Sergeant Wild.

'It's a bit rummy,' Wild explained over the wire, when Bobby got through to him. 'A lady came in last night about that Tudor Lodge. Says she lives next door.' (Bobby remembered, with some alarm, the patient watcher he had noticed at a near-by window the day before.) 'Says she used to see Miss Barton at night sometimes moving about, though she never gave anyone a chance to speak to her. Then she says, too, there used to be a light in the upstairs windows quite often, but there hasn't been recently, or any sign of the old woman herself either, and as the lady had seen us knocking – seems she saw you there yesterday, or so she says – she thought she would have a closer look herself. And when she was in the drive, prying around – only she doesn't put it that way – one of the windows on the ground floor next the front door on the left hand opened, and she saw a young man inside.'

'A young man?' Bobby repeated.

'She gives quite a good description of him – quite smart-looking, she says; quite the gentleman. Only – this is the funny part – she says he had a pistol in his hand, and was looking at it. What do you make of that for a yarn?'

'Sounds funny,' Bobby agreed. 'Is she sure it was a pistol?' he added, with arrogant masculine incredulity. 'Could it have been a cigar lighter, do you think?'

'Well, there's that,' admitted Wild, 'but she tells a good clear story, and she seems to have noticed everything about him from the colour of his tie to the shape of his nose. We think, here, we had better have a look round. Nothing in it, most likely, but you never know. Like to come along, if you can be spared, as you were with me when that girl came to the door? – and then there was that business about Con Conway.'

'Thanks awfully for telling me,' Bobby exclaimed eagerly. 'I'll come, if I can possibly wangle it. I'm sure it ought to be looked into.'

Probably the fact that he was a bit of a favourite with Superintendent Mitchell accounted for his success in obtaining this permission without too much trouble, though not without a sombre warning that if it turned out a wild-goose chase, and he proved to have wasted his morning and the time a hard-up country paid him for, then he must not be surprised if he found himself assigned to the next over-time job that came along.

Bobby reflected bitterly – though without saying so aloud – that probably that would have been his luck anyhow, especially if the job in question were rather specially dull, and, anyhow, the conviction that there was about Tudor Lodge something that needed investigation was growing ever stronger in his mind. Con Conway first and his strange panic, and then that young girl almost swooning with fear, and next the shop assistant on whom too the house had its influence of terror, and now this odd tale of a young man with a pistol in his hand.

Once he had the desired permission, it did not take him long to get to Brush Hill, where his ardour was a little damped by finding that the Inspector in charge didn't seem much interested.

'Old lady getting her friends to look her up at last,' he suggested. 'And there's a lot of young chaps like playing about with pistols – some of 'em don't even know they have to have a licence and are liable to a penalty without.'

But Wild had plainly been impressed by the story told by their visitor of the night before. She was a Mrs Rice, and as her husband was a wireless operator on one of the Australian boats, and so was frequently away for long periods at a time, she had a good deal of leisure, and spent a good deal of it at her window, surveying the activities of the world in general and of her neighbours in particular. Her story had been well and clearly told, and her account of the young man she had seen a really good one. She described him as tall, slim and dark, good-looking, with a small Grecian nose over a small well-shaped mouth with 'beautiful teeth' (Mrs Rice had grown almost lyrical over those teeth, which had evidently impressed her a good deal), and a round, slightly prominent chin. She spoke of his thin, dark, eager face, and of his well-knit, athletic form, and of a certain grace and ease in his bearing. She had noticed, too, his smart well-cut lounge suit ('West-end, if you ask me,' said Mrs Rice), his soft grey Trilby hat, and fashionable pigskin gloves. She had even noticed, and could describe his necktie ('wanted someone to choose it for him,' commented Mrs Rice – 'yellow and green in bars, it was, with blue and red spots, a fair horror, beats me how a smart young fellow, quite the gentleman, could go and spoil himself like that'), and equally well the pistol he had been holding, so that Bobby's tentative theory that it had really been a cigar lighter had to be dropped. Mrs Rice described it as small, with a gleaming mother-of-pearl handle, and it was clearly a revolver, not an automatic, and probably of a somewhat old-fashioned type.

All this had been carefully noted down, and, after Bobby had read it, he and Wild started off, the Inspector giving them a last sardonic warning to be careful what they did, and to mind they kept each other out of mischief.

'You haven't got a search warrant in your pockets, you know,' he reminded them; 'and remember, you'll easily get yourself into trouble if you try any breaking and entering and it turns out not justified.'

'Oh, no, sir,' protested Bobby. 'I'm sure we never thought of anything like that. We'll just have a general look round and see if Mrs Rice has anything more to say.'

'Well, perhaps its best not to let people have a chance of complaining we don't pay any attention to what they tell us,' admitted the Inspector, returning to his pile of reports and returns he was busy filling up.

But his observations had their effect on Wild, who began to look a little uneasy, and when they got to Windsor Crescent enquired, uncomfortably, how they were going to begin.

'We'll knock first,' Bobby said. 'All things in order.'

But to Bobby's knocking no answer came, and Wild said:

'You can knock for donkey's years, but you'll never get an answer – no one ever does.'

'No answer is a kind of answer just as not being is a kind of being, as someone once said, once upon a time,' Bobby observed. 'How about having a look at the side door?'

'May as well,' agreed Wild, 'but, if you ask me, there's nothing in it, except the old party's gone dotty living alone, and the young chap Mrs Rice saw was a doctor fetched in to have a look at her – very like by that smart little girl me and you saw, if you remember.'

Bobby agreed carelessly that he remembered her more or less clearly, but couldn't agree that the young man Mrs Rice talked about was likely to be a doctor.

'Why should a doctor be carrying a pistol?' he asked.

'Well, I suppose,' agreed Wild, 'it's more pills than pistols they use to finish you off with.'

Pleased with the good old fruity flavour of this jest, he went, quite willingly, with Bobby round to the side of the house. There everything appeared as it had done before. Bobby looked inside the outbuilding near the back door, and peered into the basket hanging there, wherein Humphreys' assistant had deposited the bread and tinned milk he had delivered. The basket was empty now, so presumably Miss Barton had come down later on to get her purchases. Bobby went back to the side door, and, while Wild looked on without much interest, he knocked. There was still no answer, so he tried the handle and found the door secure. He left it, and went to the still unmended window the football had broken. He said to Wild:

'How about getting in here?'

Wild hesitated. In the portly maturity of his twenty-two years' service he had no taste for scrambling through windows, even those on the ground floor. But Bobby was already on the sill.

'It can't have been open for years,' he said. 'The catch has rusted into place.'

But, if the rust of so many years had fixed the catch into place, it had also eaten its strength away, and as Bobby struggled with it, his hand through the gap the football had made, it gave way suddenly, breaking in half. With some difficulty still, Bobby forced up the reluctant sash and then stepped inside.

Within, the walls were black with the dust of years, the floor was covered with a damp and rotting oilcloth, and on the accumulated dust that covered it could be seen distinctly a trail of small footsteps, where, presumably, the girl they had seen there had come to retrieve the football she had returned to them. Neither table nor chairs were to be seen, but an old-fashioned mangle stood near one wall, and a small bracket supported one of the circular knife-cleaning machines, once so necessary an adjunct to every house. Both articles were so wreathed in cobwebs as to be hardly recognisable. In a corner stood the sink wreathed in cobwebs too, and with taps black with age and neglect.

'No one's been getting water here,' Bobby reflected. 'I wonder how they've managed? – bathroom, perhaps.'

The decrepit door, hanging insecurely on one hinge, the other having apparently crumbled away, stood half open. Bobby went through it and out into the passage, where, too, dust and grime lay everywhere, and cobwebs hung festooned on every side.

For a moment he stood still, and then, with the full force of his lungs, he shouted:

'Is there anyone here? Police making enquiries. Anyone here?'

His voice echoed strangely through the empty rooms and deserted passages, but no answer came. Only the spiders scuttled on the walls and the moths fluttered to and fro, and the astonished mice peeped from their holes to discover what was happening. Twice he repeated his summons, shouting with all his power. When he still got no reply, save that of the universal silence into which his loud cry entered and was lost, he went back to the side door. It was provided with a self-locking latch, easily opened from within. He opened the door, and said to Wild, waiting outside:

'I've been calling, but no one answered.'

'I heard you,' Wild said. 'Enough to wake the dead, it was.'

'It takes a lot to wake the dead,' Bobby answered,

shivering a little in spite of himself, for this strange, drear place was having its effect upon him.

'Well, what's the next move?' Wild demanded.

'Better have a good look round,' Bobby suggested.

'Suppose someone comes along, and wants to know what we're up to?' Wild asked uneasily. 'What'll we say?'

'Acting on information received, we felt it our duty to make enquiries to assure ourselves all was in order and no assistance required,' replied Bobby promptly. 'That's all.'

'Got a gift for telling 'em, you have,' Wild said, with grudging admiration, as he entered the passage. 'Comes of all this education, most likely. What's that noise?'

'Mice, that's all,' answered Bobby.

They walked along the passage, and entered a large room it led to that had evidently been the kitchen. It presented the same picture of utter desolation. At one side stood an enormous old-fashioned cooking range, and there was a huge open dresser occupying almost all one wall. There was an open knife-basket standing on it, containing knives of which rust had eaten away the blades, and spoons and forks that were quite black. On the floor, before one of the shuttered windows, was a broken bird-cage, that had apparently dropped when the cord whereby it had been suspended had rotted through. By the light of the electric torch Bobby was using in these dim places whence shutter and blind had excluded the light of day for forty years or more they could distinguish a pinch of dust at the bottom of the cage – all that was left, they supposed, of what once had been a pet canary, decayed there into that tiny residue. In this room, too, cobwebs hung everywhere, and spiders scuttled to and fro in alarm at so unwonted an intrusion upon their quiet. In one corner was a door, covered with cobwebs like a curtain. Bobby pulled it open, and found it admitted to a larder or pantry with many dishes, all empty, still standing there.

'Do you notice there don't seem to be any chairs, or any table either?' Bobby remarked.

'I never saw such a place in my life,' asserted Wild.

In the range, there were still a few cinders, or, rather, remnants of them that crumbled at a touch, and Bobby wondered to himself how long it was since last a fire had been lighted there to spread its friendly warmth through this dank place. They went back into the passage, and found another room that must have been a butler's pantry. There was a sink here that had evidently been in use at a not-too-distant date, and was probably where water had been obtained. Against one wall stood a safe. The door was open, and it seemed empty.

'Silver all gone,' Wild remarked. 'That's been seen to, anyhow.'

There were other domestic offices – all of them in the same state of neglect, all showing the same accumulated dust of years. They found some steps leading down to cellars, one evidently intended for coal, but swept quite clear, with not a trace of any coal left in it. Another had apparently been used as a kind of laundry, for it contained another mangle, and an old-fashioned stove for heating irons, and of a third the door was locked. Bobby hazarded a guess that it might be the wine cellar, and that possibly it might still hold wine though it had no appearance of having been opened for many years. Another cellar seemed to have been used chiefly for rubbish, empty bottles and jars, some rotting garden-hose, something that looked as if it had once been a sewing-machine, and so on.

'If you notice, there's no wood lying about,' Bobby observed. 'It looks to me as if anything with wood in it had been broken up, and the wood used for fuel. I shouldn't wonder if that isn't why Humphreys was never asked to supply any coal. The way the cellar's cleaned out looks to me as if what coal there was was used up first, and, after that, any wood that was handy. Strikes me that's why there don't seem to be any chairs or tables – they've all been smashed up for fuel, too.'

They went back up the steps, and then through to the

front of the house. Here, again, Bobby shouted, at the full strength of his lungs, to know if anyone was in the house, and again he got no reply.

Here, too, in this that had evidently been the part of the house occupied by its owners, there reigned everywhere the same complete desolation and neglect. Spiders and cobwebs were in full possession, and everywhere could be seen evidence of the ravages of damp and rust that for more than a generation had had their way unchecked. In one place, part of the ceiling had fallen, but evidently years ago, for the heap of plaster on the floor was black with age and covered with dust, and the scantling its fall had displayed was hidden under a curtain of cobwebs. At the back of the house, running nearly its full length, was the drawing-room, a fine, well-proportioned apartment, furnished in the style that was generally approved half a century ago – that is, with a great number of small, spindly chairs and occasional tables, a mahogany sofa, with a back and headpiece in carved scroll work, and an abundance of china ornaments, photograph-frames, and so on. The sofa itself and the armchairs still showed the antimacassars of the period, and on the open piano still stood a piece of music – a copy of Mendelssohn's 'Spring Song'. Bobby found himself wondering how many springs had come and gone since that had first been placed there.

'If you ask me,' said Wild, as though answering the thought in Bobby's mind, sinking, as he spoke, his naturally loud and cheery voice to the hoarse whisper he would have thought appropriate in church, 'there's been nobody in here for donkey's years.'

'Looks like it,' Bobby agreed; and added: 'Do you notice how many vases and bowls are standing about? They look to me as if they had all once had flowers in them.'

It was not too easy to see clearly in the obscurity of this closely shuttered room where no light had penetrated for so many years. But Wild went tiptoeing across the floor to examine more closely the bowls and vases Bobby referred to. He came back, and said:

'It's all turned to dust long ago, but there's been flowers in 'em all. When this room was shut up, it must have been a bower of flowers.'

They went out again into the passage, and Wild, wiping his forehead, said:

'Well, this beats me; never known anything like this since I joined the force.'

The room they entered next was evidently the one that had been the library, though the books that once had lined the walls were now piled upon the floor in a damp-stained, mice-gnawn confusion, while the shelves on which they had been ranged had apparently been torn down and taken away. The chairs, too, seemed to have been broken up, for remnants of what had apparently once been leather seats were piled in a corner. Attempts, too, had evidently been made to smash up the solid mahogany table, for it had had splinters broken off it and showed other marks of blows received, but the Victorian joiners had made it to last, and apparently the effort to reduce it to firewood had been turned to furniture of lighter make. From under it Wild produced a small hatchet, with an edge much used and battered.

'Looks like what was being used,' he observed. 'One way of getting firewood – smashing up the happy home all right.'

They went next into the room at the front of the house in which Mrs Rice said she had seen the dark young man with the pistol in his hand. It had probably been intended for the breakfast-room, and here all the furniture, or rather all of it that could be burnt, seemed to have disappeared. Against one wall lay a rotting pile of the upholstered seats and backs of chairs and so on, and in one or two places parts of the floor boarding had been pulled up, or attempts made to do so.

'Burning the house down bit by bit to keep herself warm

– that's what she was doing,' observed Wild. 'Well, I've never seen anything like this,' he repeated.

In the middle of the room, and reaching right across the floor to the inner wall, was that great pile of papers, circulars and unopened letters that Bobby had had a glimpse of before.

'Take some sorting out,' Bobby remarked, thinking ruefully of that pile of anonymous letters he had recently dealt with, and aware of a chilly fear that, if the need arose, he might very likely be allotted the job of going through this enormous accumulation.

They went back into the hall, and across it, and opened the door of the dining-room.

'My God!' Wild muttered. 'Look at that.'

Down the full length of the room ran a table, or, more probably, two or three put together, laid with linen that had once been white, with glass that once, no doubt, had shone, with silver now almost perfectly black, with plates and dishes, wine-glasses, decanters. At one end, the fire-place end, another table ran at right angles to the first, and on it stood an enormous five-tiered wedding-cake, crowned with Cupids and bells. Thanks to the thick coating of sugar covering it, and the fact that the stand on which it was placed had a stem spreading outwards at its summit, so that mice had not been able to climb up, this cake was the one thing in the house that appeared to have been able to resist the passage of the years. But for the thick dust that lay on it, and for a web a spider had spun from its culminating Cupid to a decanter near, still full of wine, it looked much as it must have done when it had first been placed there with pride and joy and laughter, symbol of present festivity and of happiness to come.

'My God!' Wild said again, more loudly; and a little mouse that had been sitting upright on the table, as if paralysed with surprise and indignation at this intrusion on its traditional privacy, gave a sudden squeak of protest and vanished in an angry scutter.

Chapter 9

THE SARATOGA TRUNK

GHOSTLY and strange beyond imagination showed in the dim light of that long-deserted room this table spread for a meal no guest had ever sat to, whereon the food and the drink had waited while the long years passed and wars and empires thundered to their end, where the empty chairs still stood in line ready to welcome the bridal party who never came, where the busy spiders span their webs about the five-tiered wedding-cake.

'Poor soul!' Wild said, below his breath, at last. 'Poor soul! But no police affair, and nothing we can do.'

Bobby did not reply, and Wild moved forward and slowly walked the length of the table behind the ranged chairs, and then came back to where Bobby stood.

'Hadn't we better go?' he asked. 'Somehow I wouldn't much like it if she came back and found we had been nosing round.'

But Bobby seemed hardly to hear; he was still deep in his own puzzled thoughts till, at last, he roused himself enough to ask:

'Do you think this explains it?'

'Well, don't it?' Wild retorted. 'Anyone can see what happened. Everything was ready, everybody all dressed up, most likely they went off to the church, and then something went wrong – the man never turned up, perhaps. Funked it at the last moment, and did a bunk, or else another woman waiting at the church to say he was married already – I've known it happen. The man who plays a trick like that wants shooting – only shooting's too good for him, and the woman often takes it hard like. It ain't so much being made a fool of, it's being – well,

mocked, if you see what I mean, so there's nothing ever
after you feel that you can trust.'

'I daresay a thing like that would take some getting over,'
Bobby agreed.

But he did not move, for his thoughts were still busy,
and Wild went back to look at the table again.

'Wine still in the decanters,' he said. 'There's what looks
as if it was an ice-pail, over there, with bottles of champagne
still in it. I wonder what the stuff's like now? Anyhow,
that's why the safe in the butler's pantry was empty – all
the silver laid out here, and all black as night, too, glass
and silver and all. Worth money, I should say. The table-
cloth's all rotten though, and the serviettes, too – moth,
most like. Lend me that electric torch of yours, will you?'

He took the electric torch Bobby had been using, and
by its light examined closely the dishes standing on the
table, untouched since first they had been placed there so
long ago. In some of them was visible a brown and crumbling dust, all that was left of the foods they had once contained. On others the mice had evidently held high revel,
bones they had gnawed clean lying where the busy little
creatures had deserted them when they offered no more
nourishment. And, over all, the ceaselessly working spiders
had spread their webs, as Time spreads its web of oblivion
over all the works of man.

'Mice been enjoying themselves here,' Wild remarked
presently. 'Must have been real, good, first-class tuck-out
all ready, and then the young man turned up missing,
and the girl shut the door, and all the guests went home,
tongues clacking like one o'clock, I'll be bound; and looks
as though not a soul had ever opened that door since until
you and me. First of all the food would go bad, and then
it would all dry up, what was left of it, and all the time the
mice as busy as you please, and after them the spiders.
If you've seen enough,' he added, to Bobby, 'what about
clearing out? Gives me the shivers in here, for it's more
like being in a grave than's right and proper before you're

dead. And now we know all about it, and why the poor old soul took to living the way she does, we've nothing more to do that I can see.'

'We hardly know all about it, do we?' Bobby said slowly. 'We know how it began, perhaps, but we don't know what made Con Conway run for his life the other night, or why that girl we saw here was in such a panic, or why the young chap Mrs Rice talks about was walking round with a revolver in his hand.'

'A place like this is enough to put the wind up anyone,' declared Wild. 'Why, I've a sort of feeling myself that, if we don't look out, past days will catch hold of us so we'll never get free again.'

'Yes, I know,' answered Bobby, shivering a little himself. 'But that's not the sort of fear that sends a man like Con Conway panicking through the streets full tilt, or makes you walk about with a revolver in your hand. And, whatever it was that scared them all, they all experienced it at different times and on different days. So, either it was something different each time – and what could happen in a house like this to frighten different people so badly on different days? – or else there is something here more than a wedding-breakfast laid out forty years ago and never eaten, something that frightens out of their lives everyone who sees it. And what can that be?'

Wild looked worried.

'Well, putting it like that – ' he conceded. After a pause, he added: 'I've never seen anything like this before – never.'

'I think we had better have a good look round,' Bobby said.

They closed the door of the room, and went back into the hall and up the stairs, whereon the rotting, mould-grown, moth-eaten carpet showed, however, some signs of occasional use.

On the first floor they entered, in succession, the two large bedrooms; each with a small dressing-room attached, that occupied the front of the house. All four apartments

presented the same spectacle of moth-eaten, mice-infested
desolation, with cobwebs and spiders triumphant everywhere, as though they knew the final victory was theirs.
Apparently a good deal of the furniture these rooms had
once held had been broken up for fuel, and even some of
the flooring had met the same fate, as had the door and
shelving of one or two cupboards. In one room where the
flooring had suffered most quite a big patch in one corner
having been pulled up, the carpet had been rolled right
back, preparatory, apparently, to further activities in the
same line.

'The old lady must have been getting pretty handy with
her little hatchet,' Wild remarked. 'She would have had
nothing but the four walls left, in time. Looks as if she
meant to have a good go at the floor here.'

'It's been swept carefully,' Bobby remarked. 'Do you
notice? From the door, right up to the gap in the floor
where the boards have been pulled up, the carpet's been
swept clean. I wonder what that was for?'

'Something came over the poor old crazy soul and made
her, I suppose,' Wild remarked.

They went into other rooms on the same floor; and, in
one at the back, noticed a kind of path, trodden quite
plainly across the rotting, moth-eaten carpet to the window.
It was an inch or two open, and from it they could see over
that wilderness to which the garden had reverted in the
course of forty years, so that the very paths were no longer
distinguishable, where, on what once had been the lawn,
weeds and grass grew knee-high, and even two or three
self-sown hawthorns flourished bravely.

'Look down there,' Wild said, and pointed to where,
below the window, against the side of the house, was an
enormous heap of wood-ash, some feet high and broad.
'When she had to clear out her fire, she must have just
brought the ash through here and tipped it out of the
window. It's a wonder anything of the house is left at all.'

'I expect very little wood would last her a long time,'

Bobby remarked. 'A chair a week, or something like that. I wonder how she got rid of her old tea-leaves, and so on – and the empty tins of condensed milk Humphreys says he supplies her with.'

'The tea-leaves would go down the drain,' suggested Wild. 'Most likely she dumped the old tins in the street.'

But, when they left that room and opened the door of the bathroom next to it, they found the tins there, hundreds of them, piled up till there seemed hardly room for any more.

'Never seen anything like it before,' Wild murmured. 'No, never. Lord, what a heap! What a life!'

'I am wondering where she can be now?' Bobby said.

'Gone away with some of the folk you saw here,' Wild answered promptly. 'And what scared 'em so, and made 'em look the way you say they did, was just their knowing they had to do it – and no wonder, with all this the way it is.'

'What about the revolver that last chap was carrying round with him, if it's like that?' Bobby asked. 'And what about Con Conway's scare?'

'Nothing to show,' Wild pointed out, 'Con was ever here at all, or knew anything about the place. It may have been something somewhere else put the wind up him.'

'Possible,' agreed Bobby. 'But a bit of a coincidence, all the same; and I like my coincidences explained, when possible. We ought to get hold of him somehow, and ask him to explain,' said Bobby, with a gleam in his eye, for it was not only of possible explanations he was thinking, but also of a little chat about that now recovered silk umbrella.

They continued their search, and in the last room they entered they found, at last, signs of recent occupation. It was a small room, plainly intended to serve as dressing-room to a larger apartment from which it opened. It was the room, Bobby thought, of which on one occasion he had noticed the window open, and when he looked out he saw that a gutter-pipe ran close by, so that Con Conway, with his ape-like agility, would have found no difficulty in climbing up to it. If so, it might be that, after entering through the window – but why should he want to enter an old deserted place like this? – he had met with some terrifying experience. Or else, perhaps, while looking in he had seen something that had been enough to send him in terror-stricken flight – but, yet, what was it conceivable there could be here to throw him into such an intensity of fear?

To one side stood a small iron bedstead, whereon was heaped an untidy and unclean confusion of blankets and other coverings. Against the wall opposite the window was an enormous Saratoga trunk of a kind much in favour fifty years ago, when travellers voyaged more heavily burdened than now. In the corner next to it lay a small heap of clothing - a seal-skin coat, very old and worn bare, the fur, indeed, nearly completely worn away, a woman's dress of old-fashioned make, and also very worn, one or two other articles of attire, all very old and used, and in-cluding a pair of ancient buttoned boots so badly worn they were nearly falling apart as they lay.

'Old things of hers she couldn't wear any longer and just flung 'em down there out of the way,' suggested Wild.

In the small fireplace were recent wood-ashes and an empty copper kettle, and in a corner near by was a heap of broken bits of wood. They seemed to have formed part of a chair, and evidently were intended for fuel. A few pieces of crockery, and some spoons, knives, and forks, were on a small table, and nearby was a battered old tin trunk that Wild reported, when he had looked inside, held an end of a loaf, very stale, a packet of tea, nearly finished, and a half-empty tin of condensed milk.

'Gave up everything else, pretty nigh,' Wild remarked, 'but not her tea – makes the old party more human like to think of her still enjoying her cup of tea, don't it?'

'That can't be the loaf I saw Humphreys' man leaving,'

Bobby remarked, in a puzzled voice. 'It's too stale, and she would hardly have got through the rest of it so quickly. That tin's been open some time, too – there was a new one with the fresh loaf he was bringing. What's become of it, and the loaf, too?'

'Took 'em with her when she went – why not?' Wild answered. 'No use leaving good food behind to waste.'

'She seems to have left plenty behind,' Bobby remarked. 'I wonder where she is – what can have become of her?'

'In some asylum or home, or somewhere like that, where her friends have put her – and time, too,' Wild answered. 'Look at this.'

He had picked up an old, high-heeled slipper that had been lying on the floor, near the door. Now yellow with age, it had evidently been white satin once. It seemed, however, to have escaped the moth and damp that had affected nearly all the other fabrics in the house, and indeed, everything else as well, and Bobby, turning it over in his hands, said:

'Look how down the heel is – it must have been worn a good deal. It can't have been lying aside somewhere, never touched, like everything else here.'

'No,' agreed Wild thoughtfully. 'No. Looks as though it had been worn quite a lot – sort of seems to go with the wedding-cake downstairs, don't it? Part of the bridal dress, very like.'

'If it is, I expect we shall find the rest somewhere about,' Bobby remarked.

'Perhaps she kept all her finery, and put it on sometimes,' Wild suggested. 'I've read something like that somewhere – about some man never turned up on his wedding-day, and, ever after, the girl would put on her wedding finery on the anniversary, once a year, on the same day, and sit and wait for him. Perhaps it was like that with her; and, if Con Conway did pay a visit here, that's what he saw and what scared him.'

'I think there must have been more than that,' Bobby said slowly.

He had noticed a small box that looked like a jewel-case lying on the floor by the side of the big Saratoga trunk. He picked it up. It was empty, but also, quite plainly, it had recently been forced open. The broken lock and the lid smashed right across were evidently both injuries that had been inflicted only a short time ago. He handed it to Wild.

'What do you make of that?' he asked.

Wild took it and examined it carefully, and began, now, to look more grave.

'Opened forcibly, and not long ago,' he said. 'Question is, was there anything in it, or was it empty?'

They stood for a moment or two, gravely considering the open case, and finding no answer to their question. Wild said:

'That might account for Con Conway; jewellery's always his game.'

But Bobby shook his head.

'I went through his pockets,' he said. 'He had nothing on him. Besides, this looks as if it had been broken open quite recently, not so long ago as when I saw him, and then, too, if he had collected anything worth having, he wouldn't have been drawing attention to himself by running the way he was.'

'My idea is,' persisted Wild, who, when he had an idea, did not give it up too easily, 'when they came to take her off to the home or asylum where she is now, she told them about some bits of stuff she kept in this case. Wouldn't be worth much, most likely, but she wanted to take her bits of things with her. She hadn't got the key, though, and couldn't find it, so they just broke it open.'

'What for?' Bobby asked. 'Why couldn't they take the box as it was?' He stooped down and picked up from the floor a small object he had just noticed. 'Is that a bead?' he asked, holding it out. 'Or is it a pearl? I don't think you often get a shine like that upon a bead; look at the light on it.'

Wild touched it almost reverently, and for a moment or two he was silent.

'It does look like a pearl,' he admitted; 'and a jolly fine one, too.' He tried to test its weight on the end of a piece of paper. 'If it is, it ought to be worth three figures or thereabouts,' he decided.

'It was lying on the floor there, just by that Saratoga trunk,' Bobby said.

'Well, let's see what's inside there,' Wild remarked.

He went across to it. He threw back the lid.

'God! My God!' he screamed. 'There's a dead man here.'

Chapter 10

MISS BARTON'S DISAPPEARANCE

THE crash of the falling lid that Sergeant Wild let slip from his startled hands almost drowned the loud cry wrenched from him by that sudden, dreadful sight. Bobby, too, absorbed in contemplation of the small, shining object he had just picked up, and the odd thoughts its discovery had roused in his mind, troubled still, in addition, by a doubt whether it was really a pearl of price or merely a manufactured bead, had not been paying his companion's activities much attention, and did not at first take in the full significance of his cry.

'What's that?' he said vaguely. 'Dead man? Where's a dead man?'

He was half smiling as he spoke, for he supposed at first that Wild was making some sort of obscure joke, since, indeed, had he been asked, he would have said there was no place here where a dead man could be, no place less likely in all the world than in the neglect and dirt and solitude of this old deserted house. But when he looked

round and saw Wild's ashen face, the gesture he was making with a shaking hand at the trunk by the side of the
room, Bobby realised that here was no question of any
pleasantry. All the same, it was in tones of complete bewilderment that he stammered out:

'A dead man? Why? Where? Dead ...?'

'In there,' Wild said, and pointed to the trunk.

He made no effort to approach the trunk again, but,
with a quick movement, Bobby crossed the room to it
and flung back its lid.

Within, he saw the crouched, the shrivelled, the almost
mummified figure of a man, huddled there in a ghastly
similitude of life, and yet in some way proclaiming, too,
that here death had brooded for years in terrible con-
cealment.

Bewildered and shaken, almost disbelieving his eyes that
showed him what so incredibly was there, Bobby stood in
silence, gazing down at the motionless body, and trying
to collect his thoughts the abrupt horror of this discovery
had scattered for the moment. The body was fully clothed,
and seemed, as far as could be judged from those shrivelled,
sunken features, to have been that of a young and good-
looking man. Peeping over Bobby's shoulder, Wild said,
in a whisper:

'Look at his head; the top of his head.'

Bobby nodded. Already he had seen and noted the small,
round hole there that told where a bullet, fired apparently
directly from above, as by someone crouching in a tree
or leaning over stairs, had penetrated downwards through
the skull, through the brain. Wild spoke again:

'Did the old woman know? She must have known.
Why did she never tell?'

'She must have known. How could she not have known?'
Bobby said, and the same thought and picture came into
both their minds – of that strange old woman passing in
this narrow room from youth to age in an existence that
had before seemed bizarre and pitiable enough, but

now had taken on an aspect of almost unbelievable horror.

'She must have known,' Bobby repeated. 'Think of it, living alone for forty or fifty years with – with That.'

'Where is she? What's become of her?' Wild said, looking all around as if expecting to perceive her now in some equally strange, incredible hiding-place.

'We must report at once,' Bobby said.

'What's it been?' Wild asked. 'Suicide, accident ... murder?'

'I never heard of a man shooting himself down through the top of his head like that,' Bobby said slowly. 'Besides, that shot was fired from some distance. If it was only accident, why was the body hidden? It looks to me like murder – murder long ago.'

'There's that wedding feast downstairs no one ever came to,' Wild said slowly. 'Seems to me perhaps this accounts for that ... I thought at first it meant the man had funked it at the last moment, as they do at times, and let the girl down, but now –' He made a gesture with his hand towards the shrivelled body in the trunk. 'Is that the man?' he asked. 'Is that why he never came to his wedding?'

'It looks as if it might be that,' Bobby agreed. 'Perhaps there was a quarrel, or she found out something ... perhaps, then, she hid the body in that trunk she may have bought for the honeymoon tour, and dressed for her wedding and waited, while the guests all came and wondered why he didn't, and said how cruel it was to treat a girl like that, and then one by one they went – and left her alone; alone with her trunk and – That.'

'Eh, now, then,' Wild muttered, 'if it was like that, what a thing to happen; what a way to live.'

And they were both silent, trying in a kind of haze of incredulous amazement to realise that something of that nature must have been; to imagine the existence led all through the long and solitary years, for a full half-century, perhaps, by this woman in her lonely room, her sole companion the dreadful occupant of the Saratoga trunk. There she had lived with her appalling secret from the day when the wedding festivities had been made all ready till now when at last had come to light the secret of that murder of long ago.

'It don't bear thinking of,' Wild said, at last. 'Enough to drive you dotty ... no wonder she went like she is. Where is she now, though?'

'We must make sure she's nowhere in the house,' Bobby said; 'and then, I suppose, we had better get along and report.'

'Most likely she's gone off with one of the parties you've seen here,' Wild suggested. 'Perhaps with the smart-looking girl that was here that other time. Can they have known, any of them? I can't hardly believe, myself, that poor old thing could ever do such a thing. I saw her once – a little thin faded wisp of a woman you could have blown away as soon as look at.'

'I daresay she wasn't always like that,' Bobby said. 'I daresay, then, she was – different. It's forty or fifty years ago, and in forty or fifty years ...'

He left the sentence unfinished, his hot and lusty youth brought, as it were, for the first time face to face with the supreme mystery of time that slips by like a dream and yet bears all substantial things away.

'That's right,' agreed Wild. 'When you're young, you're different; and very likely she was too, same as you say. Can she have known we were coming, and bunked off because of that?'

'How could she have known, when we didn't know ourselves?' Bobby asked. 'Besides, she had nothing to do but show herself at the window and beckon us to go away. We had no real suspicions; no search warrant; no grounds for breaking in. She was safe enough so long as she stayed here; perhaps that's why she did stay here.'

'Well, she's gone,' said Wild. 'What I'm wondering is, how the body's gone like that, all shrivelled up and mum-ified, like it is. Can she have done anything to it?'

'The doctors may be able to tell,' Bobby remarked.

All this time he had been holding in his hand the pearl – or bead – they had found. He put it down now, carefully, on the mantelpiece – on a sheet of paper he tore from an old letter he had in his pocket.

'I am wondering, if that comes in, where it comes in,' he said; and then he went across to the satin shoe they had noticed lying on the floor, and looked at it closely again, and put it down beside the pearl – or bead. 'And that – where does that come in?' he said. 'For it looks to me as though it had been worn.'

'Most likely she just kept it out of sentiment, as you might say,' Wild suggested. 'I remember my old woman kept a piece of our wedding-cake for years, till our youngest but three found it and ate it, and, after that, the two of us had to stop up with her all night, her being green in the face and yelling so we almost thought she was going to peg out, same as all the neighbours hoped so they could get to sleep again.'

'It does look as if it were part of the wedding dress,' Bobby agreed. 'Only, it looks as if it had been a good deal worn, and there doesn't seem to be anything else of the sort lying about – no bridal veil or wreath, or even another shoe. You know, it's just struck me, perhaps it's that trunk scared Con Conway, if she ever opened it. If he climbed up to that window and was looking in, and she opened the thing, and he saw what was in it, it would give him a large-size scare.'

'Why should Con be trying to break into a place like this?' demanded Wild; 'all dirt and damp and just one old woman living in it. Conway goes where the big stuff is.'

'Yes, I know,' Bobby agreed. 'Only, there's that,' he added, nodding towards the pearl – or bead – he had placed on the mantelpiece. 'If that's what I think it is,' he said, 'and if there were more of the same sort in the old jewel-case someone's been smashing open recently, or, for that matter, if Con Conway only thought so – well, he would be after the stuff quick enough.'

'That's right,' Wild confessed. He went across to look at the bead - or pearl - again. 'Looks a bit of all right,' he said. 'But one of our chaps - Turner, I think - saw the old party later that same night, and she seemed O.K., and didn't say a word about having been robbed or anything.'

'Conway may have come back again later on,' Bobby suggested. 'Or, if he had been too badly scared for that, he may have passed his story on to some pal or another. It's just possible that's what that girl was doing here – the one we saw, I mean. I'm sure there was someone else in the house at the time, in spite of what she said.'

'She looked all right,' Wild said doubtfully. 'Of course, some of 'em do – some what's mixed up with the Con Conway sort, I mean. Their stock-in-trade to look O.K.'

'It's only an idea,' Bobby went on slowly, 'but it's possible someone after the pearls calculated it would be easier to win the old lady's confidence and get admittance to the house by the help of a smart nice-looking girl. Only, then, what has that fellow with the pistol Mrs Rice says she saw got to do with it? And what's become of Miss Barton herself? Has she gone into fresh hiding because she was afraid of her secret getting known? Or has she been taken away by friends, or what's happened? We had better make sure she's nowhere in the house, and then one of us can report while the other waits here in case she turns up - or someone else.'

'We've looked everywhere already,' Wild remarked.

'Not in the attics,' Bobby reminded him.

But when they ascended the stairs leading to the second and top floor, the dust that lay thickly everywhere, covering the landing like a fall of snow, and obviously undisturbed for many years, offered good proof no one recently had visited these upper portions of the house.

They went downstairs again, and Wild proceeded to report while Bobby waited, smoking a cigarette, till presently Mrs Rice, who from her accustomed post of observation at her window had been an interested spectator of as much of all this as she could see, appeared and introduced herself. So Bobby was very polite and amiable, and thanked her warmly for the assistance she had been, and then proceeded, very gently, to see if she had any more information she could supply. All they knew at present, he explained, was that Miss Barton wasn't in the house, and there was nothing to show what had become of her. Of the grisly discovery that had, in fact, been made, he said nothing as yet, for discretion is the first of all departmental virtues, but he explained that it was feared some accident might have happened, and enquiries would have to be made at the hospitals and elsewhere to see if she could be traced. He added that if Mrs Rice could tell, or had heard or seen anything likely to help in the quest, he hoped she would be sure to give full information of it at once.

So Mrs Rice explained, on her side, that she wasn't one to interest herself in other folks' business, and, if it was gossip Bobby wanted to hear, it was somewhere else he would have to go. This firmly established, and by Bobby fully and frankly accepted, Mrs Rice went on to admit that those who did like talking about their neighbours' affairs talked a good deal about Miss Barton. It seemed there really was some vague story current in the neighbourhood about her having been crossed in love when she was a girl, though this story was but a feeble one, flickering, indeed, to extinction, since it seemed difficult to associate that flitting, ghost-like form with any tale of love, or to relate the sad, eccentric, solitary existence of the half-crazed old woman with any suggestion of youth and joy and passion. Impossible, indeed, most seemed to have found it to imagine her as ever young at all, yet, indeed, spring flowers for us all, though winter waits behind, and for Bobby there was evidence enough in the dreadful discovery they had made in the room above that strange and awful passion had once held sway in this old, sad, moth-eaten, mouse-ridden residence.

Mrs Rice, however, gave no hint that anyone had ever suspected Miss Barton of possessing any money, or of there being anything worth stealing in the house. None, indeed, of the stories about her seemed to have been of a nature likely to attract gentlemen of Con Conway's profession.

Further talk revealed that Mrs Rice had observed and been much interested in the appearance of the girl who had on one occasion opened the door to Bobby and to Wild. Mrs Rice knew all about that, and, indeed, Bobby was soon convinced that not much that had happened during the last few days – or probably at any other time – in that neighbourhood had escaped her attention.

She had been a spectator, for instance, from her vantage post at her window, of Bobby's brief encounter with Humphreys' assistant making one of his regular bi-weekly calls with the bread, the tea, the tinned milk that, with occasional matches and candles, seemed to have been all Miss Barton had needed during her long years of solitude.

Mrs Rice had not seen Miss Barton for some days, but there was nothing unusual in that – often a week or more would pass without any glimpse of her, and then the little worn old woman would be seen again, slipping, like the shadow she almost seemed, up or down the Tudor Lodge drive on one of her rare excursions into the outer world.

'One had only to say a good night to her,' declared Mrs Rice, somewhat resentfully, 'and she would be off like a mouse bolting back into its hole when it sees a cat – and there didn't seem much more to her than a mouse either. A good meal, and plenty of them, was what she wanted, but what could you do when she scuttled away the moment anyone spoke?'

'Nothing,' Bobby ageed, and when he asked what Miss Barton generally wore, the answer so interested him that he went upstairs and brought down the worn seal-skin coat and old black frock and other things that had been lying by the side of the Saratoga trunk.

Mrs Rice identified them instantly, recognising, especially, the worn seal-skin, and an old-fashioned bonnet, with strings, that had formed part of the pile.

'Well, now,' she exclaimed, handling this last item. 'Never once have I seen her not wearing that – I used to say she went to bed in it, and I daresay she did, too; and my hubby said once – when he caught sight of her for a minute, slipping along up the garden path to the house, just like a leaf the wind was blowing – that someone ought to give her a good price for it, so it could be put in the London Museum along with the other funny things people used to wear,' said Mrs Rice, proudly conscious of her own quite up-to-date attire, with a butterfly bow of which the ends could almost have met behind her back, bare arms except for gloves whereof the gauntlets nearly reached the elbows, stockingless legs, and a hat like a saucer perched insecurely on a head cropped like a convict's.

'And the seal-skin coat,' Bobby asked; 'you can swear to that, too?'

Mrs Rice could, So, she supposed, could everyone else who had ever seen Miss Barton. The quaint old bonnet and that seal-skin worn nearly smooth were not things anyone could forget once they had been seen.

'Well, she doesn't seem to be in the house now,' Bobby remarked; 'so she must have got a new outfit before she went out.'

Mrs Rice fairly giggled at the idea of Miss Barton in a new outfit. It seemed so funny somehow. However, there were Miss Barton's clothes, and no Miss Barton, so evidently she must have changed her attire – a point Bobby thought of interest.

But now Mrs Rice went on to tell an interesting story of how she had seen a stranger looking at the house a few days ago – she couldn't be sure when, she was one of those persons always a little vague about dates, but she thought more than a week ago, though it might not have been as long as that, or, again, it might have been longer still. She had noticed, specially, that he was wearing plus-fours, a form of garment much favoured by Mr Rice when at home, and one in which a gentleman always looked a gentleman, provided, of course, he had the legs for it. But for his plus-fours suit she would have thought the stranger an enterprising house agent on the look-out for possible business – house agents sometimes came to try to get Tudor Lodge on their books for selling or letting – or even a man delivering circulars, little they cared whether they pushed their circulars into an occupied or unoccupied house. The plus-fours suit, attire seldom seen in Brush Hill except on Sundays and holidays, and the way in which its wearer had hung about staring up at the house as if specially interested in it, had attracted Mrs Rice's attention so much that she had watched him for some time. Unfortunately he had been wearing a peaked cap, pulled well down over his face, and she had not been able to see his features very plainly, and could give little description of them, or, indeed, of him, except, always, for his suit of plus-fours in well-cut tweed. Unfortunately, too, a smell of burning from her kitchen across the landing had summoned her post haste to attend to the cake she had in the gas-oven there. When she returned – the cake, fortunately, little the worse – the plus-fours stranger was still there, indeed, but in the act of departing. Mrs Rice had watched him cross the street towards Osborne Terrace, and immediately afterwards she had also seen Miss Barton come slipping out from the side door in her usual silent, ghost-like fashion, almost as though she were following the plus-fours stranger.

Mrs Rice had not seen the stranger again. She could not say for certain whether or no she had noticed Miss Barton on any later occasion, but was quite clear she had never once seen her except wearing the seal-skin coat and the bonnet Bobby had just displayed.

'If I had seen her in anything else,' declared Mrs Rice,

'I should have thought the end of the world had come.'

Nor had she seen any other stranger near the house, but, obviously, others might have been without her knowledge.

'I'm not like some,' Mrs Rice explained, a little proudly. 'I'm not at my window all day long, just staring. Of course,' she added with perfect justice, 'no one can help seeing what's going on before their own eyes.'

Bobby agreed that that was indeed impossible, and, in reply to other questions, found that Mrs Rice had been an interesting spectator of the arrival of the girl who had opened the door once to himself and to Wild. Mrs Rice had observed every detail of that interview, and also had watched, earlier, the girl's arrival, had noticed that she seemed nervous and had hesitated a good deal, apparently, and not unnaturally, disliking the deserted and gloomy appearance of the house. Finally, she had gone round to the side door, which had immediately been opened for her, before she had time to knock even, exactly as though she had not only been expected, but watched and waited for. The description Mrs Rice gave of her, and especially of her clothing, was extremely good and clear – a fact of some importance, since it suggested that her description of the young man of the pistol whom she said she had seen would be equally accurate, and that her account of his tie, for example, was probably as exact as her exhaustive tally of the girl's frock and accessories.

'A smart little three-piece,' she said, adding loving detail: 'and all to match – bag, scarf, and gloves – all very smart; she looked a real tip-topper, and might have stepped straight, that very minute, from behind the counter of one of the big West-end shops.'

To her story of the young man with the pistol she had nothing to add, but there could be no doubt of its having been actually, and in fact, a small revolver that he had in his hand, for on that point, as on others, she was clear and precise.

Apart from these three visitors, however, and, of course, excluding Bobby himself and Sergeant Wild, and various routine callers, such as the occasional postman delivering an 'or occupier' circular, the bill distributor, too tired and indifferent to care whether he deposited at an inhabited or uninhabited house his announcements of the 'unparalleled, unrepeatable sacrifices' some drapery firm was making in its altruism, or Humphreys or his assistant making their usual delivery calls, and so on, Mrs Rice had seen no one. Nor could she remember having seen Miss Barton since the day of the visit of the plus-fours stranger, or even, since then, any light at any of the windows of Tudor Lodge. But she added, spontaneously, that Miss Barton was so small and slight and shrunken her comings and goings were hardly more noticeable than those of a withered leaf blowing to and fro along the drive. Then, too, it was often dusk when she made her rare appearances outside the house, but it was very unusual for no flickering candle-light to show during the evening at one window or another.

In answer to a final question Bobby asked, Mrs Rice declared, with emphasis, that she would certainly be able to recognise again both the pretty girl of the smart 'three-piece' and also the young man of the revolver. But the stranger in plus-fours she had only had a glimpse of, and that, too, at a moment when the daylight was failing. She admitted, reluctantly, that she hardly thought she could be sure of knowing him again; and then they heard the sound of an approaching car, heralding the arrival of Superintendent Mitchell and his assistants.

Chapter 11

THE SEARCH BEGINS

IT was not only one car that arrived, but two, and the already simmering excitement of the neighbourhood rose to boiling-pitch when from the first car there descended Superintendent Mitchell, a doctor, and Inspector Ferris, and from the second car a photographer, finger-print expert, and two C.I.D. men, together with Sergeant Wild, for whom they had called at the Brush Hill police-station. True, of these, only Sergeant Wild was in uniform, but this sudden irruption in his company of all these official-looking persons, mostly 'out-size', presented no difficulty of interpretation to the Windsor Crescent onlookers.

The cars had drawn up exactly in front of Tudor Lodge. One chauffeur remained on guard at the entrance to the drive, in order to keep in check the rapidly growing crowd. The other was stationed at the front door, to act there as a second line of defence. The rest of the party entered the hall, where Bobby was waiting with Mrs Rice, who by now was enjoying herself as thoroughly as the artist watching a crowd before his Academy picture, as the author surveying a special 'window display' of his new book, as the actor acknowledging yet another call before the curtain.

Bobby introduced her to Mitchell, who, without her quite understanding how, cut short the long and detailed story she was preparing to tell, got the gist of it out of her by two or three well-directed questions and then disposed of her by instructing one of the C.I.D. men to take her statement in full.

'In full, mind,' said Mitchell, firmly, to the C.I.D. man. 'I'm sure Mrs Rice realises how important it is she should mention every detail, no matter how small and unimportant she may think it, and how necessary it is to get it down in writing before anything's forgotten.'

Slightly bewildered, a good deal flattered, a little wistful as she gradually realised that she was thus missing the opportunity she had been looking forward to of seeing all over mysterious Tudor Lodge, which she understood was about to be searched again from top to bottom in case Miss Barton were still there, only somehow, somewhere, concealed – for as yet, of course, Mrs Rice knew nothing of the dark discovery made – she found herself escorted back to her own domain ('can't ask a lady to stop around in all this dust and dirt,' explained the C.I.D. man amiably), and there was torn between the joy and interest of delivering a monologue to an attentive young man, who took it all down in shorthand, and her intense longing to know what was going on in Tudor Lodge, and what, indeed, as she comprehensively phrased it, 'everything was all about'.

'And now that good lady's out of the way,' Mitchell had said, with a sigh of relief, as he saw her shepherded safely back to her own quarters, 'carry on, Owen'.

In succession Bobby showed the dining-room with its strangely pathetic, strangely dreadful wedding feast that for half a century or so had waited the guests that never came, the drawing-room where the little brown heaps of dust were all that remained to tell of the flowers that on that day so long ago must have made it a bower of beauty and sweet scent, and then upstairs, while the dust rose up in clouds and the moths flickered to and fro and the spiders scuttled on the walls, to the room where stood the Saratoga trunk with its grisly occupant, the shrivelled shrunken casket of what once had held the spirit of a man.

'What do you make of that, doctor?' Mitchell asked, as they stood clustered in silence around the trunk, of which Bobby had lifted the heavy lid.

'Never seen anything like it,' the doctor answered, unconsciously echoing Sergeant Wild. 'That bullet wound in the head shows how the poor devil was killed, but I don't quite know how to account for the mummified condition of the body – not off-hand.'

'Shall you be able to say how long the body's been like that?'

'Not much nearer than "many years," I don't suppose,' the doctor answered. 'Quite outside my experience, though – perhaps a closer examination may show something. Don't altogether see why the body should have gone that way. It might be due to the heavy lid shutting off all air – that Saratoga trunk is practically airtight – and then, if the room's been used for living in, with a fire and all that, the atmosphere would be drier than elsewhere; possibly there's been a kind of drying effect. Curious, though. Quite possibly there's some other cause been operating. I can't say for certain as yet.' He paused and turned to Owen. 'Do you say an old woman has been living here in this room with – with That?' he asked, nodding towards the poor shrivelled remnant of humanity they had now extracted from the trunk and laid as decently as they could upon the floor.

'It looks like it, sir,' Bobby answered; and for a little they were all silent, trying to realise what that lonely life must have been, dragged on through all the passing years with such a secret for companion by day and by night.

'Never seen anything like it,' the doctor repeated; and then: 'That room downstairs with the tables laid out, and a wedding-cake and all – was this the chap?'

'Looks as if it might be that way,' agreed Mitchell. 'Looks as if everything was got ready, and, when he never came, there they were all waiting and wondering and whispering – and only she knew why, she and the Saratoga trunk. And, when they had all gone, she must have come up here all alone, for she wouldn't dare let anyone else in the room, and ever since –'

He stopped abruptly. He was not a man easily moved, for his long experience had known many tragedies, but now his voice was shaken, and he put up a hand as in a defensive gesture, as if to keep off thoughts that were past endurance. Ferris said, from behind:

'It don't bear thinking of. Enough to give you dreams all night.'

'No wonder, anyhow,' remarked the doctor, 'that she lived all alone. No wonder she didn't dare let anyone else in. I wonder if the others in the house, her family or friends or whatever they were, knew what had happened, and if that's why they all cleared out and left her to it?'

'It might have been that – they may have suspected something,' Mitchell remarked. 'But how has she managed to live? She must have got money somehow.'

'We found this on the floor, sir,' Bobby said, showing the pearl – or bead – he had placed on the mantelpiece. 'I don't know if it's worth anything, but it looks as if it might be. And we found this box with the lid broken,' he added, producing it. 'If that is a real pearl, she may have had jewels she's been selling, and that's all that's left now. Perhaps that might be why she felt she had to make a change – because she had nothing left to sell.'

Mitchell was examining the pearl closely. He knew something of precious stones, and was soon able to decide that it was not only genuine, but a very fine specimen, probably worth well over three figures.

'If she's been selling much of this sort of thing,' he remarked, 'we ought to be able to trace it.' He picked up the jewel-case, if that is what it was, that Bobby had produced. 'Broken open quite recently,' he remarked. 'What was that for?'

'Just possibly,' Bobby suggested, 'if someone's been to fetch her away, they wanted to see if any of her jewellery was left, and if they were in a hurry or impatient, or perhaps the old lady was a bit excited and couldn't find her key, then the lid was smashed to save time.'

'Possible,' agreed Mitchell, 'Only, she certainly wasn't quite at the end of her resources with a pearl like this to sell.'

'Then there's this, too,' Bobby went on, producing the white satin shoe they had noticed lying on the floor.

Mitchell examined it carefully.

'Looks like part of the wedding outfit,' he observed. 'The heel's a bit down, too. Looks as if it had been worn quite a lot – the satin is nearly through at the toe as well.'

'I remember reading once,' Inspector Ferris put in, 'about a case something like this, and the poor old girl who had been jilted on her wedding day used to dress up in her bridal togs every time the anniversary came round.'

'It may have been like that here,' Mitchell agreed. 'Notice any more of a bridal costume anywhere about?'

'No, sir, but of course we weren't looking for anything like that.'

'It's a point to see about,' observed Mitchell thoughtfully. 'Make a note of it; it might turn out important. If that shoe is part of a bride's outfit, the rest of it ought to be here, too; and if it isn't –'

He broke off, evidently considering some idea that had occurred to him, and Bobby, making the note as ordered, wondered what Mitchell had in his mind. For his own part he did not see at the moment what an old bridal dress had to do with it, or how its absence or presence could affect the present puzzle of what had become of Miss Barton. She could, he supposed, hardly have been wearing it when she disappeared.

'What's your theory, Owen?' Mitchell asked abruptly.

'Well, sir,' Bobby answered slowly, 'I thought it might be that Miss Barton's friends or relatives had begun to wonder about her, and the young lady we saw had come to see if she was still alive – or perhaps to find out what had happened to the house. I suppose it must belong to some-one, and be worth money still.'

'But I thought,' Mitchell pointed out, 'she told you she wasn't any relation?'

'There is that,' Bobby admitted. 'But there might be some sort of connection, perhaps. Anyhow, from what Mrs Rice says, she was expected; so, either she had been here before – but Mrs Rice says she seemed to be a stranger to the place, and, also, she is quite sure she hadn't seen her before, and Mrs Rice is a lady who doesn't miss much of what goes on – or else there had been letters. The young lady was very nervous, and seemed very upset, when we saw her, but I suppose that might be natural enough in a house like this. Enough to upset anyone, especially if they had seen –' He paused and looked down at that withered thing upon the floor round which they were all clustered. 'It is possible,' he went on, 'she managed to persuade Miss Barton to leave here, and that she found some place for her where the old lady could be looked after. Or it's possible Miss Barton thought she had better find a fresh hiding-place herself – if it's the fact Con Conway had seen inside the trunk and that's what frightened him. Perhaps that is why the girl we saw came here; perhaps Miss Barton sent for her to take her away somewhere where she thought she would be safer now her secret was known to someone else. Or, of course, she may have gone away by herself to some new hiding-place.'

'Would she go like that and leave the trunk behind, and what she knew was in it?' Mitchell asked doubtfully. 'After so many years ...? What about the man in plus-fours Mrs Rice says she saw? Or her story about a young man with a pistol? I suppose she's not just telling fairy-tales, is she?'

'Oh, I don't think so, sir,' Bobby answered. 'The plus-fours man very likely has nothing to do with it – just a stranger curious why a house was standing derelict like this, or, it might be, a house agent on the look-out for new property to get on his books. And if Miss Barton has gone to some friend or relative, the young man with the pistol may be someone come to fetch something for her, or even just to look round. Possibly, if she had some more jewels left, he came for them. He may have had to break open the box to get them if he had no key, and, if the jewels were valuable, that might be why he brought a pistol.'

'I don't see why he couldn't put the jewel-case in his pocket, if that's what he was after,' observed Mitchell, 'instead of breaking it open and dropping pearls worth three figures. And, even if he had a pistol with him, I don't see why he should be flashing it about in a perfectly empty house, or why he should be looking at it in the way Mrs Rice describes. Not much use speculating, though, till we know more about the facts. I don't know that there's much in the clothes she usually wore being left behind here. If someone came and fetched her, they would be very likely to provide her with some sort of new outfit; and if she were bolting, in a scare, to a fresh hiding-place on her own, because she thought it was known what was in the Saratoga trunk, it would be natural for her to try to dress differently.'

'There's one thing certain,' observed the doctor suddenly. 'It's been murder all right enough; no man could very well himself put a bullet right down through the top of his own head.'

'Not much doubt of that,' agreed Mitchell. 'She'll have to be found; though whatever she did so long ago, and whatever made her do it, she's paid for long since by the life she's led. But murder is still murder, no matter how many years past; and we've our duty to do, and we'll have to try our best to find her. Anyhow, no one will want to hang her now, but, all the same, I almost hope we don't succeed.'

Chapter 12

FULL CRY

ALL the customary routine had now to be gone though: innumerable photographs to be taken, sketches to be made, the finger-print expert let loose, the coroner informed, and so on; and in the midst of it all there arrived, first, a fast motor-car containing the crime expert of the *Daily Announcer*, and then, hard upon his wheels, more fast motor-cars containing all the other crime experts of all the other national papers. Already, in some mysterious fashion – probably by black magic – all Fleet Street knew that something sensational had happened in the Brush Hill district, where hitherto the most exciting event ever known had been the scene in which a leading local Fascist (*aetat* 18) had exchanged rude repartee with a prominent Communist (*aetat* 17½) of the neighbourhood, both of them probably destined to be good sound solid Tory voters before many more years had passed.

But these journalistic gentlemen knew well enough that Superintendent Mitchell did not depart hurriedly in a fast car for remote suburbs without good reason, and were not to be satisfied with mere words. So Mitchell decided that, after they had promised on their journalistic faith – an undertaking more sacred to their hard-boiled, hard-bitten souls than an oath under seven seals – not to release the story till leave was granted, they were to be given full details, and even allowed to take as many photographs as they liked.

'You see, boys,' Mitchell explained to them himself, with the amiability he always showed to journalists – though they little guessed, or cared, what he sometimes said about them, when they weren't there – 'you see, boys, we want, if we can, to get on the track of the old lady who was living here before the friends she's gone to, or who have taken her away, if that's the truth of it, have any idea we are looking for her. As soon as this gets known, most likely it'll be ten times harder to find her. Also, there's just the chance that, if we lie low, someone may come back here.'

'How long do you want it held up?' the *Daily Announcer* man asked anxiously.

'Not practicable more than a day or two,' Mitchell answered, thinking to himself that, if only the black magic of the newspaper men had been a little less efficient, he might have held it up much longer.

'Right-oh,' said the *Daily Announcer* man. 'The best story,' he declared enthusiastically, 'since – since –' He paused, searching his memory for the last comparable announcement with which the Press had been privileged to shake the nation to its depths. 'Since Larwood said he wouldn't play in our garden any more,' he declared at last, and all his colleagues agreed that it was so.

So then they departed to their note-taking, their photographing, their interviewing, though the petition put forward by one of them – that the poor shrivelled body should be replaced in the Saratoga trunk so that a snap could be taken of it, *in situ* – Mitchell declined to accede to, thereby showing, it was generally felt, a deplorable lack of right feeling of what was due to the great British public; his plea in excuse – that even so poor a relic of humanity as this should be treated with respect – being regarded as weak sentimentalism, and a proof of the softness of the age. However, they were all pleased and excited at the prospect of having such a story to present to their editors, and at being allowed to photograph everything they wanted to, till, in the room where that sad wedding feast had stood in solitude and neglect so many years, the flashlights flared like summer lightning by the sea on a hot August evening, while the cameras clicked ceaselessly, and the poor spiders were driven almost to distraction. Also, the gentleman who had first made the suggestion about the Saratoga trunk accepted Mitchell's decisions very meekly, and, indeed, supported it warmly, only revealing, when all his colleagues had departed, that the splendid idea had occurred to him of himself crawling into the now empty trunk and getting his assistant to photograph him in the exact position in which the body was when found. Thus his proud editor was able to feature the now famous photograph on the front page, marked, with justifiable pride, 'Exclusive to Us', and thus was a 'scoop' effected of which Fleet Street still talks with admiration and awe.

All this being settled, and Inspector Ferris being fully

competent to attend to the further detail of the usual
routine, Mitchell departed, taking with him the pearl – or
bead – Bobby had found, and beckoning to Bobby himself
to accompany him.

'First thing,' Mitchell explained, 'is to make sure whether
this pearl thing is the genuine article or not.'

After that he lapsed into silence, for he was a man who at
times could sit without uttering a word, and at others
would pour out an unbroken torrent of speech. The only
remark he made during the rest of the drive was when he
said once, more to himself than to Bobby:

'You know, that satin shoe may mean a lot.'

'Yes sir,' agreed Bobby dutifully, though wondering
how or why.

Outside a well-known jeweller's establishment the car
stopped, and Mitchell alighted and entered the shop. He
came out again in a few minutes.

'Valued at two hundred, or a little more,' he told Bobby.
'That is, buying price – selling price probably three times
as much, but I didn't ask about that. As one of a well-
matched necklace, it's value would go up fifty per cent, or
possibly more. If the old lady has been living by selling
little things like that, it shouldn't be difficult to trace the
transactions. Have to go into that. Anything you can think
of you would like to follow up yourself, Owen?'   ·

'Well, sir,' Bobby said slowly, 'I think one of the first
things to do is to try to get in touch with Con Conway, and
bribe him or coax him or third-degree him till he tells us
what did really scare him that night I met him. I expect
when he knows we know about the Saratoga trunk he'll
be willing enough to talk, and it's a fair chance he may have
something interesting to tell us, if he noticed any special
details, as quite likely he did.'

'Elusive sort of bird, Con Conway,' Mitchell remarked.
'How do you propose to set to work to find him?'

'I might begin by making enquiries of people who may
have been in touch with him recently,' explained Bobby,

looking abstractedly out of the window. 'Anyone known, for example, to have been in possession of any article – an umbrella, for instance – Conway may have had in his hands recently, through having pinched it, and so on.'

Mitchell turned a cold official eye upon the young man.

'As for umbrellas,' he observed, 'what makes you think Con Conway mightn't simply have left it at the Yard one day for you, with his compliments and thanks for the loan of it?'

'Yes, sir. Did he do that, sir?' asked Bobby.

'I only said "might",' retorted Mitchell. He paused, and his cold official air gave place to one of slight embarrassment. He signalled to the driver to stop.

'There's a tube station over there,' he remarked. 'Ever hear of a place called Tooting? Improbable sort of name, but if you hop out here and take a tube or tram or a bus, according to taste, and if it's going the right way, you'll probably get there in time. If you do, you can ask the local men if anything's been seen of a chap answering Con Conway's description, possibly run in recently for obstructing the traffic by trying to sell bananas and apples from a barrow in the street – fast traffic for motorists being more important than cheap stuff for housewives or an honest living for a fellow like Con Conway.'

'Yes, sir,' said Bobby, and hopped out accordingly.

The journey to the improbably named district known as Tooting duly accomplished, Bobby soon found, as indeed he had expected, that he had been put upon a hot scent, but, unfortunately, one that ended abruptly, as abruptly as when, in full cry, the hounds are checked when the cry goes up 'Gone to earth' – though in this case an earth of which the locality was not known. For at the local police-station the Sergeant in charge knew all about Conway, except where he was now.

'Pushed a barrow for one week-end,' he said. 'I knew him again at once – I was at Cannon Row last time he was brought in. Of course I didn't let on. Next thing I heard

was that he had sold barrow and fruit to another man for
half its value – said he was fed up with the job and he was off
to Manchester, where he knew of a £10,000 pearl necklace
he could pick up for the trouble of climbing a gutter-pipe.
So we told Manchester they had better keep their eyes
skinned.'

'You told Manchester to keep their eyes skinned?' repeated Bobby, slightly alarmed. 'What happened?' he asked
anxiously.

'Oh, they just thanked us, and said they'd do their best,
but they knew Manchester wasn't London, which, of course,
it isn't, and never could be,' agreed the Sergeant. 'And then
there was something about a thanksgiving service I didn't
quite follow, and so I told 'em to keep a special eye on any
locality likely to be harbouring £10,000 pearl necklaces,
and they said there weren't none their way, and hadn't
been, not since cotton went bust. All Manchester pearl
necklaces come from Woolworths nowadays, they say. But
they thanked me, and wanted to know if I could go and
help them, but of course I couldn't do that.'

'No, you couldn't, could you?' agreed Bobby, offering a
silent little thanksgiving service of his own that he wasn't
likely to have anything to do with Manchester until this
passing episode had been forgotten.

'I told them to watch out for Butler, too,' continued the
other. 'You know Slimy Butler? Behind most of these
jobs, and behind that last one Con Conway did – the one
he was brought in for with the goods upon him and got
ten years, and then that there blessed Court of Appeal let
him off because at the trial the judge happened to allow
one witness repeat a bit of hearsay or something of the sort.
It cut no ice one way or the other, but the Appeal Court
said it might have affected the jury, if they noticed it,
which they probably didn't, and if they thought it important, which wasn't possible. Just hair-splitting, I call it.
Us chaps sweat our livers out bringing in a notorious
criminal like Con Conway, and then the ruddy lawyers

turn him loose again just on a silly technical point like that.'

'Too bad,' agreed Bobby absently, for he was thinking his hardest.

'Heart-breaking, I call it,' said the Sergeant. 'What I say is, when you get 'em, keep 'em. Makes the force a laughing-stock, if you ask me, and encourages men like Con Conway to think they can always get away with it.'

'Something in that,' agreed Bobby. 'I suppose these men selling stuff from barrows buy it at Covent Garden, do they?'

'Cheap lots that have got left over,' the Sergeant said. 'Sometimes they get stuff from a grower near London who's got more on hand than he can deal with comfortably. But generally it's Covent Garden.'

So Bobby thanked him and returned to headquarters, and afterwards went home and went to bed, though first, not without a heavy sigh, setting his alarm-clock for half-past three.

At that strange, unearthly hour the alarm-clock duly sounded, but probably would have failed to waken Bobby had he not taken the precaution to place the clock on top of an overturned tin bath. Thus it did awake him, though not till it had awakened first everyone else in the house, so that it was in an atmosphere charged with malediction and hate that ·Bobby threw a blanket over clock and bath, and dressed and let himself out into the street at that sad hour which combines all the drawbacks and disadvant- ages of both day and night into one enormous yawn.

However, when he arrived at Covent Garden it was to find everyone there brisk and lively, and apparently quite unaware of the unsuitability of the hour. Bobby could only suppose, rather crossly, that custom had hardened them to it, as use is said to harden eels to skinning.

He had provided himself with a photograph of Con Con- way, and patient and persistent enquiry, diversified by many hairbreadth escapes from charging trucks and backing lorries seeking whom they might annihilate, discovered, at last, a porter who first plainly recognised the photograph, and then firmly denied that he had done so.

'Police, ain't you?' he asked, with an appraising glance at Bobby's stalwart, upright form. 'No, I don't know him; take my dying oath I never saw him. What's he done?'

'Nothing,' answered Bobby promptly. 'We only want to find him because he can give us some information we are quite willing to pay him well for. It'll mean a pound note, most likely, for him, if you can help us find him.'

The porter admitted, though with some distrust, that that did make a difference. Finally, after a little more persuasion, he agreed he recognised the photograph as that of a man who had been to the market once or twice recently. The porter had noticed him because, though a new-comer, he seemed to have an eye for a bargain, and had made one or two good purchases. For instance, the porter remembered having helped him with a load of Australian apples he had bought cheap as they were on the point of going bad.

'There was too many for one load,' the porter explained, 'so he stored about half or more, and then when he came back he got rid of the lot – gave 'em away, so to speak. I asked him what he was doing that for, and he said the competition was too strong down Tooting way, and he was going to try his luck in Glasgow – competition too strong in Tooting, and so he's going to try his luck among them Scotties – ha, ha, ha,' laughed the porter.

'Ha, ha, ha,' laughed Bobby, and thanked the porter, and offered him a shilling, which was refused, for the good man was even yet not quite easy in his mind, and wouldn't risk accepting what might turn out to be blood money earned by betraying some poor devil to the authorities.

But a cigarette and a drink he had less objection to, and then, his debt discharged, Bobby returned to Scotland Yard to ask permission to take the next train to Glasgow. This was granted, though not by Mitchell, who was not expected on duty that day till afternoon, and, on his way to Euston, Bobby reflected that he would give quite a lot to know where Con Conway had got the money from to pay for his Covent Garden transactions and his Glasgow fare.

'I may have a nasty suspicious mind,' Bobby admitted, reflectively, 'but, all the same, I shouldn't wonder ...' and then left the sentence unfinished, even to himself.

Chapter 13

GLASGOW HISTORY

THE sky was a cloudless blue, the sun shining brightly, when Bobby reached Glasgow. The sky was still a cloudless blue, the sun still shining brightly, when Bobby, his enquiries completed, took the train back to London. These facts, being taken directly from Bobby's own diary, in which they are carefully recorded, are beyond doubt or denial.

On his return Bobby was informed that the Superintendent was expecting him, and so proceeded at once to Mitchell's room with the pleasant knowledge that he had a success to report and even something more as well.

'You found Conway, then, I understand?' Mitchell greeted him. 'What on earth is he doing in Glasgow?'

'Well, sir, it's happened this way,' Bobby explained. 'I got track of him all right in Tooting. It seems, sir, from what I can make out, he had managed to touch some kind, soft-hearted gentleman for a' – Bobby just managed to smother a laugh – 'for a tenner, sir; no less. Must have been a very kind, very soft-hearted gentleman,' said Bobby, quite failing now to conceal an enormous grin.

'Never mind that,' said Mitchell testily. 'Get on with your story.'

'Yes sir,' said Bobby. 'Only a tenner – to Con Conway! I ask you – Yes, sir, as I was saying,' he went on hurriedly, when Mitchell made an impatient gesture to indicate he was not in the least interested in 'tenners', or in soft-hearted gentlemen, either, 'Con used it to get a start selling fruit from a barrow.'

'Well, I suppose that's what it was meant for,' grunted Mitchell. 'I suppose he didn't say who he got the money from, did he?'

'No, sir. I asked him, but he said he had taken his dying oath not to tell.'

'Oh, well,' observed Mitchell indifferently, 'if he had promised, of course he couldn't. You didn't press him?'

'Oh, no, sir,' answered Bobby. 'Though, if only I knew who it was, I should like to warn him to watch out when a man like Con Conway tries to touch him. No good being soft with his sort, that's a mug's game.'

'So it is,' agreed Mitchell, with emphasis.

'I should like to see one of Con's sort getting a tenner out of me,' declared Bobby, with a grim smile. 'If that soft-hearted gentleman knew a bit more, he would know the Con Conways let you down nine times out of ten, and it's best to keep your pockets closed against them.'

'Suppose,' observed Mitchell coldly, 'you tell me what you did in Glasgow, if you've quite finished your general observations.'

'Yes, sir,' said Bobby. 'Sorry, sir, only it did seem funny to think of anyone trusting Con just because he pitched a yarn about wanting a chance to run straight.' Bobby gave a superior smile, and Mitchell began to put some papers away in the wrong drawer, and then took them out again. 'So when he got his tenner out of the soft-headed – that is, soft-hearted, gentleman, but it's much the same, whose name he wouldn't tell, he bought a barrow and some apples or something, and started peddling in Tooting. Then Slimy Butler turned up.'

'Slimy Butler?' repeated Mitchell, sitting upright, and

speaking in a very dismayed voice, for Slimy Butler was only too well known as an organiser of big thefts and burglaries, helping in carrying them out and in disposing of the booty, but himself remaining so carefully in the background that never yet had it been possible to bring any offence home to him. Worse still, by far, he was known, more than once, by half tempting, half bullying them back into their criminal ways, to have frustrated attempts to help released convicts who had seemed likely to make an effort to run straight for the future. 'If Slimy Butler got to know about Con, and got after him, it's not much wonder if he's gone wrong again,' Mitchell admitted gloomily.

'No, sir,' agreed Bobby. 'Especially as it seems Slimy Butler knew about some job Con had had a hand in some years back, and was threatening to give information, if he "went back on his pals", as Slimy chose to call it.'

'Some day, perhaps,' observed Mitchell, 'I'll get hold of Slimy. I only hope I never get a chance to push him under a motor-bus. I might be tempted to do it.'

'So then,' Bobby explained, 'poor little Con – he hadn't much chance against that big bullying brute of a Slimy Butler – sold his barrow and load to another man for half value, and vanished from Tooting, though not before he told a man he was having a drink with he was fed up barrow-pushing, and knew where he could pick up a £10,000 necklace for the trouble of swarming up a gutter-pipe. I wonder,' said Bobby, with the most superior smile that even Oxford at its most superior could produce, 'what the soft-hearted gentleman of the tenner would think if he heard that.'

'Probably think his head was a deal softer,' growled Mitchell. 'Anyhow, if a job's done Manchester way, we shall know who to look for, and that'll mean another ten-year stretch for Conway, a big success for the Yard – and a big failure too. Only what's he doing in Glasgow, if the job's in Manchester?'

'Well, it's like this,' Bobby explained. 'You see, it seems

the soft-hearted gentleman knew Con had been let off by the Court of Appeal because it was felt that just possibly he hadn't had a perfectly fair trial, even though there was no doubt about his guilt. So the soft-hearted gentleman put it to Conway – as he had had a square deal himself, oughtn't he to try to give a square deal back, and didn't he owe it to the judges, who had let him off so as to be quite fair, to play up? Apparently Con admitted he felt a little like that, and he said, as between gentlemen, he wanted to show the three old geezers in wigs that he appreciated it. Only, he had to live, and after two nights on the Embankment, and two days without anything to eat to speak of, you don't care much what you do. But then the tenner came along, and Con was getting a fair start with his barrow when Slimy Butler turned up, and Con said he felt that put the lid on Tooting for him. So he told a whacking lie about Manchester and a pearl necklace to put Slimy off and cleared out for Glasgow.'

'Why Glasgow?'

'He has a sister there, who had promised to help him if only he would try to keep straight. When I found him – I had his photo with me, and I soon got on his track – he had bought another barrow and done a fair deal in grape-fruit, and seemed quite cheery and hopeful. It almost seems as if that soft-hearted gentleman's tenner might turn out a good investment.'

'More than he deserves,' declared Mitchell. 'I suppose Conway stuck to it he wouldn't tell who it was?'

'Oh, yes, sir,' answered Bobby. 'Even when I made a guess, he wouldn't say, and when I said most likely the soft-hearted gentleman's initial wasn't in the first half of the alphabet from A to L, or even in the second half from N to Z, he wouldn't answer. But he did want to know if I got my umbrella back all right – though I don't know what made him ask that – and then he had the impudence to say he never could stand being preached at.'

'Don't blame him,' said Mitchell. 'Being preached at

just naturally brings out all the worst there is in all of us. Whenever you are tempted again to preach –'

'I'll remember my umbrella sir,' Bobby promised meekly. 'And more especially,' he added, looking rather rueful now, 'how Con said he hoped it would be a lesson to me, because even if one gentleman did stand another the price of a doss that didn't give him any right to hand out uplift as well. So I said if ever I got him alone on a dark night I would give him uplift all right, but I would let him off if he told me just what it was scared him so bad that night. But he shut his mouth tight and said there was nothing doing; and then I said it would give Mr Mitchell a leg up in his work if he did, and Con said that was different. He asked me if I had seen tales in the papers about someone they call on the evening placards "The Mad Millionaire". It's somebody who every now and then gives away money at random without anyone having any idea who it is. Sometimes it's to "down-and-outs" on the Embankment, or it's thrown to men queueing up outside a Salvation Army centre. It's always managed so no one can ever spot where the money comes from, but Con heard as a kind of joke that one man had thought he had been clever enough to track the donor home, and then at the last moment found out he had only been following a poor old woman who lived all alone at Brush Hill, and who must have been passing by accident when the money was being distributed – it was pound notes in envelopes on the Embankment seats that time. But Con has got some brains of his own, and it struck him this yarn about the old woman might be worth following up, even if the first fellow hadn't thought so. He went off to Brush Hill, and when he found there really was an eccentric old woman living in the district he thought he would have a look at her. There was a light in a window of the house where he had been told she was living, and a gutter-pipe that passed near the window. So he shinned up it, and when he looked in he says he saw a tiny little old, old woman, dressed up like a bride – white satin and wreath of faded orange-blossom and a long lace veil – and then, while he was still staring, she opened the Saratoga trunk, and Con saw what was inside. He was pretty well scared out of his senses already, but what finished him was that she turned round and saw him and beckoned to him to come inside. He says she called something about having been waiting for him or expecting him, and now at last he had come – and if you ask me, sir, I think Con was so scared he made sure if he wasn't off pretty quick she would have him shut up inside a trunk, too. I suppose it really was a pretty weird sort of scene – the open trunk, the dead man in it, the old woman in her bridal array, all half visible by the light of one guttering candle. Anyhow, Con slid to the ground and made off as fast as he could, half persuaded she would follow and catch him if he didn't look out.'

'I suppose it was enough to give him a bit of a scare,' Mitchell agreed.

'He wasn't anxious to tell anyone,' Bobby continued, 'for fear of being asked what he was doing up that gutter-pipe. And he says she was wearing round her neck, hanging down over her bride's frock, a pearl necklace he will swear was worth ten thousand at least, and probably more.'

'The dickens she was!' Mitchell exclaimed. 'If that's right ...'

'Con was quite positive about it,' Bobby said. 'I think it's been a good deal on his mind. What he said was, it wasn't fair to blokes like him for old parties what was dotty to be going round with bits of all right only waiting to be picked up what any honest fence would stump up five thou for on the nail. I think myself that's partly why he went off to Glasgow, so as to be as far away from temptation as possible.'

'Shouldn't wonder,' agreed Mitchell. 'It does sound as if that's where the pearl you found came from. Bad enough when a woman's missing, makes it worse when there's a £10,000 necklace vanished as well. I don't like the whole thing,' he burst out. 'I don't understand what's been happening, and I don't much want to find the poor old thing herself, and yet I've a feeling that we must.'

'No one will want to be hard on her, after all these years,' Bobby said.

Mitchell looked at him gloomily.

'Likely enough the fellow in the trunk deserved all he got,' he said. 'And, if she killed him, she's paid for it, living like that. Paid in full, perhaps - yet, is murder ever paid in full? But I don't like it about that necklace. Do you think Con talked about it to anyone?'

'He said not, sir. I think I believe him.'

'I'm thinking about that young man with the pistol – who he was, and where he comes in,' Mitchell said slowly. 'And why is there only one satin shoe left of the bride's dress Con says she was wearing? Can you tell me that?'

Bobby looked a little vague, for he did not at the moment quite see that what had become of the bridal dress mattered very much – it was Miss Barton herself, not her clothing, they had to find. Mitchell went on, referring to some papers on his desk:

'We've traced sales of jewellery to Allen & Wildman, the Bond Street jewellers, that look like deals with Miss Barton. Allen & Wildman say they have been buying for something like forty years from a mysterious client who answers very well to Miss Barton's description. She used to come every year or two - never bargained; wouldn't give any name or address: took what was offered in gold at first, and latterly in pound notes, and went off. It rather looks as if she made it a practice to keep enough for herself for a year or two - the way she lived she can't have spent more than two or three bob a week - and gave the rest away.'

'That would mean she is probably "The Mad Millionaire" of the evening-paper placards?' Bobby asked.

'Almost certain, I think,' Mitchell said. 'One way she had of making amends, I suppose. Apparently the jewellers never made any enquiry. They had been buying stuff from her for so long, and there had never been any trouble, so they began to take it for granted it was all right. Possibly they made enquiries at first, but there's no record. They have promised to get out full details as far back as possible, but some of their early books were destroyed in a fire a few years ago.' Mitchell paused, and drummed on the table with his fingers. 'Well, we know now what scared Con Conway. But has he told all the truth? For him a necklace like that would be like a saucer of cream shoved under a cat's nose. Had the girl who opened the door to you seen the same thing, and is that what frightened her – or was it something else altogether? And what about the fellow in plus-fours Mrs Rice saw hanging about Tudor Lodge? Was he just a curious passer-by, or was he someone who had heard about Con's experience and had come along to see what he could pick up for himself? And then, what about the young man with the pistol? And why have none of them come forward now the papers have splashed the story – especially the man in plus-fours, if he was only an innocent passer-by? They can't all three of them be afraid of being asked what they were doing there, can they?'

It was a question to which, as Bobby knew not what response to make, he offered no reply.

Chapter *14*

NEWSPAPER INTERLUDE

THE newspapers had indeed 'splashed' the story to good purpose, and the public imagination had been deeply stirred by the tale of the woman whose romance of so long ago had ended in so tragical a manner, who for so long had guarded so terrible a secret, who now, it seemed, was identified with the unknown benefactor whose showers of gold and notes had at intervals during recent years fallen like the manna of heaven upon the desolate and the out-cast of London, and who, finally, had vanished from human ken.

Public sympathy was almost entirely on her side. A flood of correspondence descended on the papers, on the Home Office, and on Scotland Yard, suggesting, imploring, almost commanding, that no further official action should be taken. It had all happened so long ago, the writers of these letters urged, the penalty paid by that long life of solitude and privation had been so great, surely now the veil could be drawn over the past. Other correspondents suggested that there was and could be no proof of what had actually happened. It might well have been a case of accident or suicide, they argued, or, if it was murder, then someone else might have been the assassin. In fact the picture of the solitary recluse dressed in the wedding attire of her youth, of the marriage feast spread and ready to which no guest had ever sat down, had moved profoundly the soft heart of the great British public.

The climax was reached when the author of the tremend-ously, almost fantastically, popular 'Up the Garden Path' series reconstructed the probable course of events in an article that doubled the circulation of *Sunday Photos* – already well into its fourth million – and caused so many tears to be shed that no wonder the Air Ministry was able to report, next day, the breaking of a ten-days' drought.

The theory thus put forward was that the unfortunate inmate of the Saratoga trunk had committed suicide in a moment of passionate, unbearable ecstasy because he had felt that their love was too perfect a thing to be soiled by contact with the common life. Alternatively, as the lawyers say, the writer suggested accident. This, he pointed out, would account for the position of the wound in the crown of the head. The victim had been prostrate in reverent adoration at his mistress's feet when a loaded revolver had been discharged by some unlucky accidental movement and the fatal wound inflicted.

The *Daily Announcer*, fulfilling its function, as a great national moulder of opinion, to follow with loud cries of leadership whithersoever the public happened to wander, supported in a very clearly and closely reasoned article the theory of accident, and a prominent member of Parliament suggested that the police might well turn their attention from their efforts to hound down a most unhappy and unfortunate lady to protecting motorists from the wanton efforts of the undisciplined pedestrian to hamper them by getting in their way.

Public sympathy, it is true, received a slight shock when it was announced that the mummified condition of the body was – in part, at least – due to the presence of arsenic in large quantities. A heavy dose must have been taken, declared the report of the Home Office analyst, shortly before death. But as the *Daily Announcer* – after a brief pause to make quite sure which way the cat of public feeling was going to jump – pointed out, in a special article by the 'Up the Garden Path' author (bribed away from *Sunday Photos* by a kind of film-star fee), this discovery in no way affected the accident theory, since every day cases are reported of poison drunk in error, and obviously did not touch the suicide theory, since a broken heart may turn as well to arsenic as to pistol. In a peroration which has become almost a classic for its grave and solemn beauty and the tender restraint of its language, the writer made the final suggestion that possibly the arsenic had been administered after death in order that the body of the loved one might be preserved – eternal companion and everlasting symbol of 'what might have been'.

'All of which guff,' observed Mitchell, reading it with keen appreciation, 'ought to make someone come forward. No one can believe now that the old lady is in any danger of the gallows – why, it's all odds, when we do find her, the paper will offer her a complimentary banquet and a cheque for ten thousand for an article on "How I Did It" – film rights reserved.'

But in spite of all these demonstrations of public sympathy, in spite of all appeal, in spite of all the exertions of all the crime experts of all the national papers, in spite of all the police themselves could do, in spite of all the help given them by amateur investigators, in spite of the fact that no woman of sixty or seventy – at least, of those who looked their age instead of looking sixteen or seventeen as most of them did – could venture out in public without attracting immediate attention, no further information could be obtained.

The newspaper men consoled themselves for their own failure by bitterly criticising that of Scotland Yard, and by publishing long, and always 'exclusive', interviews with everyone concerned. *Sunday Photos* revenged itself, not too effectively, for the virtual abduction of the 'Up the Garden Path' genius by whisking away Mrs Rice to a remote country cottage where none but their own reporters could find her, and the *Daily Announcer* man complained bitterly to Bobby that someone must have 'done the dirty', too, about Humphreys, the little local shopkeeper, who for year after year had supplied every week the missing woman's meagre wants.

'Kidnapped,' said the *Daily Announcer* man bitterly, 'that's what it comes to. The neighbours say the shop was open as usual one day, and next morning the shutters stayed up – and have stayed up ever since. Seems to be no one there. Can't get hold of the assistant who used to work for him, either.'

'Why not?' Bobby asked. 'Has *Sunday Photos* nobbled him, too?'

'No, he's keeping out of the way on his own, apparently. From what I can make out, Humphreys caught him at the till, and threatened him with the police, so he's taken care to be missing ever since. Funny thing is, the landlord says the rent was in arrears until recently, and then

Humphreys cleared it off and paid two quarters in advance. What do you make of that?'

'Sounds as if business had been picking up,' observed Bobby cautiously.

The newspaper man made sounds indicative of disgust at so prudent a response.

'Not giving anything away, are you?' he commented. 'The landlord says he's never known it happen before, but, naturally, he didn't object, or ask any questions. Can't you people find out what's become of the little blighter?'

'I've been run off my legs the last few days,' Bobby responded. 'I didn't even know Humphreys had cleared out. But I don't see what good he would be to you. We took a statement from him, you know, long ago. I don't think he had anything useful to say. He never seems even to have seen Miss Barton, and so long as he got his weekly order and his weekly pay he never gave her a thought – her order wasn't big enough to interest him much. Even if you found him, there's nothing you could get out of him.'

The *Daily Announcer* man looked at Bobby pityingly.

'It's a poor journalist,' he said, 'who can't make a thundering good story out of nothing, only, of course, you've got to have their signature to confirm, in case it's challenged. In fact,' he added reflectively, 'I prefer it when they've nothing to say. You're less' – he paused, searching for a word – 'less – trammelled,' he concluded triumphantly, having found one at last. 'Less trammelled – that's what you are. And if one of those blighters from *Daily Intelligence* or *Sunday Photos* spot him first, they'll call it a scoop, and a nice telling off I shall get.'

Bobby had no consolation to offer, but he did think it worth while to go round to Humphreys' shop and make a few enquiries. He remembered the little man had talked of selling his business in order to buy another in Bournemouth; apparently he hadn't sold, but closed down, and had even paid two quarters' rent in advance. This last fact, when

Bobby had confirmed it, seemed to him so unusual that he reported it to Mitchell.

'I thought it might be worth following up, in case there's something in it,' he explained.

'What?' asked Mitchell.

'I don't know,' Bobby answered. 'It's hardly probable, but there is just the chance that when Miss Barton left Tudor Lodge she went to Humphreys and asked him to help her find a fresh hiding-place. She had money, most likely, and would be able to offer him good pay – that is, assuming she hadn't already sold all her jewellery.'

'It may be worth looking into,' agreed Mitchell. 'Lord knows, there isn't much we've got we can follow up! How can you trace people when about the only description you have is that the girl was a pretty blonde with fair hair and blue eyes, all togged up in the latest style – and, thank heaven, England stands where it did so far as pretty girls go, and pretty girls still stand where they did so far as the latest thing in togs goes. Then about the one man all we know is that he wore plus-fours, and wasn't seen very clearly; and about the other that he was young and dark, and sported a pistol and a rather specially lurid tie.' Mitchell paused, and began again to drum upon the table, as was his habit when some new idea struck him. 'Might be something in that,' he said musingly. 'Not that a lurid taste in ties is much to trace a man by. But first, what about Humphreys? It's a bit odd he should have vanished, too, and odder still that he should have paid two quarters' rent in advance and yet closed down the business. How do you propose to start tracing him?'

'Well, sir,' Bobby explained, 'he talked rather a lot about Bournemouth, when we saw him – as if he meant to go there if he ever got money enough. He told us he had done well with garden-stuff, and had worked up the business a lot since he had gone in for that as a new line. He boasted in the same way to some of his neighbours as well.'

'How do you mean, garden-stuff? Greengroceries?'

'No, sir. Seeds, tools, artificial manures, garden lime, lawn sand, and so on. Doesn't sound a profitable line in Brush Hill, but he told everyone he had done very well with it.'

'Well, we'll try Bournemouth,' Mitchell said. 'It'll be easy enough to find if any new business has been opened, or any old one taken over, by a man named Humphreys, or answering his description. Draw up as complete a description as you can and let Ferris have it, and I'll tell him to carry on. May as well try other seaside places as well. Shouldn't be much difficulty in finding him. He can't have any reason for lying low, unless, of course, Miss Barton really ran for it because she thought her secret was known now the Saratoga trunk has been seen open. She was more or less in touch with Humphreys through her purchases, and she may have gone to him and given him money to help her to some fresh hiding-place. Perhaps that's how he got the money to pay rent in advance, and why he only put his shutters up – he means to come back and start again some day.'

But Bournemouth was drawn blank. So were all the other towns, at the seaside and elsewhere, where enquiries were made. Nowhere did it seem that any new business had been opened by anyone answering the description of Humphreys, and once again the investigation was at a complete standstill. The newspapers began to lose interest, discovering new amazing sensations to proclaim in their headlines, and Bobby, going home after another long and tiring and utterly futile day, found himself staring into a hosier's window, attracted, in spite of himself, by a remarkable collection of ties of patterns so strange, of colours so startling, of designs so staggering, that the general impression was that of one of Euclid's propositions, gone insane through studying Einstein, crossed by a neo-post-impressionist turned Bolshevist.

But then, with a certain relief, Bobby understood that it was merely a collection of 'old boy' ties he was looking at, and he remembered vaguely that Mitchell had once said something about a 'specially lurid tie' there might be 'something in'. He had not seemed to follow up the remark, but now from that almost incredible tumult in the shop-window Bobby's eye gradually selected a pattern of green and yellow bars spotted with blue and red. As though drawn by the awful fascination of the thing, Bobby entered the shop and enquired about the particular brainstorm that had attracted his attention.

'St Polycarp's, sir,' the assistant told him, not without pride. 'Supposed by school tradition to represent what St Polycarp said during his martyrdom on the grid-iron – not the orthodox story, I'm told, but much cherished by the school.'

'I don't think I know it,' Bobby said. 'Where does it hang out?'

'In the Bicester country, sir,' the assistant explained. 'One of the smaller schools, but very well thought of, and very ancient – founded by Edward the Confessor for the sons of destitute lepers, but limited by later statute to two hundred pupils. Always a waiting list, because only boys of the very best and wealthiest families are admitted, and besides, owing to the rich endowment, very low fees as well.'

'Interesting,' said Bobby. 'I'll take that one, please.'

'Yes, sir,' said the assistant hesitatingly. 'Very chaste line of ties here, sir, only half the price.'

'But I want that one,' said Bobby.

'Yes, sir; just so, sir,' said the assistant. 'Beautiful thing here, sir – in purple and gold, very restrained and gentlemanly, only three and nine.'

'But –' said Bobby.

'Yes, sir; exactly, sir,' said the assistant. 'The secretary of Old Polycarpians is very particular, sir, in asking us not to sell to any but Old Boys. Now here, sir, is a very tender, chaste design –'

But Bobby stretched out a long arm, captured the

atrocity they were talking about, dropped the three half-crowns it was valued at on the counter, and walked out, and the assistant turned despairingly to a colleague.

'Can you beat it?' he demanded. 'Doesn't even know where St Polycarp's is, and then buys their tie to swank around in – well, I ask you. No wonder,' said the assistant, shaking his head moodily, 'there's all this Communism and Socialism about. What we want is the Blackshirts – they'd soon put a stop to that sort of thing.' He fingered, lovingly and softly, another Polycarpian tie. 'Swell,' he murmured. 'Might borrow it for to-night, now I'm taking Gladys Amelia to the new Mae West picture.'

Chapter 15

GHOSTLY PURSUIT

THE registrar of St Polycarp's, that ancient and honourable foundation, was a major and a reverend, as was only suitable, for St Polycarp's bestowed upon Army and upon Church an almost equal approval – and that is saying something, for there was not much except St Polycarp's that St Polycarp's really approved. He was also an Honourable, which was almost equally suitable, since the House of Lords was the one institution to which St Polycarp's paid real deference. When Bobby appeared he was on the point of setting out for a round of golf – St Polycarp's concentrated on golf, considering football slightly vulgar, cricket a trifle colonial, and tennis a bit international, and considering itself called upon, in these slack days, to set its face steadily against the vulgar, the colonial, and the international.

On Bobby's explaining his errand, the registrar showed himself a good deal worried. For him the world consisted

of two great divisions – the recognisable, who were Old
Boys, and the unrecognisable, or, in Indian parlance,
the untouchable, who were not. Bobby he did not quite
know how to place, for Bobby was undeniably an Old
Boy, though only of the minor, on the fringe, variety,
but still within the pale, while yet, as a sergeant of police,
he could scarcely be so considered. A confusing world,
it has become, sighed the registrar, and, indeed, values
are no longer as once they were – simple and clear cut and
plain for plain and simple and clear-cut minds.

The registrar therefore offered Bobby a cigarette as an
Old Boy, as a police-sergeant omitted to shake hands with
him, and continued to show much hesitation over Bobby's
request to be informed of the names and addresses of those
boys who had left the school in recent years.

The head master had to be consulted, a phone message
put through to the noble lord who was chairman of the
governing board, and nearly half a day wasted before at
last the information Bobby required was put at his disposal.

Fortunately St Polycarp's was a school as small as it was
exclusive. Only about forty boys departed every year.
Therefore, if Mrs Rice's estimate of the age of the young
man she had seen could be trusted – and Bobby had much
faith in Mrs Rice's powers of observation, trained as they
were by long hours at her window, keeping an eye on her
neighbours' comings and goings – then, during the ten
years that covered the probable date of his leaving the
school, there were, roughly speaking, about four hundred
names to be considered. But a good many of these could
be eliminated at once. One or two had died, some were
known to be abroad, or it was remembered that the description of tall, dark and good-looking could not possibly
apply to them – 'Tubby Brown', 'Carrots Smith', and
'Cross-eyed Jones' were, so to speak, automatically dis-
qualified.

In the end Bobby was left with a list of about a hundred
names and addresses to work on, of which he was able to

tick off about twenty as clearly coming within the tall, dark, good-looking ambit, and, not dissatisfied with his day's work, Bobby took his leave, though not till the registrar had warned him to remember that, unhappily, not all who wore the old school tie did so of natural right.

'There are painful cases,' the registrar admitted. 'I myself have seen, serving in a grocer's shop ...' He paused and shuddered slightly, but went on bravely enough. 'I spoke about it ... a regrettable insolence was shown ... even Old Boys themselves. ... One informed me recently, appearing to consider it humorous, that his jobbing gardener always wore an Old Polycarpian tie, as coming from the neighbourhood. ... He refused to take action in the matter, on the ground that Old Boys were a jolly sight easier to find than working gardeners who knew their job. ... Subversive ideas are so widely spread to-day, one fears the wearing of a tie is no longer conclusive proof. ...'

'That's the snag,' admitted Bobby gloomily. 'But our job is mostly all snag. We just go on bumping our heads against stone walls in the hope that one day we shall find a soft spot. In the wall, I mean, of course,' he added hurriedly.

All this had taken so much time that it was past midnight before Bobby got home. In the morning he presented himself and his list to Mitchell, and, being told to carry on, proceeded to go systematically through his score of possibles. One he found had been in gaol that day, and another getting married. A third was playing cricket for his county, and a fourth occupied attending an inquest on an old woman who, while trying to cross the road, had got in front of his new hundred-mile-an-hour sports car (fortunately the coroner and the jury had been very nice about it, and had tendered him their deepest sympathy), and for various other reasons quite half of the rest of the list could be disregarded.

Five or six of the others had addresses in or near London, and Bobby put Mrs Rice – rescued from the clutches of

Daily Intelligence, but promise made that no other paper should be allowed to know about her – in a car, and took her round to visit them all in succession.

One was demonstrating golf clubs in a big London stores. 'No,' said Mrs Rice decidedly. 'His nose is a snub.' One was in a lawyer's office in New Square. 'I said good-looking,' Mrs Rice pointed out, with some severity. 'What that young man has is more a calamity than a face.' Another was run to earth in a Chelsea studio. 'No,' said Mrs Rice, still more decidedly. 'There wasn't any of that wild look in the eyes about the one I saw.' Yet another was an officer in the guards. 'No,' said Mrs Rice. 'But I'm glad to have seen him,' she added simply. The last held some position in a wireless factory but could not be seen, as he had left early in order to test at home details of a new invention of his own he was endeavouring to persuade his employers to take up. They got his address, however, and found it to be beyond Purley, involving rather a long ride. However, Mrs Rice had no objection; it was not every day that she was treated to long motor-drives, and when they reached their destination the first thing they saw was a tall, dark, good-looking young man strolling from an outbuilding at a little distance up to the house.

'That's him,' said Mrs Rice.

Bobby drove on, a little to Mrs Rice's disappointment, for she had hoped to see the handcuffs clapped then and there on the young man's wrists. However, Bobby explained he wanted her to have a closer view, so as to avoid any possibility of a mistake, and would she mind calling at the house and trying to collect a year's subscription to the local parish magazine. This errand Mrs Rice, after a little persuasion, accepted, and returned successful, but slightly embarrassed by the possession of the shilling the young man had meekly yielded up to pay for the delivery of the magazine in question.

Bobby was a little puzzled by this problem, too, for he had not anticipated that such prompt success would be achieved, or achieved upon a cash basis. However, Mrs Rice had been able to confirm her identification of the young man as the one she had seen at Tudor Lodge.

'I could swear to him anywhere,' she declared emphatically.

They were passing the church now, and Bobby noticed a clergyman, standing in the porch, and thought it would be a good opportunity to get rid of the shilling. So he stopped the car and alighted, and handed the coin to the clergyman, explaining that he had been asked to give it him as a subscription to the parish magazine for Mr Aske, of such an address.

The clergyman accepted the shilling, but looked exceedingly bewildered.

'Very curious; very strange,' he murmured, regarding the coin with an air of blank amazement. 'Miss Aske, Mr Aske's sister, is honorary secretary for our magazine, and receives all subscriptions – why didn't he give it to her? Besides, he's a subscriber already – nineteen times.'

'Nineteen times?' repeated Bobby, awestruck, for, indeed, he had never heard of such a thing as one young man subscribing nineteen times to his local parish magazine.

'I understand,' explained the clergyman, feeling that explanation was needed, 'that Miss Aske asked her brother for a list of all his greatest friends, and then gave him a postal subscription to each one of them, as her present to him last Christmas. So it is indeed gratifying that now he should require another.'

'Yes, isn't it?' agreed Bobby, retreating towards his car. 'Rather ... awfully jolly to have a sister like that ... my word. ... Well, I must be off ... so glad to have been any use.'

With that he 'stepped upon the gas', as the classics say, and vanished in a cloud of dust, like one of Homer's deities when it got too hot for them too, while the clergyman still stood regarding the shilling in his hand as if it might go off bang any moment.

'And that,' said Mrs Rice coldly, when Bobby had slowed down a little and she could hear the things he was saying to himself, 'that is not at all the kind of language I am accustomed to.'

'I beg your pardon,' said Bobby contritely. 'I was only thinking aloud.'

'Thinking, you may call it,' observed Mrs Rice, still more severely, 'but, if so, I'll ask you to remember no gentleman ever does.'

'Very true indeed, Mrs Rice,' agreed Bobby, much impressed. 'Very true, and sums up at once the whole secret of England's greatness.'

Mrs Rice, flattered both by this remark and by the meekness with which her rebuke had been received, said no more, and Bobby stopped at the nearest police-station, where he arranged for his passenger to be conveyed back to London, and himself discovered, to his great content, that, by a happy coincidence, the number of Mr Aske's car was known, he having recently been summoned and fined for leaving it unattended while he bought a packet of cigarettes.

So Bobby grew very busy at the phone. All round his messages flew, and a plain-clothes man, hastily dispatched to watch outside the house Bobby and Mrs Rice had just left, reported that Mr Aske's car, N.B.G. OOX, had just started out, and was being driven Londonwards at a high speed.

Then the phoning grew fiercer still, and then began a curious chase, a ghostly immaterial pursuit that would have been impossible and inconceivable only a few years back.

Young Aske drove his car sometimes fast, sometimes slow, sometimes he swung back upon his tracks, sometimes he shot straight ahead, occasionally he stopped dead, and then, starting again, followed an eccentric track, first towards Croydon, then back to the country, then Epsom way, and finally in the direction of Town. For that, after so many, so careful, so cunning precautions, it was still being followed, trailed, or shadowed seemed to young Mr Aske quite out of the question. He had dallied on lonely country roads, he had speeded in crowded areas, he had lurked in side-streets, and never once had he seen anything suspicious or anything to suggest that he was under observation or being followed, or, indeed, that there was any possibility of his having been tracked.

For, indeed, it did not enter his mind that every policeman he passed, dawdling indifferently down the street with nothing more to do apparently than direct old ladies on their way or inform inquisitive children of the right time, was in fact keeping a keen look-out for his car, or that, recognising its number, they made haste, the instant he had passed, to phone in a report.

To Bobby, sitting with the receiver at his ear, these reports came in quick succession. On a map spread open near, one of the local men marked with a pin the erratic course of the car, noting down, too, the time of each report, and thus, invisibly observed, immaterially tracked, was followed in ghost-like fashion young Mr Aske's car till it came to a standstill outside a block of flats. By it presently passed the policeman on the beat and opined that it was obstructing traffic. The porter protested indignantly that it was doing nothing of the sort, but agreed to fetch the owner from Flat 27, where he was visiting. Equally indignant, Mr Aske appeared; the policeman, agreeing that he had been overzealous, withdrew both his complaint and his abashed self. Mr Aske exchanged a few words of severe criticism of the force with the porter, and then returned to Flat 27; and faster and nearer, on the motorcycle with which he had been supplied, Bobby stormed along. When, presently, he arrived, the uniformed man was waiting for him round the corner.

'Car still there,' he reported. 'Driver in Flat 27.'

So Bobby thanked him, and, in his turn, proceeded to Flat 27.

Chapter 16

DOROTHY YELTON'S STORY

THE flats, one of those new blocks that recently have sprung up in London like mushrooms in a field after rain, were provided with all the latest improvements, from refrigerators to lifts. In a lift, therefore, Bobby ascended to the third floor, where No 27 was situated, for though, from a professional point of view, he disapproved of lifts as giving unfair facilities to the shadowee to escape the attentions of the shadower, at any rate he much preferred them to three flights of stairs.

He knocked at the door of Flat 27, and, when it opened, he was not much surprised to find confronting him the fair-haired, very pretty girl who also had opened the door for him the first time he had knocked at Tudor Lodge. He was not sure whether she knew him again, in which doubt he did less than justice to her memory for faces. She did not say anything, but she looked startled and alarmed, and still more so when he showed her his card.

'I am sorry to trouble you,' he said, 'but I am investigating a matter in which we think you may be able to give us some assistance.'

She was looking really frightened now, though not with that pale extremity of terror she had shown when he saw her before. As she was still silent, he went on:

'I expect you have read in the papers that Miss Barton, who used to live at Tudor Lodge, has disappeared.'

'But I can't tell you anything. I can't, really,' she broke out. 'I don't know anything at all about her, or where she is.'

'I should like to ask you a few questions, if you don't mind,' Bobby continued. 'I think Mr Aske is here, too, isn't he?'

'Oh, oh! How do you know that?' she stammered.

'It is our duty in the police to know things,' he explained gravely. 'May I ask you to be quite frank and open with us? I am sure it will be best, in the long run, for everyone.'

'But I don't know anything,' she protested again.

He was looking at her closely, wondering very much what connection there could be between her and the strange and tragic recluse of Tudor Lodge, and what errand it was had taken her there the day when he had seen her – perhaps the first visitor the house had known since that morning when the wedding guests had assembled for the wedding that had never taken place.

'I think it was you who opened the door to us, and gave us back a football?' he said.

She nodded a frightened admission, but still did not speak.

'May I come in?' he asked.

She stood aside for him to enter, and he crossed the threshold into a dark little square space the flat management called 'the lounge'. From it two or three doors opened, and she pushed one back. It admitted to a large cupboard – the flat management called it 'spacious reception room' – already nearly crowded to suffocation by a tall, dark young man, who did not strike Bobby as particularly good-looking, and who, observing Bobby with marked disfavour, said, addressing the girl:

'Oh Lord, the blighters have got on to you, too!'

Bobby followed the girl into the room – to give it the courtesy title it generally received. On a small bookcase he noticed a photograph of a man in plus-fours, with a bag of golf clubs at his feet and a general air of looking down his nose that made Bobby feel certain he spoke with a pronounced Oxford drawl. He noted the fact, and stored it away in his memory, noticed, too, that there was nothing to suggest the presence of an old lady, and then Aske said again, speaking to him this time:

'How the dickens have you managed to get here? You were out at my place just now?'

'We have means of information,' Bobby said impressively, or so he hoped. 'I am an officer of police –'

'Knew that all right,' grumbled Aske. 'Spotted that as soon as I saw the way you were staring all round, like a cod on a fishmonger's slab. And, of course, when you sent that old girl along touting for a sub to the parish magazine my kid sister messes up every month ...'

Bobby deflated, so to speak. He had been feeling rather pleased with himself for having been able at last to find these two for whom the search had been so long, and till now so unsuccessful. But the parish-magazine stunt had not, he felt, been a very brilliant coup, and he decided, hurriedly, to pass it over as lightly as possible when making his report. It was partly to change the subject that he demanded abruptly:

'Is Miss Barton here?'

'Oh, no ... oh, poor thing, I wish she was,' the girl exclaimed. 'At least, I mean ... I mean, if it was all right. ... Oh, I do think that you might leave her in peace now.'

'Have you any idea where she is?' Bobby asked. 'Or where she is likely to be?'

'Oh, no,' she answered; and Aske echoed: 'Not the foggiest.'

'I didn't even know she had gone, till I saw it in the paper,' the girl added; and once more Aske echoed: 'Same here.'

'Didn't you also see, at the same time, a request that you should come forward and tell what you knew?' demanded Bobby severely.

'Yes, I did, and I just wasn't going to,' retorted the girl, suddenly indignant. She looked a little like an angry fairy defying an intruding cheeky puppy dog (which is what Bobby felt like) to do his worst, and she was so evidently trying so hard to make herself appear tall and imposing that Bobby was aware of a naughty impulse to push forward a chair for her to stand on, that she might look taller still. She continued: 'If I did know, I wouldn't tell or anything; and Mr Aske wouldn't either, would you, Mr Aske?' And this time Mr Aske's rumbling echo came back:

'Not on your life.'

'I've my duty to do,' Bobby observed.

'I don't see why,' retorted the girl simply.

'Much better chuck it,' agreed her faithful echo.

'I don't care what she did all that long time ago, or who she did it to, either,' the girl went on. 'It's years and years and years; and I do so hope you'll never, never find her – never!'

'Same here,' said Mr Aske, and this time reaped the dazzling, rich reward of a grateful smile.

'Murder has apparently been done,' Bobby reminded them. 'At least, it looks like it – and murder is still murder, even after fifty years. It is police duty to find Miss Barton. It is your duty to give what help you can.'

'Nothing doing,' said Mr Aske firmly.

'Besides, we don't either of us know anything at all,' the girl added. 'I told you so before, and it's true.'

'Not a thing,' confirmed Mr Aske.

'I take it you probably know why you were at Tudor Lodge, and what took you there that day I saw you,' Bobby remarked dryly. He turned sharply upon Aske: 'You were seen in the house, too. You were carrying a pistol!'

'I suppose that old girl of yours spotted that, did she?' Aske enquired coolly. 'Well, sorry to disappoint, but there's nothing in it. I picked the thing up in the hall. I've got it at home now. You can have it, if you like – quite harmless; it wouldn't go off if you tried from now to doomsday, not unless it was taken to pieces and cleaned and assembled again. The trigger's rusted in; it can't have been touched for –'

'For forty or fifty years?' Bobby asked.

'Well, I don't know about that,' Aske answered, more soberly.

'You should have handed it to us,' Bobby said, severe again, and then turned once more to the girl. 'I think it would be best if you were quite frank about what you know,' he said. 'I'm afraid it's bound to come out. You'll have to tell, in the long run, and I don't think you need be afraid of what will happen to Miss Barton. I don't suppose anyone will want to press the case, but it has got to be cleared up.'

'Don't see why. Don't see why you can't chuck it,' Aske grumbled.

'Got to keep the rules,' Bobby answered. 'It's the same in everything; you must stick to the rules or you get into no end of a mess. Besides, once anything is reported to Scotland Yard, there's nothing can stop it – except an Act of Parliament. It's simply got to go on – like day and night, or a broadcast talk, or the traffic down the Strand, or one of Noel Coward's plays.'

A little more persuasion, and at last the girl consented to tell her story.

Her name, she explained, was Yelton – Dorothy Yelton – and she kept house for her father, John Yelton, a member of the firm of Yelton & Markham, metal merchants, founded by her grandfather, John Yelton the first, and his younger brother, James Yelton. The brothers had made a successful start, but had both died young – her grandfather while her own father was still a child. During his minority the business had been carried on, less successfully but competently enough, by the manager, Henry Markham, father of the present junior partner. Then came the war, when the firm, after a moderately successful but uneventful existence since its foundation, prospered exceedingly – they were days, indeed, like those of Solomon, when 'silver and gold were nothing accounted'. After the war, however, the partners, in common with many others, had committed the twin errors of supposing that, as war meant a boom, peace must mean a treble boom, and, again like many others, of failing to understand that war merely leaves behind many bills to pay. So they launched out magnificently into superb far-reaching enterprises, in which they lost all they had gained, and more also.

Indeed, Bobby was able to infer that the firm was distinctly in low water, and that that explained a recent move from the house in the country to this flat, whereof the chief recommendation was that it had a 'W' in its postal address. It was from their former country home which her grandfather had built, and where the family had lived ever since – Dorothy herself had been born in it – that a letter sent there had been forwarded to the flat, asking Dorothy to come to Tudor Lodge, and making a reference that at the time seemed hard to understand to a Mr Yelton the writer had known many years before.

'Your grandfather?' Bobby asked, startled. 'You don't mean ... do you mean ...?'

'Not my grandfather,' Dorothy answered in a low voice. 'He died of pneumonia when he was quite young. My father was his only child. But he had a brother, the brother who helped him start the business. He was called James, and he disappeared, and no one ever knew what had become of him. It was on the eve of his wedding-day. Everything was ready, and then he just vanished, and no one knew what had happened. They thought he must have gone abroad. There was another woman, and she said he had promised to break the marriage off and marry her instead, so everyone thought he had run away because of the muddle he had got into. Grandmother always said he would turn up again, most likely with another wife altogether, but he never did.'

'It looks as if ...' Bobby began, and paused, his own voice not quite steady, so much was he affected by this tale of ancient sorrow, and the suggestion of strange tragedy that it had led to.

'I think so,' Dorothy almost whispered. 'I think it's almost certain ... I think that must be my great-uncle you found.'

They were all three silent for a little, and then Dorothy went on in the same half-whispered tone:

'When I went there ... to Tudor Lodge, I mean ... she told me ... I ... the letter seemed so funny I thought I must find out what it meant, and father thought so, too ... it was addressed to "Dorothy", but I think now perhaps it wasn't for me, but for grandmother ... she died just after the war ... but I think it was meant for her ... when I got there I thought perhaps it was all a mistake or a hoax of some sort ... then Miss Barton came down to let me in at the side door, and she looked so thin and frail and old I wasn't frightened any more ... at least not much ... and it all seemed so dreadful in that old house, and I thought how terrible it was anyone should be living like that, and she ought to be taken away somewhere where she could be looked after. ... I can't think how she can have managed.'

'She had been selling her jewellery, hadn't she?' Bobby asked.

'Yes, I think so. I don't know. She had a great pearl necklace she showed me. It must have been worth ever so much. It was beautiful, only it made everything else look more dreadful still. She began to tell me about great-uncle, and how they were in love ... she kept saying he did love her ... and then she found out he was in love with another woman too ... and that he was planning to leave her ... even though everything was ready ... her dress and the wedding-cake and everything ... she said several times the invitations had all been sent and people were coming ... and she talked about the wedding-cake ... she said when she was looking at it where they had put it on the table in the dining-room, and everyone was saying how nice it looked ... then it came into her mind quite suddenly that she would never let him go ... she made up her mind all at once, just as if it had been made up for her and quite settled ... she said it seemed like that, not as if it were something she wanted to do herself of her own will, but more as if it were an order from somewhere else and she just had to

do it ... and she sent him a note to ask him to come to her
room that night, only to be careful not to let anyone know.
... I think from what she said they had done that before ...
I think my great-uncle can't have been a very nice man,
and he had persuaded her they needn't wait because they
were really married already, only just for going to church
... he must have been to her room secretly before, and he
came again that night ... and he hadn't let anyone know,
or let anyone see him. ...' Dorothy paused, and put up her
hands to her eyes as if to shut out something that she still
saw. She resumed: 'It was when she was telling me that,
that she opened the Saratoga trunk. ... I saw ... there was
a kind of horrible, awful likeness to father. ... I just couldn't
move or speak or anything. ... She shut the lid again, and
she said first she gave him some poison in a glass of wine ...
and he lay down on the floor and was very ill and all
twisted up, but he didn't die ... so she took a pistol she had,
and shot him through the top of his head while he was
on the ground or trying to get up. ... She hid the body in'
the trunk, and no one ever knew ... at least she says she
thinks some of them knew ... only they never said, but
they all went away and left her there alone, and she thinks
that was why ... because they knew or just guessed, perhaps,
but they wouldn't say because of the scandal ... and she
just went on living there ... alone ... with It ... and then,
just as she had finished telling me, we heard an awful
noise downstairs, and she said, ever so quietly: "Perhaps
he has come back. I always thought he would, and the
other night I saw him at the window and I beckoned to
him, only then he went away, but now, perhaps, he's
come back again." ' Again Dorothy paused and shuddered.
'That made me ever so frightened again,' she said, 'because
then I knew she was mad.'

'She could hardly have remained sane,' Bobby said
gravely, 'living as she had done for so long.'

'Then she began to tell me, again, how they loved each
other,' Dorothy continued. 'It was dreadful. ... Oh, you

can't imagine how awful it sounded. She talked just as though he were still alive and she had simply been waiting for him as you might wait for anyone who had been away for a day or two. She said she had her wedding dress ready, and the wedding breakfast was all ready, too, and you know I had seen it ... on the table in that room downstairs, all covered with spider's webs, all withered away ... but she seemed to think it was just as it had been when they finished laying the table ... and I felt I couldn't bear it any longer, but I should go mad as well if I stopped another minute, and then, just as I was going, you knocked at the door.'

Chapter 17

MR ASKE'S STORY

THE strain of telling her strange and ghastly story, of living over again those dreadful moments at Tudor Lodge, was evidently proving too much for Dorothy. She was fighting hard to retain her self-control, but looked as if she might collapse at any minute. Fortunately Aske, who had been indignantly fidgeting for some time and looking as if he were only hesitating between committing a violent assault upon Bobby and carrying Dorothy off in the best 'Young Lochinvar' style, relieved the situation by compromising on a third course – that of suggesting that she should go and lie down. That set her off into a paroxysm of hysterical giggling, and Aske looked quite hurt and offended.

'Well, that's what mother always makes my kid sister do when she's more tangled up than usual with the parish magazine accounts,' he explained.

Dorothy went on giggling hysterically. Bobby suggested a glass of water. Aske improved on this with the idea of a cup of tea. Dorothy omitted to be grateful for either suggestion, but disappeared into her bedroom, emerging presently looking a little as if she had dipped her head in cold water and appearing considerably calmer.

'I'm so sorry,' she said, 'only you can't imagine ... it was all so terrible and no one could possibly help feeling most awfully sorry for that poor old thing, sitting there like a ghost, like the shadow of a ghost, and telling in her tiny, tiny voice what she did all those unhappy years ago. Oh, dear, don't people get themselves into frightful muddles?' she sighed.

She seemed quite composed again now, but Bobby thought it would be just as well to ask her no more questions for the present. That what she had told him was the truth, and the exact truth, he was quite convinced. There had been in her story an accent of sincerity impossible to mistake, of a genuine experience imprinted in all its vivid terror eternally upon her memory.

But he was not quite so sure that she had told him all the truth. No doubt it was her own kinsman who had been the victim of this distant crime, but a great-uncle one has never seen is but a shadowy relation, and it was not difficult to tell where her sympathies lay. Bobby felt it more than probable that she would have been willing enough to give help and shelter to the poor old woman who had so long and so painfully expiated her ancient crime. He would not have been greatly surprised, indeed, to find that Miss Barton was, in fact, somewhere in the flat at that very moment, though he hardly thought it very probable. He turned to Aske, feeling that while Dorothy was recovering herself it would be a good opportunity to put a few questions to the young man.

'I don't quite understand,' he said, 'how you come into all this. Do you mind explaining how you came to be at Tudor Lodge that time when Mrs Rice saw you there, and if it was your first visit?'

'Does it matter if I do mind?' Aske asked somewhat

sulkily. 'You seem to think everyone's got to tell you everything you choose to ask.'

'Not tell me,' Bobby reminded him gravely; 'not me,
but the King. It is the King's peace that we believe has
been broken, and that it is our duty in the police to see it
kept, or, if it is broken, then to see that the penalty is paid.'

'Oh, it has, it has – enough to satisfy anyone,' Dorothy
cried, interrupting. 'Oh, why can't the poor old woman
be left alone now? ... Aren't her memories enough – her
awful memories?'

'I can't see for the life of me why you can't leave her
alone,' agreed Aske.

'It is not for any of us to decide,' Bobby answered. 'There
is an inquest to be held, for one thing. Anyhow, we've our
duty to do.' He turned back to Aske. 'How was it you came
to be there? Did you know anything about Miss Barton
before?'

'No, not a thing; never heard of her till I nearly ran her
down one night, near the new County Hall,' Aske explained
slowly. 'I had been out in the car rather late, and, coming
home across Westminster Bridge, an old woman got right
in front, trying to cross the road or something. I pulled up
short just in time, and I hooted to warn her and it made
her jump. By a bit of bad luck, there was a banana skin
some fool had thrown down, as if Westminster Bridge
wasn't enough of a death-trap without that. She put her
foot on it when she jumped, and went over rather a smack,
so I stopped and got out and picked her up. She was pretty
badly shaken, and I thought perhaps I might as well give
her a lift home if it happened to be my way – of course,
there wasn't a policeman anywhere near; there never is
when you want one.'

'Never,' agreed Bobby contritely. 'I've noticed that
myself – it's our speciality. We're only there when we aren't
wanted. Go on, please, Mr Aske.'

'I asked her where she lived,' Aske continued, 'and she
didn't want to say. Well, she wasn't fit to be left alone;

she looked so old and frail. So I just told her if she wouldn't
say where she lived I should have to call the police to look
after her or else take her to St Thomas's across the road.
That seemed rather to scare her – of course, now I know
why – and she coughed up it was Brush Hill. I shoved her
in the car, started, and on the way she fainted. I had the
scare of my life. I made sure she was dead, and I was going
to be stuck with a dead woman in the car in the middle of
the night. Luckily she came round. I wanted to knock up a
doctor, but she swore she was all right again and I wasn't
so sure what a doctor would say if I hauled him out of bed
at that time of night to see an old lady who seemed quite
brisk and lively again. Then, when we got to Brush Hill,
she gave me another shock by fetching out a roll of one-
pound banknotes – quite a fat roll.'

'Could you tell about how many?' Bobby asked.

'No; there might have been fifty or a hundred or thereabouts,' Aske answered. 'It's rather hard to say. She
wanted to give me a fistful – not just one or two, but a
regular fistful she pulled out, without counting, just as if
they meant nothing to her. Of course, I wouldn't have
them, and she said a funny thing. She said: "Why not? I
only get them to give away"; so then I felt more certain
still she was a bit potty. And she said: "I've given away ten
times as many tonight." And I told her she had better
hang on to them while she had them and get someone to
look after her.'

'Can you say what day this was?' Bobby asked.

Aske kept no diary and had made no note, but he was
able to fix the date within a day or two, and Bobby said:

'I can't be quite certain without checking it to make sure,
but I think it was that afternoon she sold a diamond brooch
to a Bond Street firm of jewellers for £475, and, if so, when
you saw her on Westminster Bridge she must have been
coming away from leaving pound notes on the benches
all up and down the Embankment. She seems to have made
a practice of selling her jewellery from time to time, keeping

just as much of what she got as she thought she needed for a year or two and getting rid of the rest. She used to push pound notes through letter-boxes in poor streets or throw them to "down and outs" waiting to get into a Salvation Army shelter or anything like that – I suppose, perhaps, it was a kind of expiation, too. The papers used to talk about "The Mad Millionaire" and splash the story in headlines whenever it happened, but they never traced her or found out who she was. I suppose anyone who saw her hanging about the Embankment just thought she was one of the ordinary derelicts there.'

'Well, she certainly didn't look like anyone able to hand out pound notes galore,' Aske agreed. 'It fairly took my breath away when she pulled out that fat wad she showed me. It was a darkish sort of night, and when we got to Tudor Lodge I could make out it was a pretty dismal, desolate-looking sort of place, but I didn't see what it was actually like. I don't know that I should have wanted to leave her there alone if I had. I went round with her to the side door and I said something about did she live there all alone, and she said no, she had a friend she lived with, but he slept so sound nothing would ever waken him. I said if she would let me I would jolly soon rouse him out, because of course I had no idea what she was getting at. She said something about forty-three years that made me more sure than ever she was off her chump, and then she went on talking about having seen someone at the window who had come for her, so she knew it wouldn't be long now before she joined him, after he had been waiting for her all those years. I can tell you I was beginning to sweat a bit. I didn't feel one tiny bit happy, standing there in the dark, in the shadows of that old house, listening to all her weird talk. I said I must be going, and I said she ought to get someone to look after her, and then she said in quite a different way, as if she had suddenly come back into the real world, would I wait while she wrote a note to someone she knew and would I post it for her. I thought that was just what was wanted, and if she did that, then I could get her off my chest. I shouldn't have to feel responsible for her any more. So I waited all right, and she gave me the letter and began talking rot about how kind I had been. Of course, I hadn't done anything really except give her a lift, and you jolly well don't have to have a car long before you find out that's chiefly what it's for – giving other people lifts. But there was something about a pearl necklace she had been going to sell but now she would like to give it to me instead. Of course, I didn't take it very seriously, and I told her it was awfully kind of her but I must really be going, because they would be waiting up for me at home – they know better, in point of fact, but I had to say something to get away. So then she took the key out of the door and gave it me, and said if when I came again I couldn't get any answer, then I was to open the door and let myself in. I didn't want to argue with her any longer and I did want to get away, and so I took it – I thought it would be easy enough to send it back through the post. But I remember I did ask her how she was going to manage without it, and she said she had another; the door had two keys.'

'You are sure she said two?' Bobby asked quickly.

'Quite sure,' Aske answered. 'She said now we had one each, one for her and one for me. Then I cleared off, and when I looked at the letter she had given me I saw she had forgotten all about the stamp. So I put one on myself, and I noticed it was addressed to "Dorothy Yelton." '

'It's my name,' interposed Dorothy, who had been listening intently, 'but I think it was really grandmother she meant.'

'The address,' Aske continued, 'was at a little place I knew quite well. It's not far from where we are, and I've often driven through it – you have to if you are going west – so next time I was out for a bit of a spin I called at a pub near there and had a drink, and they told me some people called Yelton had been living there, but had moved, though only a short time before, so any letters sent them would probably reach them all right. They told

me what the London address was, and, as I didn't feel any
too easy about the whole thing, I thought I would call and
make sure they really had got the letter I posted. That's
how I came to know Miss Yelton and her father.'

'I see,' Bobby said. 'Did you send the key back?'

'No. When I called here I had a talk with Miss Yelton
about the old woman. Miss Yelton said she wasn't any
relation, and I could see she was very upset and troubled
and worried, and that she didn't know at all what to do.'

'Oh, I didn't,' exclaimed Dorothy fervently. 'I couldn't
think what was best – I felt it wasn't right to let her go on
living like that, and yet if I told anybody, then it would all
come out. I was most awfully grateful when Mr Aske said
he would go and see her again.'

'I went as soon as I could,' Aske continued. 'I had to
wait a day or two, because I had a chance to go up to
Yorkshire to see a man I'm trying to interest in an invention
of mine I want to bring out, if only I can get the capital
to develop it. But as soon as I could I went back to the
house. I couldn't get any answer when I knocked, so I let
myself in with the key she had given me. There didn't
seem to be anyone there, and I didn't get any answer
when I shouted. But I noticed a pistol lying on a chair in
the hall. Well, I didn't much like the look of that, when I
remembered that wad of banknotes I had seen or her talk
about the pearl necklace she said she had. So I picked the
pistol up and went into one of the rooms, and opened the
window so as to have a good look at it – all the house was
dark and in shadow, you know. But it was all right about
the pistol; it was all choked with dust and rusty; hadn't
been handled for years. I suppose that is when your Mrs
Rice saw me.'

'Probably,' agreed Bobby.

' I didn't go upstairs or in any of the other rooms,' Aske
continued. 'I knocked at one or two doors and shouted
again, but nobody answered, and I thought the old lady
must either be out or else she had gone away. I put the key

she had given me down on the table in the hall and let myself out by the front door and went off. I told Miss Yelton, and we were still wondering what we ought to do when the papers came out with the full story. And then we knew still less what to do, and finally we made up our minds to keep quiet. I don't know what you may think your duty is, but I don't see that it is any duty of ours to help you find her. I jolly well hope you don't, for that matter. What good will it do, anyhow, supposing you do?'

Bobby made no attempt to answer that question. He was deep in thought. As before, he felt fairly well convinced that Aske was speaking the truth, for he had told his story with an accent of sincerity it was difficult to believe was only assumed, and he had told it, too, with a wealth of detail that clearly suggested memory more than invention. But again, as before, Bobby was less convinced that the full truth had been told. The tale was complete perhaps as far as it went, but he could not shut his eyes to the possibility that it went further still. He said:

'When you left Tudor Lodge, did you fasten the back door?'

'It was on a latch; it caught when you shut it,' Aske explained. 'I left by the front door, though.'

'Have you told me all you know?' Bobby asked abruptly.

They both assured him that they had.

'I don't see we could have helped you even if we had told you all about it, as you make out we should have done,' Aske insisted again. 'I'm not pretending we're keen on your finding the poor old soul – why should we be? Why should anyone, for that matter? But I do say there's nothing we know about her, either of us, or where she is, or anything we could do to help you spot her, even if we wanted to. Of course, the moment I saw you messing round the house I knew you had got on to us somehow, and so I came straight along to warn Miss Yelton. I thought if you were on me you were most likely on her, too.'

'Of course,' said Bobby.

'Jolly glad you dropped on me first,' Aske observed.

'Gave me a chance, anyhow, to warn her to be ready for you.'

'So it did, didn't it?' agreed Bobby, resisting the temptation to explain that it was Aske himself who had shown the way to the Yelton flat. 'I suppose you have no objection to my looking through the flat to make sure Miss Barton isn't here?' he added to Dorothy. 'Someone must be giving her shelter, and, considering the life she's been living and her mental state, it's a little difficult to understand where she can be.'

'I suppose you'll be wanting to send a search-party to our place next, to see we haven't got her tucked away in the coal-cellar or somewhere,' grumbled Aske.

Bobby indicated placidly that that was quite likely. Every possibility had to be considered. Meanwhile, if Miss Yelton had no objection – they would be sure to ask him when he returned to the Yard if he had been through the flat, and he would like to be able to say he had. Miss Yelton had no objection – looked rather amused, indeed – and duly conducted Bobby round the flat, where, as a matter of fact, there hardly seemed room for a mouse to hide, much less a woman. So then he apologised for the trouble he had given them, feared they would be troubled again, as most likely superior authority would consider further interviews required, and so took his leave, returning to headquarters in a somehwat thoughtful mood and very much wondering if he had heard all there was to tell.

Chapter 18

FRESH TRAIL

ON his return to headquarters Bobby was lucky enough to find Mitchell as comparatively disengaged as superintendents of the C.I.D. are ever likely to be. Bobby's account

of his success in tracing and identifying two of the mysterious strangers seen at Tudor Lodge, and of the stories
they had told him, was listened to with a good deal of
interest, and, when he had finished, Mitchell commented
slowly:

'Well, it's something to know what two of them were
doing there, and their stories sound as if they were telling
the truth, but do you think they have told it all?'

'Well, sir, I've been rather wondering that myself,'
Bobby admitted. 'Anyhow, I'm quite sure of one thing –
whether they know, either of them, anything more about
Miss Barton or not – they haven't got her there, not in the
flat. I went all over it.'

'No, I don't suppose she would be there,' Mitchell remarked. 'They may know something about her, though
they don't want to tell.'

'That's the trouble in this case,' Bobby observed, somewhat ruefully. 'No one wants us to find her, and no one's
going to help.'

'Do you want to yourself?' Mitchell flashed at him,
and Bobby answered, rather stiffly:

'I know my duty, sir.'

'But is the heart in it?' Mitchell asked; and then, without waiting for an answer: 'I'll tell you whose heart is in it
– mine is.' He spoke with an abrupt, somewhat startling
energy. His face had taken on the grim expression that
Bobby knew well – the look of the man-hunter, hard upon
the trail, who will never slacken or weary till his task is done,
his end achieved.

Bobby sat silent and bewildered. He could not imagine
what made Mitchell speak with so fiery and intense an
energy. He knew well the Mitchell who would spare neither
himself nor others to vindicate outraged law – to see that
by road and by path all might go in safety upon their
lawful business, the weak as well as the strong. But he could
not for the life of him imagine why Mitchell should feel
like that in the matter of this search for an old and lonely

woman that, as Bobby knew perfectly well, no one else at the Yard was following up with any real energy. Indeed, failure to bring it to success Bobby himself was quite prepared to regard with complete resignation, even though he intended, as he had said, to do his duty. But why Mitchell should have spoken with such energy was beyond Bobby's comprehension, especially as till now that energy and resolution he generally showed had been less marked than usual. As though he were answering Bobby's thoughts – and, indeed, it may be that he was, for he had an uncanny power of reading what was in the minds of others – Mitchell said:

'You think it won't matter much if we can't find out what's become of a harmless old woman? Well, are you so sure she's harmless?'

'Sir?' said Bobby astonished.

'Only God knows what was in her mind when she left Tudor Lodge,' Mitchell went on, 'but one thing's certain – she wasn't in a normal state. Suppose she thinks she is escaping from enemies; suppose she has it in her half-crazed mind that she's got to defend herself, and possibly her pearl necklace, from pursuers, enemies; suppose she still has a supply of that arsenic she used on James Yelton fifty years ago; suppose she starts making use of it again.'

'Good God, sir!' exclaimed Bobby. 'You don't think –'

'I think it's a distinct possibility,' Mitchell answered gravely. 'I've been talking to – .' He mentioned the name of an eminent medical man, the chief Home Office consultant in such matters. 'He thinks there's more than a danger. Once a poisoner, always a poisoner; and when in a mind already half-crazed there are nearly certainly ideas of persecution, escaping pursuit, self-defence, and so on, the danger is ten times greater.'

'But we don't know that she has any arsenic in her possession,' Bobby said.

'It is certain a very big dose was given James Yelton; it is what helped to preserve the body – that and the conditions under which it was kept,' Mitchell answered. 'If she used it so freely, it is at least possible she had access to a large quantity. The stuff was easier to get in those days than it is now. There is the chance that she still has some in her possession, and, if she has, she might easily make use of it to protect herself against the pursuit she very likely thinks has chased her from her refuge in Tudor Lodge. I shall be a good deal easier in my mind when we know what's become of her. Apart from other possibilities,' he added abruptly.

Bobby was silent. It was a new idea to him, this of the half-crazed old woman all the world felt so sorry for, as a potential danger to the community. Yet he saw the risk was a real one.

Her secret she had guarded so long was disclosed to. the world, but she might well feel she still had her life to defend, and even her pearl necklace, last of her possessions, as well. He sat silent, contemplating an aspect of the affair quite new to his thoughts, and Mitchell went on:

'If they've told you the truth, these two we've got tabbed know nothing about where she is now. There's still the man in plus-fours Mrs Rice talks about – I suppose neither of these two know anything of him?'

'Well, sir,' Bobby said slowly, 'it's not much to go on, but I noticed in Miss Yelton's flat a photograph of a man in plus-fours. I understood he was her father. I thought perhaps it might be as well if some excuse was made to ask him a few questions.'

Mitchell nodded thoughtfully.

'In a case like this, can't neglect even the off chance,' he remarked. 'Miss Yelton would naturally tell her father about her visit to Tudor Lodge, and it would be quite natural for him to go there to see for himself. The firm is reported hard up, isn't it?'

'Yes, sir.'

'Quite so,' observed Mitchell. 'Well, we've information now that they paid off certain liabilities the other day and reduced their overdraft at the bank very considerably – apparently they have made payments to the extent of about seven or eight thousand pounds. It seems that's about what the pearl necklace Con Conway described might bring in if it had to be disposed of in a hurry. Of course, that may be another coincidence.'

'Yes, sir,' agreed Bobby doubtfully.

'Another reason for trying to find Miss Barton as soon as possible,' Mitchell said. 'If it's her necklace which has provided the money Mr Yelton seems suddenly to have got hold of, what has become of her? There's no record of anyone else having been seen near the house, is there?'

'No, sir. Of course, that's not certain, but Mrs Rice strikes me as a lady who doesn't let much escape her, and she is quite clear she has seen no one else, except, of course, Wild and myself, and the people like the postman and bill distributors, and so on, and the man who used to deliver her groceries twice a week.'

'Vanished too,' observed Mitchell, 'and no trace of him so far. Spent all his life in the shop there – made his living by it – and now he closes it down and disappears. Only it seems as if he had been preparing for something of the sort, by the way he kept talking about how well he was doing with his new garden line, and how he might be selling out soon at a good price. That doesn't hang together with the idea of a sudden flight with Miss Barton. Besides, if she's gone with him, that means three of them, and three in a group should be easy to trace. Anyhow, I think the next step indicated is to find Mr Humphreys and make sure about him.'

'We've been trying to, haven't we, sir?' Bobby asked meekly.

'We have,' admitted Mitchell. 'Complete wash-out so far – that's why we must go on trying. Any ideas on how to set to work – outside the usual routine, I mean?'

Bobby admitted that he hadn't.

'What about making some enquiries among commercial

travellers?' asked Mitchell. 'I suppose a good many of
them must have seen him and known him – I got Mrs
Mitchell to ask at the shop where she goes, but I gather
they told her commercial travellers are to customers in the
ratio of ten thousand to one, and that the shop keeps one
assistant whose sole duty is to say "No" to them. Try to get
in touch with any travellers who had Humphreys' shop on
their round, and see if you can find out anything that way.
Another thing. Humphreys has worked all his life, long
hours, and plenty of them, and no outside interests that we
can hear of. Unless he has got started in a new shop – and
new shops, and shops with changes of management, have
been fairly well combed now – he'll be at a bit of a loose
end, and he is described as a talkative sort. So it's a fair
chance he may be doing the daily buying of what he and
his wife want, and might easily get chatting with the shopkeeper and explain he had been in business, too – get gossip-
ing, you know, as two of a trade will. You might have a
try at following that idea up.'

'Yes, sir,' Bobby said again, though with some hesitation,
for the chance of meeting with success on such lines seemed
to him small enough.

'A strange case, altogether,' Mitchell continued, talking
half to himself now. 'It's caught the public imagination –
they're all on her side, too. Can't wonder, I suppose,
considering the way the papers have been letting themselves go. I give you my word, Owen, I saw a fat old boy in
the tube, yesterday, wiping his eyes over that last article
in the *Daily Announcer*. Fairly sniffling he was. If we find
her living with Humphreys and Mrs Humphreys in some
quite country village, and try to arrest her – upon my
word, I believe there'll be a riot, and meetings in Hyde
Park, and Lord knows what.'

'Yes, sir,' agreed Bobby.

'There's quite a lot of pressure coming along to make
us give up looking for her,' Mitchell said slowly. 'It means
public feeling's pretty strong when you get both the *Morning*

Intelligence and the *Daily Announcer* barking up the same tree. The worst of it is, if we don't find her we shall get laughed at as incompetent muddlers, and if we do find her we shall be howled at for heartless bullies. So you'll remember to be careful what you do.'

'Yes, sir,' Bobby said again.

'Though perhaps there won't be any need,' Mitchell added. 'There's always that chance as well – that when we find her there won't be any need for care.' He began to look among the papers on his desk. 'There's a long letter from Allen & Wildman's manager this morning,' he said. 'They found a note somewhere in one of their books to the effect that Miss Barton was connected with "Barton's of Hatton Garden", and it seems there are still one or two old boys in Hatton Garden who remember "Barton's" well enough. It was a firm in a biggish way at one time, and one man even remembers the last partner, and can say he was a widower with one daughter. He went out of business rather abruptly – apparently about 1890. He closed down in Hatton Garden, and nothing more was seen or heard of him by any of his old associates. It is at least a fair guess that he knew or suspected what had happened, couldn't denounce his own daughter, couldn't stand the knowledge, possibly was afraid of being implicated himself and went abroad to America or Australia, taking his money with him, but leaving his stock of jewellery to the daughter for her support. He may have died years ago; he is spoken of as elderly then. Anyhow, he can hardly be living still. That is why no enquiry was ever made by Allen & Wildman as to where Miss Barton got the jewellery from she was selling. Originally they knew her father had held a good stock for trade purposes, and afterwards it was supposed no questions were necessary as she was an old and well-known customer. One of the Hatton Garden dealers was even able to produce an old boy who had been his father's clerk, and who remembered Mr Barton's last big transaction before he went out of business having been the purchaser of a fine pearl necklace, valued at five figures. At this distance of time he couldn't give any details, but he was quite sure of the main fact and said he had often wondered what had become of that necklace, as you didn't often see one like it. And he agreed the pearl found at Tudor Lodge might well have been part of it – they all agree it has certainly been part of a necklace. And I would give a good deal to know where that necklace is now.'

'Would not Miss Barton naturally have taken it with her?' Bobby asked.

'If she has, all the more necessary we should find her as soon as possible,' Mitchell said. 'This is no sort of world for half-crazed old ladies to be wandering about in with pearl necklaces in their possession valued at five figures. I would like to know, too, what clothes she was wearing. The things she was always seen in are those she left behind. Had she a new outfit? If she had, what was it? Where did she get it? Who bought it for her? Ferris has been working along those lines, but he's drawn a blank every time. Then there's the old wedding dress it seems clear she was in the habit of putting on at times. What's become of that? Did she take it with her? She can't possibly have been wearing it, surely, or someone would have noticed her. Besides, there's the one shoe that was left behind.'

'That looks a little as if the wedding dress had been packed up in a hurry,' Bobby remarked.

'It might suggest something else,' mused Mitchell, and Bobby told himself that remark, and the tone in which it was made, meant there was some idea working in Mitchell's mind that would probably come to fruition soon.

Quickly Bobby decided to go over the whole case again, in his mind, from the very start, to see if he could not discover what it was Mitchell was apparently beginning to find significant.

'Well, carry on,' Mitchell said, turning to his papers, with a nod of dismissal. 'Call on Mr Yelton first and have a talk with him, and see if that suggests anything, and then work the commercial-traveller idea – and if you can guess why Humphreys has been telling lies about making a good profit on selling garden-stuff, don't forget to let me know.'

'No, sir,' said Bobby, puzzled, and withdrew.

Why, he wondered, should Mitchell be beginning to attach importance to the fairly obvious lies Humphreys had told about those mythical profits of his from his newly-developed trade in garden-stuff? Very likely he boasted just for the sake of boasting, or to impress customers or creditors with the increasing prosperity of his business, or it might be some prospective purchaser of the shop.

'I suppose Mitchell can't possibly have got it into his head,' Bobby thought smilingly, 'that Humphreys started dealing in garden-stuff so as to have a spade handy in order to bury the old lady in the Tudor Lodge garden after he murdered her? Only, unless he has some such notion, what's he worrying about Humphreys' garden trade for?'

Chapter 19

BUSINESS CONVERSATIONS

YET this idea, though he dismissed it at first as absurd, since he scarcely thought it possible to cast the mild, timid, conventional little suburban grocer that was Humphreys for the part of the first murderer, kept recurring again and again to Bobby's mind. It was at any rate certain that Mitchell saw something significant in Humphreys' chattering tarradiddles about the big profits earned by his new line in garden requisites, and Mitchell's somewhat slow-moving but generally sure mind was one of which the ideas were seldom expressed till they had been tested and found good. Bobby made up his mind that as soon as he could snatch a spare moment he would visit Brush Hill again and have another look at the garden of Tudor Lodge – though, indeed, if Mitchell's suspicions were moving in that direction, it was hard to understand why he had not at once directed that a search should be made.

But that would have to wait. Bobby's first duty was to pay a visit to Mr Yelton. The offices of Yelton & Markham were situated close to the Tower, and certainly they did not, Bobby thought, give a very great impression of prosperity, or suggest that any share of the some thousands Mitchell had somehow got to know had recently been disbursed by the firm had been expended on renovations. Not that this general air Bobby thought he perceived of a losing fight waged against adverse circumstance was due merely to the fact that the premises seemed in the last stage of decrepitude, as if they had known neither paint nor repair for decades, and that the interior of the office was dark and shabby and poorly furnished. Bobby was well enough aware that in the City of London there are firms whose activities are world wide, whose bankers treat them with anxious deference, but whose headquarters suggest those of an insolvent rag-and-bone merchant.

What was significant was that about Yelton & Markham's office there seemed to hang a general air of somnolence. There was no coming and going, no bustle of activity, no ringing of telephone bells; the staff seemed to have little to do and not to think that the doing of it mattered greatly. Even the junior clerk who came forward when Bobby entered had a slight air of surprise at seeing him, as though visitors were rare.

Nor did he seem a very intelligent junior clerk. He appeared quite unable to believe that it was Mr Yelton Bobby wanted to see, and made various efforts to usher him instead into Mr Markham's room, explaining that, though Mr Markham had been away ill, he was now back again at work. It rather looked, Bobby thought, as if so few people ever wanted to interview Mr Yelton that the junior clerk could not believe it was not really Mr Markham who was wanted. Bobby was also inclined to guess that during the absence, owing to this recent illness, of Mr Markham, Mr Yelton had not handled what business there was with any conspicuous success – even though, apparently, there had been a windfall, according to Mitchell's information, of several thousands of pounds. Finally it emerged that, anyhow, Mr Yelton was not in at the moment.

'Then I'll wait for him,' said Bobby with decision, and the junior clerk gave it up with a general air of being accustomed to treat difficult problems like that, returning thereupon contentedly to his desk in the corner and his former occupation of playing noughts and crosses with himself.

Luckily it was not long before Mr Yelton arrived. He seemed a physically brisk, vigorous man of middle age and middle height, but with the somewhat dull and vacant eyes of a man not much used to thinking. He would probably have been happiest, Bobby guessed, in some routine outdoor occupation – he would have made a first-rate sergeant-major, for instance, or even general in time of peace; and, after all, it is in time of peace that most generals function – but hardly the type likely to do well in the intense competition of modern business; and, indeed, his chief triumphs had been won upon the links, for once he had even done well in the Open, and always he cherished the secret belief that had circumstances been propitious he might have achieved a great position in the game. Characteristically, he expected circumstances to be propitious, and, if they were not, considered that a fully sufficient reason for failure.

A curious thing, however, that Bobby noticed at once, and that worried and bothered him greatly, was that he found in Mr Yelton an odd, teasing, troubling resemblance to someone he had once seen. Yelton himself, he was sure, was a complete stranger, but yet there was a kind of family resemblance, as it were, to someone he had seen on some

previous occasion. Whether it lay in some resemblance
of feature, or in some trick of manner, Bobby could not
determine; and he was at any rate sure that it did not lie
in any family likeness he and his daughter bore to each
other, for there seemed no feature in which there was any
resemblance between the child and the father. Bobby
made a mental note to find out if Mr Yelton had any male
relatives, and, if so, to get a look at them all in turn.

Another thing Bobby noticed – and that confirmed his
previous impression that the business was in none too
prosperous a state – was that while he was talking to Mr
Yelton they were not once interrupted. No letters were
brought in for signature; no phone bell rang; no one came
knocking at the door for instructions.

A placid life, Bobby thought, business men seemed to
lead, and he wished he had nothing to do but doze in an
office all day instead of chasing wild geese up and down
the country.

Mr Yelton seemed disposed, however, to be both frank
and communicative in his drawling, somewhat irritatingly
superior way, though of course a certain loftiness of manner
is only natural, and even to be expected and approved,
in a 'plus' man living in a world composed chiefly of
rabbits. He admitted at once that he had paid a visit to
Tudor Lodge, but denied emphatically that he had either
entered or attempted to enter the house, or that he had
had sight of, or speech with, its unhappy inmate. His
daughter had told him about her nerve-racking experience,
and a natural curiosity had taken him to have a look at
the house on his way back from a golfing afternoon. He
agreed, too, that from the first he had felt it was most likely
the dead body concealed in the Saratoga trunk was that of
his uncle, his father's brother, who had disappeared so
mysteriously.

'A bad lot, I'm afraid,' Mr Yelton said frankly. 'It wasn't
only the two women he had promised to marry – he had
played himself into the rough with others as well. One

particularly bad case was with the daughter of one of the
staff – most destressing case altogether. My father did his
best to make up. There was money trouble as well – one
of those men who can never drive straight, you know. I
expect the family and everyone else was extremely relieved
when he scratched. Of course, no one had any idea what
had really happened. They just took it he felt bunkered for
keeps and decided to vanish. Most likely what they were all
most afraid of was that he would turn up again. They were
always expecting him to, but he never did, and now 'of
course we know why.'

In answer to further questions, Mr Yelton agreed that
he knew very well that, strictly speaking, he ought to have
reported his daughter's discovery to the authorities. He
quite recognised that, but he hadn't in the least felt like
doing so. What was the good of raking up old scandals?
Besides, the publicity would have been most distasteful
to his daughter, who had already had one bad shock and
was in no condition to face all the fuss and excitement
which would have resulted. It was not as though there was
any vindictive feeling against Miss Barton. The poor old
creature had suffered enough for what she had done, and
her victim had met no more than his deserts. Anyhow, Mr
Yelton had not seen then, did not see now, what harm there
could be in adding another week or so of delay to the forty-
five years that had gone by, and Bobby was again aware
of a general impression that Mr Yelton solved in the same
way most of the problems life presented to him – that is,
by doing nothing. A weak, well-meaning man, Bobby
summed him up, and no more of the stuff of which deliber-
ate, cold-blooded murderers are made than was Humphreys
himself. Though, of course, one can never tell, Bobby
reminded himself; psychology is no exact science, and
the human soul has strange and dark and sometimes
dreadful qualities that slumber in it till emergency awakes
them.

Mr Yelton went on talking. No good purpose would have

been served by saying anything about his daughter's experience, he insisted. Then the paper came out with the news that the discovery had been made independently of any action of his or of his daughter's, and that had been rather a relief. For his part, he did not see why the whole thing could not be dropped. What was the good of harrying a feeble old woman on the edge of the grave, or of raking up old family scandals?

One thing he made quite clear, speaking with an air of sincerity that impressed. Neither he nor his daughter had the very least idea what had become of Miss Barton – though he admitted also that, even if they had known, they would probably not have been in any hurry to communicate their knowledge to the authorities.

'Let it drop, let it alone,' he kept repeating. 'Pick up and concede the hole,' he urged.

Another point he was emphatic upon was that they had not breathed a word to anyone about the affair or their connection with it. They had discussed it between themselves, of course – and naturally with young Aske; but, then, Aske had known all about it from the beginning. It was he to whom had been entrusted the letter that had in the first place taken Dorothy to Tudor Lodge.

'The old scandal is still remembered in the office, and outside, too, I expect,' Yelton said, somewhat moodily. 'Not likely I was going to start all that beastly gossip all over again.'

He agreed, too, that Dorothy had told him about the pearl necklace Miss Barton showed her. But he had not paid that story much attention, though it was true there was a vague family legend to the effect that James Yelton had probably been willing to marry Miss Barton only in order to lay his hands on her jewellery. Her dowry was to have been, apparently, a good share of the jewellery in which her father was said to have his capital invested, and possibly this pearl necklace might be a relic of that legendary store. Certainly Dorothy had insisted that it looked tremendously valuable. But then, she knew nothing about jewellery, declared Mr Yelton with all a father's dogmatism, and as likely as not the thing was only imitation. Imitations were often good enough to deceive experts, much more young girls like Dorothy. (Mr Yelton suffered from the usual male-parent delusion that young girls don't know much, whereas in point of fact they generally know practically everything.) Of course, one couldn't tell. Anyhow, he knew nothing about it. Presumably, valuable or not, it was still in Miss Barton's possession. If she had kept it safely for half a century or so, she was probably capable of keeping it safely a little longer. But Bobby could rest assured that in any case no living soul had heard about the pearl necklace, either from himself or from his daughter. It had never ever been mentioned between themselves except on that one occasion. They had not spoken of it since, and certainly not to any third person.

'No good starting all that old story all over again,' Mr Yelton grumbled.

Bobby thought he seemed somewhat sensitive about a tale fifty years old, but was inclined to accept his denial. Guilty, he would not have talked, and innocent, this disinclination to risk reviving old gossip would equally have kept him silent.

Rather neatly, Bobby now got in a reference to any relatives Mr Yelton might possess. But Mr Yelton explained that he had none. He and Dorothy were alone in the world. He grew, indeed, quite pathetic about their loneliness. It was apparently a favourite theme, for Mr Yelton was a man always profuse in pity for himself, and Bobby let him dilate upon it for some minutes, while there still persisted, as there had done in his mind all through this long and inconclusive interview, that worrying, teasing feeling he had of a vague, shadowy resemblance that Mr Yelton showed to someone Bobby had once seen. Of course, it might be merely a coincidence, due to some chance resemblance, and, indeed, it is a fact that people, complete strangers to each other, sometimes display a most strange mutual resemblance.

Mr Yelton seemed quite prepared to go on talking for another hour or two, but Bobby thought it about time to bring the conversation to a close, and so took his departure, emerging from Mr Yelton's private room into the outer office just as a tall man in top hat and morning coat was leaving it.

'Our Mr Markham,' explained the dumpy little white-haired senior clerk to Bobby. 'He has been waiting in the hope of having a talk with you, but he has an appointment with some big American people this morning and he couldn't stay any longer.'

'Anything special he wanted to say?' Bobby asked.

'Oh no, but we're all interested, naturally,' declared the senior clerk. 'Mr Yelton's looking very worried – newspaper men calling and all that. Naturally we told them nothing,' he added primly; and from one or two other things he said Bobby felt certain that the scandal, old as it was, to which Mr Yelton had referred, was still a living memory with some at any rate of his staff.

Bobby lingered to chat a little, but soon convinced himself that the senior clerk had nothing to tell and also that he was far too prudent and discreet to tell that nothing. But one thing was clear: he had great respect for the senior partner as an employer, as a golfer, for his educational qualifications – 'Eton and Cambridge,' said the senior clerk in an awestruck voice, 'and took very high honours, very high indeed,' a statement which surprised Bobby a little till he reflected that a certain knack in passing examinations is not necessarily indicative of high intelligence, and that even what intelligence is indicated may presently rust away from disuse. Presumably it was on account of this sort of social aura that seemed to surround Mr Yelton that all his colleagues of the office, from junior partner to office-boy, appeared to have adopted a somewhat haughty 'looking down the nose' kind of attitude towards the rest of the world, an attitude Bobby thought little likely to help the firm in these days of intense competition.

But for his employer as a business man the senior clerk seemed to have no respect whatever. What he said, indeed, confirmed Bobby's previous impression that the business was almost entirely conducted by Mr Markham. Even during Mr Markham's recent illness, when he had been recuperating in the Bournemouth nursing-home whither he had gone for some slight operation to be performed, he had still directed all the activities of the firm. Every night a full report had been sent to him at Bournemouth for delivery next morning, and by return had come back full and explicit directions, delivered at the office the following morning.

'Never missed once,' said the little clerk proudly, 'not even the day of the operation.'

As, however, he seemed to have nothing of very great interest or importance to say, Bobby took himself off to carry out his next task – that of searching for some commercial traveller who had known Humphreys and might possibly have either knowledge of his present whereabouts or be able to give some hint of where to look for him. And in this effort he met, for once in this extraordinarily difficult and tantalising case, with a piece of remarkable good luck.

Everyone has heard, and most people have partaken, of the 'Ninety-Nine Delights – British, Pre-Digested', that almost every hoarding crashes on the attention of the passer-by, roaring to him that they range from genuine best tinned turtle to finest superior best Brussels sprouts, and that they may be obtained from any grocer for a mere sixpence (home, sweet home size), shilling (lordly mansion size), or half-crown (Lord Mayor's banquet size). It was the well-known picture of a family, from great-grandfather to new-born babe, all hysterical with joy over a dinner-table furnished solely from the contents of these different tins that caught Bobby's eye as he left the office of Yelton & Markham, and that reminded him he had once seen an enormous pyramid of such tins in the window of Humphreys' shop at the corner of Battenberg Prospect in Brush Hill, filling it with so many bright and varied hues as no tropic sunset could have rivalled, dazzling indeed the spectator by their outward glory just as their contents made the digestive process a mere anachronism or as they replaced culinary skill by skill in the use of the tin-opener. So now, inspired by this contribution to what has been libellously called the People's Gallery of Art, Bobby took himself off to the chief office of the Ninety-Nine Delights – British, Pre-Digested – Corporation where it rears its splendid head twelve stories high in Mayfair Gardens, overlooking St James's Palace, which it reduces to the insignificance proper to a mere royal palace by the side of a palace of commerce.

And what a contrast this hustling hive of industry presented to the somnolent offices of Yelton & Markham that Bobby had just left! Here the phone bell never ceased from ringing nor the telegraph-boys from arriving. Here the most junior clerk was obviously the 'go-get' chrysalis of a millionaire, and here every typist banged her machine as if she knew the whole balance of trade hung upon the nimbleness of her fingers. Indeed, Bobby was soon thinking himself lucky to have been able to escape giving that order for the instant delivery of a thousand cases, assorted, which he felt the super-efficiency of the place must almost automatically extract from all who crossed its threshold.

However, when he had managed at last to make his business known, he was instantly shot up to the tenth floor in an express lift that didn't stop till it reached the twelfth. He was then swiftly hurried down again two floors, bustled thence through a labyrinth of corridors, only to be abruptly deserted before a maze of doors, all painted with different names and all intimidatingly marked 'Private'. However, at last he managed to reach the presence of a Mr Smithers, who proved to be in charge for 'Ninety-Nine Delights – British, Pre-Digested' of the Brush Hill district.

'Humphreys, Battenberg Prospect, Brush Hill?' repeated Mr Smithers. 'Knew him all right – got a good order out of the little rat and then he went back on it. Did a window display for him, too. Funny thing, one of our chaps was telling me he saw him the other day – said he had sold out at a good figure and retired on it. There are,' said Mr Smithers gratefully, 'lots of suckers in the world, but Humphreys must have found the champion sucker of them all. Dead-alive hole he was in – no traffic, bus route changed, several multiple branches quite close. Why, I would as soon have bought a dud ticket in the Irish sweepstakes three days after the race was over as that place of his.'

'I heard he had been doing well selling garden requisites,' Bobby remarked.

'Garden my eye!' retorted Mr Smithers. 'Of course,' he conceded, 'that's what he may have told the sucker he sold out to. I must tell our chap on that round to look the new man up. Ought to be able to sell him all creation, and St Paul's Cathedral thrown in as soon as look at him – only, of course, it will have to be cash,' added Mr Smithers thoughtfully, 'and quite likely Humphreys won't have left him any.'

'Where was it your man met Humphreys?' Bobby asked.

Mr Smithers didn't know, but said he would try to find out, and, after ringing up various people unsuccessfully, suddenly remembered that Ryder across the corridor might know. The traveller who had met Humphreys had been so surprised at seeing him, and at hearing that he had sold out his Brush Hill business at a good price, that he had repeated the story to several of his colleagues, and might have to Ryder.

Anyhow, it would do no harm to ask Ryder, and luckily Ryder was able to supply the information. It was a small village in the Cotswolds, and thither Bobby supposed, correctly, his wandering footsteps would now have to be directed.

Chapter 20

THE HUMPHREYS' STORY

To the Cotswold village concerned, therefore, Bobby was permitted forthwith to depart by motor-cycle, with instructions that if he found Humphreys and his wife there, and Miss Barton with them, then he was to take no action, but report and wait for orders. If, however, Humphreys and his wife were there, but alone, then he was to question them, and try to assure himself whether their flight from Brush Hill was in any way connected with Miss Barton's disappearance. If they had been in the village and had left, then every possible step was to be taken at once to trace and follow them.

The weather was still fine, calm, and not too hot, and Bobby felt that for once he was in luck, and that after all there might just possibly be something to be said for police work when it gave you the chance of a long leisurely ride in the sweet country air through some of the loveliest scenery in the land.

But Bobby was young, and no exception to the general rule that a motor-cycle, most modern of modernities, wakens instantly all that is most primitive, violent, and barbaric in a young man's nature, so that just as the first youth on the first horse probably thought of nothing but galloping, galloping, so the last boy on the last new motor-cycle certainly thinks of nothing but speeding, speeding, speeding. At any rate, that is what always happened to Bobby, and as soon as he had the motor-cycle between his legs there grew a feverish light in his eyes, his sole idea became to see how fast he could make the mile-posts skim by, and his long leisurely journey in the sweet country air through lovely scenery he accomplished in such a riot of dust and clamour, in such a haze of petrol and exhaust gas, in such a series of nerve-racking, neck-risking escapes, that when he reached his destination he was glad to quench his thirst in a stuffy bar-parlour, where it was at least cool and shadowed, and where the smell of stale beer and staler tobacco was, at any rate, a change from the smell of petrol and exhaust gas.

Refreshed, he went on to the local police-station, where they had been warned to expect him, and where, though he was still a full half-hour before his time, he found no less a personage than the Chief Constable of the county, Major Griggs, waiting to receive him. So much had the Tudor Lodge case stirred the imagination of the whole country, indeed, that even Chief Constables themselves were excited about it, and eager to know the latest details.

So there was a very full report ready for Bobby, who, for his part, would have preferred a less exalted personage to deal with, since a Sergeant is always at something of a disadvantage when talking to a Chief Constable. However, fortunately, the Major allowed the local Sergeant to tell his story himself, and to answer Bobby's questions. It appeared that a man who gave his name as Hutchings, but answered to the description of the missing Humphreys, was staying with his wife in the village – at a cottage where they had a bedroom and the use of a sitting-room. Their story was that they had been in business in London, and were here to enjoy a quiet change and holiday in the country. They seemed great readers of the papers, buying several every day, and Mr Hutchings, in a moment of expansion, had confided to Mr Bloomfield, the proprietor of the only grocer's shop in the village, that he, too, had been in the grocery line. He had even declared that he had made money in it – a statement which Mr Bloomfield frankly regarded as incredible, unless the grocery business was very different in London from what it was in the country. However, Mr Hutchings had ex-

plained that his had been a really tip-top establishment, doing a high-class trade and employing a number of assistants,
and these further statements had confirmed Mr Bloomfield
in his opinion that Mr Hutchings was extremely inexact in
his remarks – only, Mr Bloomfield expressed that belief by
means of a single adjective and a single noun. Consequently
Mr Hutchings' further statement – that he was looking for a
good, sound, well-established business to purchase, and
might even be tempted to buy Mr Bloomfield's, if the price
was right – had not been treated very seriously.

'High class, indeed,' Mr Bloomfield had snorted indignantly to the Police-Sergeant. 'Tip-top nothing ... four or
five smart assistants – all my eye ... bah! General stores in
a back street, if you ask me, him and his missus ran together,
with one errand-boy to help – that's more their sort.'

'Which is not so far out,' agreed Bobby, smiling, 'except
that they really had one assistant once, and so smart, I believe, they caught him at the till and had to clear him out in
a hurry. I daresay the one errand-boy was more like it, as a
rule.'

But one thing seemed quite clear. The Humphreys were
quite alone. No one else was with them, or had been seen
with them, and they had no visitors and, their landlady said,
no letters. They seemed to be well supplied with money, but
to be careful of it, even though inclined to boast of the large
sum for which they said they had disposed of their London
business.

'The odd thing about that,' Bobby remarked, 'is that, if
it's been bought, it's been bought, apparently, merely to
close it down. It's been shut ever since Humphreys left. One
day he seems to have been there, working as usual. The next
the shutters stayed up, Humphreys and his wife cleared out,
and the shutters are still up.'

'Queer,' agreed Major Griggs. 'You mean there's no one
in residence there at all?'

'Apparently not. Our men have knocked several times
without getting any reply, and the neighbours say they've

never seen any sign of life there since Humphreys left.'

'Perhaps there never was any sale, they just came away.'

'The shop was Humphreys' living,' Bobby pointed out. 'He can hardly have afforded to close down without some money from somewhere – besides, he paid two quarters' rent in advance.'

'That sounds queerer than ever,' agreed the Major. 'I mean, paying rent in advance – suggests to my mind there's something in the shop Humphreys doesn't want seen.'

'Yes, sir,' agreed Bobby thoughtfully, 'there's that.'

'You are going to have a talk with Humphreys, I understand?'

'Yes, sir,' repeated Bobby. 'Instructions were I was to put some questions to him unless Miss Barton was with them.'

'I'm afraid she's still missing, as far as that goes,' observed the Major. 'Something about a pearl necklace, too, I understand?'

'Supposed to be worth a lot of money,' confirmed Bobby, 'but that's not certain. What is certain is, a valuable pearl that looked as if it had been part of a necklace was found at Tudor Lodge, that Miss Barton was in possession of a necklace she said was valuable, and that she has been living all these years by selling jewellery. If there is any left, she must have it with her, or –'

'Or –' repeated the Major, and for a moment he, too, left the sentence unfinished. Then he said: 'It looks very much to me as if the old lady had been done in and the necklace stolen.'

'Yes, sir,' agreed Bobby.

'I suppose you've considered the other alternative – that she may be wandering about with a pearl necklace and a persecution mania, and a packet of arsenic for defence. Once a poisoner, always a poisoner, is good criminology, I think.'

'It's why Mr Mitchell is so anxious to find her,' Bobby explained. 'There's always the doubt in one's mind – whether she's victim herself, or likely to make new victims of others. I know Mr Mitchell is very uneasy. Though, after fifty years, you wouldn't think she would be likely to start again.'

'I was talking to a doctor – well-known man,' Major Griggs replied. 'I put the case to him – he thought the danger very real. He said an impulse might easily lie dormant for as long as half a century, and then, on some stimulus being given, re-awaken stronger than ever. I think the sooner it's known where Miss Barton is, and what's she doing, the better.'

He spoke with emphasis, and Bobby was aware of a momentary vision of a frail old creature passing like a decrepit and feminine Azrael through a busy, unsuspecting world, and scattering her white powder of death around her as she went. It was an imaginative but not wholly impossible picture, and the apprehension of it lay heavy upon Bobby.

'I think we shall all be glad, sir, when she's found,' he said presently. 'Only, if it's like that, it would imply that there can't be any connection between her disappearance and Humphreys giving up his shop.'

'Why should there be?' demanded the Major. 'Very likely the fellow did sell, and the new purchaser isn't ready to start yet, that's all.'

They talked a little longer, and then the Major offered to drive Bobby round to the cottage, a little distance outside the village, where Humphreys was staying. They went out, accordingly, to the street where the Major's car was standing, and, as Bobby was taking his place, Humphreys himself came out of a small shop opposite, and, for the moment, stood still and staring.

Evidently he recognised Bobby; evidently, too, the recognition had filled him with alarm, almost with panic. For just that moment he stood quite still, and then, with a little squeal of terror, turned and ran.

'No need to ask if that's your man,' remarked the Major, as they watched the little figure scurrying up the street like a frightened rabbit. 'Bit of a bad conscience, eh? Why?'

'Looks to me,' said Bobby slowly, 'as if it would be a good idea to get inside that shop of his he was in such a hurry to close down.'

'It's beginning to look more like that than the other way,' agreed the Major. 'I thought, at first, probably the old woman had gone off on her own with her necklace and her arsenic, but, when anyone runs for it like that at the sight of one of us, it generally means a pretty bad conscience. Put it like this: old woman missing; pearl necklace missing; man known to have been in touch with old woman missing, too. Shuts up his shop and vanishes, and then reappears, in small country village, with a changed name and plenty of money. Sounds nearly good enough for an arrest. Better follow him, eh?'

'If you please, sir,' Bobby said; and added: 'Only, is it possible to imagine a quiet little humdrum grocer turning suddenly into a murderer? Isn't it rather a long step from, say, putting sand in the sugar to planning and carrying out murder?'

'If you ask me,' said Major Griggs, with conviction, 'any of us is capable of anything – given opportunity and temptation. I wouldn't put it past a single bishop on the bench to do murder if the chance came his way, and there was what he thought a good reason. There's only one thing that can save us.'

'What's that?' Bobby asked.

'The grace of God,' Major Griggs answered, and then suddenly looked frightfully embarrassed and went very red, and stepped so hard on the accelerator that he nearly did murder himself on a harmless pedestrian. Whereon the Major slowed down, and added: 'In this case, if Humphreys has really done murder, quite possibly he didn't intend to at first. Just thought it was a pity a lot of money in the form of a pearl necklace should be lying useless when he could make good use of it. Perhaps he was being hard pressed. Bankruptcy quite close, perhaps. Think of the temptation. An old half-crazed woman to whom the necklace meant nothing, from whom it would be easy enough to get it away. Only it didn't turn out quite like that. And an old feeble woman is easily killed.'

'Well, sir,' Bobby remarked, 'I almost hope it's that way. I prefer it to the idea of her wandering about with a packet of deadly poison she may be making any sort of use of. But perhaps it's neither the one nor the other. There's a difficulty, too. Humphreys seems to have been in possession of money. Would he have been able to sell the necklace so quickly, supposing he had possession of it? I don't even know that it's likely he would have any idea of how to set to work to dispose of it.'

'He may have it still, as far as that goes,' Griggs suggested. 'Easy enough to get rid of it abroad, too – lots of people in Amsterdam alone who would give a good price and ask no questions. Better find out if he's been abroad recently.'

Bobby agreed, and the car drew up before a small cottage which was, the Major explained, the one where Humphreys and his wife were staying.

'Well, good luck,' he said as Bobby alighted. 'If you want any help, I shall be here an hour or two longer – I admit I shall be curious to know developments. Interesting case, so many possibilities.'

Rather too many possibilities, Bobby thought, as he reflected on that disturbing picture the Major had drawn of Miss Barton defending her necklace from dangers, either real or imaginary, by a liberal use of arsenic. Certainly it was not agreeable to think of an old woman, who must be very far from normal after such a life as she had lived, being in possession of a packet of arsenic of which already she had made use once.

Bobby's knock at the door was answered by an elderly woman, who, when he asked for Mr 'Hutchings', showed him into the front sitting-room – a typical country-cottage parlour, with a big Bible and equally big family album on the round mahogany table in the centre of the room, various souvenirs of occasional holiday trips to London and Margate and elsewhere that one felt had been landmarks in a quiet, uneventful life, and on one wall an enlarged photograph of a young man in khaki, with, underneath, framed medals, and, also framed, the conventional official telegram of the war years.

Huddling together near the window, as if to give each other support, were Humphreys and his wife, who looked just such another as her husband, timid, faded, and bloodless, and as little likely to forsake the safe paths of respectability and convention. Impossible, Bobby felt at the first glance, to suspect them of murder, and yet it is true, as the old proverb says, that the heart of man is a dark forest, and who can tell to what wild, fierce extremity the relentless economic pressure of modern life may not drive any one of us? A rat in a corner will fight, they say. The ceaseless strain of struggling against the unknown, incomprehensible, impersonal forces of modern life – economic crises, war panics, threatened revolutions, changing traffic routes, the opening of a tube station here rather than there, the decision of the directors of some huge combine to begin a rival business next door to yours – might not all that induce in quite ordinary normal people much such a state of mind as that of the cornered rat biting frantically and blindly at anything within reach? Caught in the tangle that is the world to-day, bewildered, desperate, frantic, what wild ways of escape might not even such as little peaceful Humphreys seek?

The war tried humanity too highly, and men and nations broke beneath the strain, often reacting strangely and dreadfully. Now the peace, too, tries some beyond their strength, and they, too, at times, react strangely – and even dreadfully.

Besides, there was always the possibility, as Major Griggs had pointed out, that the death of Miss Barton – if she were dead – had not been premeditated, that it had been, in fact, almost accidental.

As gently as he could, for, in spite of the terrible suspicion that hung about them, he could not help feeling a little sorry for a couple so plainly weak and inadequate, Bobby began his questioning. They admitted their identity at once – indeed, they could not well deny it. But, beyond that, they took refuge in a dull and stubborn reticence. It was true they had sold their business in Brush Hill. If it was still closed, that was none of their affair. They did not know who the purchaser was! They had negotiated with a man who described himself as a lawyer, declared he was acting for a third party, and had offered a good price, cash down. They had asked no questions – why should they? They had required no references – why should they? The money offered, in pound notes, was reference enough. They had taken the price offered, delivered the key of the establishment, and walked out, and that was all they knew – or, Bobby thought, all they meant to tell.

Altogether, a most unsatisfactory interview, and any reference to Miss Barton was met by a shaking of heads, and a blank denial of knowing anything whatever about her.

Bobby gave it up, and came away with two firm convictions in his mind: first, that the pair of them had something to conceal; secondly, that they had probably been coached by some third person, in the background, in this very effective attitude they had adopted of sulky reticence and protestations of ignorance.

But, then, so far as he knew, there was no third person in the background, at least no trace of one that he could see, and no apparent connection that he could discover between them and anyone else who had anything to do with the Tudor Lodge affair.

Bobby sighed, and presently began to wonder whether he might not have considerably underestimated the capacity and determination of Mr and Mrs Humphreys, and whether possibly they were not a good deal less simple and timid and commonplace a couple than he had assumed.

Chapter 21

RESOURCES OF THE LAW

LATE as it was when Bobby got back to town, later still when he left headquarters after handing in his report to Inspector Ferris – Mitchell had left for the day – he did not return straight to his rooms, but instead made his way to Brush Hill.

For there was still running in his mind Mitchell's hint that some reason there must have been for Humphreys' certainly untrue boasting of the large profits he had been making by the sale of garden requisites. How these apparently merely foolish lies could be connected with the Tudor Lodge mystery Bobby could not imagine, but his inability to do so merely increased the young man's uneasy sensation that there was something in this talk of garden requisites he had overlooked but that Mitchell had perceived.

It was still light when Bobby reached Tudor Lodge. For a time public curiosity had been so great that a constable had had to be stationed outside the house, to restrain trespassers, watch the souvenir-hunters – who, under the influence of their peculiar mania, were quite capable of knocking bricks out of the walls or smashing in the doors and windows to ransack the interior – and of keeping the continually gathering crowds of spectators 'moving on there, please'.

But public interest – a fire that needs continual feeding with fresh fuel – had died down. The Tudor Lodge affair had been dismissed from the prominence of front-page headlines to the obscurity of inside page bottom-of-the-column paragraphs, and the constable had been withdrawn. Bobby turned in unchallenged through the gap between the newly re-padlocked gate and the tumbledown front garden railings, and walked up the weed-grown drive. A moment or two he stood gazing up at the house where the missing woman had passed her long and dreadful and solitary existence, and then he walked on by the side of the building to where the garden sprawled its overgrown tangle of weed and grass and tree and bush.

It did not take him long to assure himself that that wilderness of half a century's neglect had not recently been disturbed in any way whatever. Everywhere the grass and the weeds showed themselves untrodden and untrampled. Across one path such a tangle of briar rose had spread itself as the legend tells protected the palace of the Sleeping Beauty from intrusion. The corresponding path on the left hand of the garden was choked in much the same way by a mingled growth of weed and creeper, and across the desolation that had once been a trim English lawn not even a cat could have made its way without leaving plainly visible tracks.

Nor was there any possibility of entering the garden in any other direction save through and across that of one of the neighbours. The vague notion Bobby had half entertained that the lost Miss Barton might have been murdered and her body buried in the garden, possibly by Humphreys using a spade taken from his 'garden requisites', had therefore to be dismissed. Whatever had become of the missing woman, her body was certainly not lying in the garden of Tudor Lodge, and, indeed, Bobby was now inclined to wonder why he had ever seriously entertained such an idea. Not but that the whole place – the gloomy, neglected, closely-shuttered house, the overgrown and deserted garden – did not suggest the tomb. No more appropriate spot could be imagined, Bobby thought, than this for the murderer to hide the awful evidence of his crime, but it was self-evident no use had been made of the garden for that purpose; and then, as Bobby turned away to go home to the bed and sleep he was beginning to feel he needed badly, he saw a light flash out for an instant in one of the upper windows of the house.

Just at first he was half inclined to think he must have been mistaken. The light did not reappear. Everything had assumed again its aspect of age-long desolation and neglect. Besides, who, for what reason or purpose, could possibly be wandering about the old house at that time? It was nearly night outside now, and indoors must be quite dark.

Still, Bobby's memory of that momentary flash of light remained vivid, and he began to run, swift and silent and light-footed, till he came to the side door of the house. It was hanging an inch or two open. Someone then, it seemed, had another key besides that in the possession of the police. He opened the door and passed within.

He felt his breath coming a little more quickly than usual. He had an idea that possibly the solution of the mystery might be within his grasp. Perhaps Miss Barton had come back to her old refuge. That was not unlikely, Bobby thought, if she were in fact still alive. He felt a little pleased with himself that he had been sharp enough – lucky enough would have been a more modest thought – to notice that momentary flash that had told of the presence of someone in the building. Or perhaps it might be her murderer returned on some grim, secret errand, and in a moment or two Bobby would find himself at grips with him in a desperate struggle for life and death.

Light-foot and silent, he ran down the passage and on into the shadowed hall, whence the stairs led to the upper portion of the house. Here it was quite dark, and Bobby went more slowly for fear of stumbling, or of knocking over a chair or something else, and so giving the alarm and the advantage to whoever might be there; and then a familiar voice hailed him from above:

'Mind you don't break your neck, Owen. Come up here. You haven't a torch with you, have you? Mine's about burnt out.'

'Oh, is it you, sir?' stammered Bobby, slightly discon-certed as he recognised Mitchell's voice.

'Who did you think it was?' retorted Mitchell with a sly chuckle. 'Miss Barton kindly come back to save us any further trouble looking for her? I doubt whether she'll ever do that, poor soul. But at any rate she's not buried in the back garden, is she?'

'No, sir,' agreed Bobby, as he made his way up the stairs. 'But I've seen Humphreys, and she's not with him, and she must be somewhere.'   •

'So you thought of the garden, eh, and remembered how Humphreys keeps talking about his big sales of garden stuff? Was that it?' asked Mitchell. 'But if he had used any kind of garden stuff in a murder – even a spade for a secret burial – would he talk so much about it – about garden stuff, I mean? Though I agree he must have some reason for lying about his sales in the way he does. I would give a lot to know what's behind that boasting and lying of his. Must be something, but I can't imagine what. Anyhow, I'm glad you spotted that light I flashed for you to see.'

Bobby did not answer. He felt slightly disconcerted to find that the momentary flash he had been inclined to applaud himself for noticing had been in fact aimed at his attention. Mitchell was standing on the landing between two rooms – the one in which Miss Barton had apparently lived during her long solitary sojourn in the house and the large front room in which some of the furniture, and part even of the flooring, had been broken up for firewood. Mitchell had a torch in his hand but it had nearly run down. Bobby produced his, and Mitchell took it and flashed its ray across the landing, sometimes directing it to the floor, where the curious kind of path swept between the two rooms on the dusty moth-eaten carpet was still plainly visible, though even in the short time that had elapsed since their first visit a covering of fresh dust had fallen.

'What made her turn tidy here and nowhere else in the whole blessed house?' Mitchell asked musingly. 'There's no sign she ever used a broom in any other spot, and yet here every grain of sawdust and every chip has been swept up. Another thing, what did she use? There's no broom about that I can see.'

No, sir,' agreed Bobby. He said slowly: 'I believe she's been murdered.'

'I almost hope so, rather than that she's wandering about with her necklace, and a packet of arsenic to defend it and herself with against anyone she suspects of following her,' Mitchell said slowly, for that was the constant dread in his mind. 'Perhaps it's neither, but a pearl necklace worth five figures or thereabouts in the possession of a half-crazy old woman is a big temptation. Why, it could be offered for sale in Bond Street to-morrow, and who could identify it? No risk in trying to dispose of it, so far as identification goes. How did you get on to-day?' he added.

Bobby gave a brief account of his visit to the Cotswold village, and Mitchell listened intently.

'Doesn't take us much further forward,' he commented. 'It looks as if Humphreys knows something he doesn't want to tell. And yet it seems hard to imagine that little rabbit of a man mixed up in it, either. That's one difficulty in this case – none of the people we know were hanging about Tudor Lodge seem of the murderer type. Con Conway's a little rat who would run from his own shadow; Humphreys is the perfect small-grocer type whose ideas of crime you wouldn't think went beyond false weights; Mr Yelton's a respectable business man who hasn't any ideas at all outside golf; young girls like his daughter aren't often murderers; Aske doesn't seem quite the type either. And yet, God knows, murder's a thing so easily done, and old Miss Barton must have been so frail, the slightest thing might have killed her – not meant at all; just a grab at the necklace, an effort at defence on her part, a scuffle, and there you are. But one thing's clear: we must have a look round Mr Humphreys' late establishment.'

'Yes, sir, I'm sure we ought,' agreed Bobby, wondering, though, how Mitchell meant to gain admittance, and if he thought his case strong enough to apply for a search-warrant.

'A strange case altogether,' Mitchell went on. 'What a

life the poor old soul must have led here all those years –
and then her excursions to throw her money away anywhere and anyhow – I expect she thought it a kind of
making up for what she had done. Strange, the things
that go on behind the walls of the houses we pass every
day.'

'The biggest snag of all,' Bobby remarked, 'seems to me
that, even if we trace the pearl necklace, there's no way of
identifying it.'

'No, and we haven't traced it yet,' commented Mitchell,
'nor Miss Barton either. Do you like getting up early,
Owen?'

'No, sir,' answered Bobby promptly.

'Then,' said Mitchell, in his most benevolent voice,
'it'll do you good to meet me at six sharp outside Mr
Humphreys' former establishment at the corner of Battenberg Prospect to-morrow morning.'

'Yes, sir,' said Bobby, suppressing a sigh and looking
a little worried.

'You might as well,' observed Mitchell, 'say "search-
warrant" out loud as merely look it.'

'Well, sir,' confessed Bobby, 'I was wondering –'

'More ways,' Mitchell remarked, 'of killing a cat than
choking it with cream. The English leasehold system is the
only known method whereby you may eat your cake and
have it – sell a piece of property and yet own it still. The man
who thought that system out is the greatest benefactor of the
human landlord the world has ever seen, and ought to have
a statue to him in the office of every estate agent in the
country. But, as someone said once, there's a soul of good in
all things evil, if you do but diligently distil it forth, and the
lease providing that the property Mr Humphreys' landlord
bought from a third person still belongs to that third person
contains a useful clause that the ground landlord's representatives may claim admittance to the premises for inspection
purposes at any hour between sunrise and sunset, and, if it is
refused, may force admission on condition that due notice

has been given and that all damage done is made good. Due notice has been given, and you and I, Owen, have been appointed representatives of the ground landlord for to-morrow only, from six till noon. If, therefore, admittance is refused us to-morrow, we shall be entitled to obtain it by force.'

'I see, sir,' said Bobby, much impressed by the remarkable resources of the English law.

Chapter 22

RENEWED SEARCH

BOBBY was outside the shuttered shop in Battenberg Prospect at a quarter to six next morning, for during his comparatively short term of service he had observed that it is as unwise for sergeants to keep superintendents and inspectors waiting as it is for constables to make sergeants attend.

The interval before Mitchell was due to arrive he spent going over and over in his mind the various points on which the Superintendent had dwelt the night before. It had been Bobby's full intention to do that the previous evening, and to give all such details careful and prolonged consideration before retiring. But when he went to his room so as to be quiet and alone for that purpose, the bed looked so inviting he thought he might as well lie down on it and do his thinking with his eyes closed. And then he thought he might as well undress first and get into his pyjamas, so as not to have to bother with toilet operations after he had finished thinking out Mitchell's points. Besides, he had heard on good authority that the problem your mind is full of when you drop off to sleep will often be found there quite cleared up when you awake. But what unfortunately happened was that slumber deep and profound overtook him the moment his head touched the pillow – not only before he had had time to think out his problems, but even before he had been able to fill his mind with them. And when he awoke the instant consciousness that overwhelmed his thoughts to the exclusion of all else was an acute awareness of the necessity of stopping, before a lynching-party arrived at his door, the clamour of the alarm clock on the top of the overturned tin bath where he usually perched it in order to reinforce its appeal.

So, what with the scramble to dress and bathe and breakfast and get to Brush Hill in good time, he had not yet been able to give Mitchell's points very careful consideration. Yet now, as he looked at them again where he had them all jotted down in careful order in his note-book, there grew very strongly into his thoughts the conviction that somewhere, if only he could find it, was a connecting-link that would bind them all together – that would, so to speak, weave from their present chaos and disorder a coherent, reasonable pattern.

Only what link could there be, for instance, between a forgotten satin shoe and a runaway grocer? Bobby was still so deep in thought, indeed, trying to fit together the pieces of this puzzle, that he was not aware of Mitchell's approach till the Superintendent hailed him from behind.

'Oh, beg pardon, sir. I didn't hear you,' Bobby exclaimed, startled, and a little surprised as well, to notice that Mitchell had apparently not come by car, for he was on foot, with no car visible; and it was, in fact, the sound of an approaching car that Bobby had subconsciously been on the alert for.

'Left the car round the corner; no use attracting too much attention,' Mitchell explained, with his uncanny gift for knowing just what other people were thinking.

He had two civilians with him, and he introduced them in turn as Mr Gardner, 'another representative of the ground landlord', and as Mr Bent, 'one of us once, but in the City now and on the way to being a big man there'.

Gardner was an elderly, important-looking person with a

worried and disapproving air, as if he wished it to be understood that he took no responsibility for anything whatever.
Bent was a younger man, not much older than Bobby, on
whom he bestowed a genial smile at this introduction, and
Bobby looked at him enviously.

'In the City now, are you?' he said. 'Lucky devil.' For to
Bobby the City was a place in which, after the carrying out
of mysterious transactions in places called Exchanges, you
retired into private life with a large fortune. 'Chance to do
something for yourself in the City, isn't there?'

'Got promotion already?' Bent said, almost simultaneously, for Mitchell had referred to Bobby as 'Sergeant', and he
looked at Bobby very enviously indeed. 'With a start like
that, you've a chance to do something for yourself in the
force,' he remarked.

Then they both gave a hollow laugh as they each thought
how little the other realised the trials and troubles of a policeman's – City man's – lot; and Bobby said reproachfully:

'You were in the force yourself once, weren't you? Then
you know what it's like.'

'Sorry I ever left it,' declared Bent, 'and I wouldn't either,
only my foot slipped.'

'Foot slipped?' repeated Bobby, wondering a little why
that should entail leaving the force.

'In the air,' explained Bent, and Bobby looked more
puzzled still.

'I don't quite see,' he ventured.

'Upwards, I mean,' Bent explained again, 'and it just
happened to contact my Inspector on the part he used when
he sat down.' Bent paused, blushing a little, for he was only
a City man, not a fashionable young society lady. 'If you
know what I mean,' he added, still blushing. 'And so I got
shot out, and lucky I wasn't given seven days' hard as well. I
had to go before Mitchell, and he dressed me down before he
sacked me so I wanted to go and jump in the Thames, only
I hated to think of polluting the river like that. But afterwards he found me a job with a big firm of accountants in

the City, and so I got leave to come along this morning when he said he wanted me.'

Bobby wondered a good deal why Mitchell had requisitioned this former policeman turned accountant, and then the constable on the beat came up. He had been warned to be in readiness, and it had been his job to make those various efforts to secure admission Mr Gardner, nervously afraid of possible actions for damage, insisted should be a preliminary to forcible entrance. Mitchell received his report and then turned to Bobby.

'No reply received, and written notice duly delivered. By the terms of the lease, forcible admission may now be obtained, all damage done to be made good. Have a look at the lock, will you?'

Bobby was something of a locksmith. It is a trade a police officer often finds it convenient to know a little about. Fortunately, in this case the lock was a simple one and presented no difficulties. In a minute or two Bobby had it open without having done it any damage, and they all entered the shop. It was very dark there, for the shutters were still up, but Bobby lighted the gas and then he and Mitchell began a careful search together, while Bent, as if he knew just what he was expected to do, dived into the room behind the shop, discovered the books of the business, and became immersed in them, and Mr Gardner, as if he had no idea what was expected of him, lighted a cigarette and looked on with his usual mildly bored, mildly disapproving air.

The search Mitchell made with Bobby's help was careful and prolonged, though Bobby, for his part, had no idea what they were looking for. But no nook or cranny escaped Mitchell's keen eyes, and, so far as Bobby could tell, nothing of the least interest was discovered, nor anything in any way out of the normal. There was proof enough, indeed, of departure having been somewhat precipitate and little prepared for, but that was all. Speaking roughly, everything of personal value or interest appeared to have been taken and everything else left.

'Nothing worth much left behind,' Mitchell remarked. 'I believe a ten-pound note would cover the lot. All the stuff's pretty old and nearly done for. Not much reason why they should worry over what they left.'

As for any apparent evidence of crime or violence committed, there was not an atom to be seen. Everything seemed to suggest, indeed, an exceedingly hasty departure, but that was all, and for a hurried departure there might of course be many reasons, all perfectly normal and innocent.

'All the same,' Mitchell remarked, 'the fact remains that this disappearing act of theirs coincides with the disappearance of Miss Barton. Any connection? Is it two disappearances with but a single cause? If so, what is the single cause? But most likely it just happened that they went when she went. It's a devil of a case, Owen.'

'Yes, sir,' said Bobby, with some feeling.

'Had to look round as carefully as possible,' Mitchell went on, 'but it's pretty certain there's nothing to help us here.'

They went downstairs again to the shop parlour, where Mr Gardner was waiting with the expression of a Christian martyr when the appearance of the lion has been unreasonably delayed, and Mr Bent was up to the neck – metaphorically – in papers and figures, and apparently enjoying it.

'Just about finished, sir,' he said cheerfully to Mitchell. 'The books haven't been badly kept – quite neat and all that. The stock's not worth much – pretty low, too. I imagine Humphreys kept it as low as he could. No accounts outstanding. I doubt if he got much credit. Nothing to suggest who the business was sold to, or that it was sold at all for that matter. No effort made to draw up a final balance-sheet that I can see, or get out the figures any ordinary purchaser would want to see. An assistant named Jones – no address – was engaged during the three weeks prior to Miss Barton's disappearance instead of an errand-boy, got rid of, according to a note, for dishonesty – there's a note, "caught at till".'

'Is the boy's address given?' Mitchell asked.

'Yes, I've made a note of it,' Bent answered. 'It's rather

curious that there's the same note about the assistant Jones –
that he was "Caught at the till and sacked", I mean. But in
his case there's no address, and it looks as if he wasn't paid
his wages the last week.'

'I wonder if he would come forward if we made a public
appeal,' mused Mitchell. 'Difficult to trace him, perhaps, if
he doesn't. Humphreys might know his address – and
mightn't. Go on, Bent.'

'Garden requisites,' continued Bent, 'seem to show a loss
in two months, since the line was started, of about three and
nine.'

'Loss of three and nine is hardly a big profit,' commented
Mitchell. 'Now, why has Humphreys been lying about that
the way he has? What made him start stocking garden stuff
at all, for that matter? Any spades stocked and any of them
missing?' he added, with a sly glance at Bobby.

'None stocked, apparently,' answered Bent.

'What about artificial manures and so on?' Mitchell
asked.

'Good stocks held but not much sold,' answered Bent.
'Ten bags of garden lime delivered, but none on hand that I
can find, and no record of any sold.'

'Wonderful what a lot well-kept books can tell about a
business,' remarked Mitchell. 'I think we've seen all there is
to see here, though.'

Mr Gardner looked pleased at this hint that their visit was
over. He fussed a good deal to make sure that everything
was left as nearly as possible as it had been found, and evidently was as nervous as ever over the risk of actions for
damages. But Bobby had opened the door so skilfully, with
so little damage to the lock, there was no trouble in closing it
again as securely as before, while within, though the search
had been as thorough as it had been without result, all had
been carefully replaced as it was before.

Then Mr Gardner and Mr Bent departed with Mitchell's
profuse thanks for their help, and Mitchell said to Bobby:

'It seems there were ten bags of lime stocked that are not

here now and yet there's no record of any having been sold.'

Bobby had become a little pale. After a moment's pause he said:

'A lot of lime like that would prevent any smell coming from a body that had been hidden away.'

'That means,' Mitchell said, 'a hiding-place where any unusual smell would most likely be noticed at once.'

'But that's almost anywhere,' Bobby said, 'almost anywhere in town or country.'

Mitchell said:

'An old broom is easily got rid of; you could throw it away and no one would notice it, or pay it any attention. We'll push on to Tudor Lodge now.'

Chapter 23

DISCOVERY

THE meticulous and quite fruitless examination of the Battenberg Prospect premises, the equally meticulous and exceedingly fruitful examination of the books of the business, had occupied so much time that by now it was afternoon, and breakfast taken at so early an hour had become for Bobby scarcely so much as a memory. Nor is Brush Hill a district in which restaurants abound, though fortunately there is no district in London in which teashops are not as frequent as quarrels in Test Match cricket. Into one of these establishments Mitchell now, to Bobby's great content, led the way, and, though it was hardly what Bobby called a meal, still, he did manage to assuage the fiercer pangs of hunger by such trifles as cold sausage, a pork pie or two, sardines on toast, and so on. Mitchell contented himself with a boiled egg and a cup of coffee, preserving throughout that slim repast a silence Bobby did not venture to intrude upon.

But as they were leaving the shop Mitchell turned to him suddenly.

'Have you thought how you would dispose of the body if you had murdered an old woman in an empty house you knew might soon be searched by the police?'

'Yes, sir,' said Bobby promptly. 'I should have a car ready. I should carry the body down and put it out of sight under the seat – I am assuming the body would be that of a tiny shrivelled-up old woman I could carry and handle quite easily. Then I should drive the car to some deserted spot in the country I had fixed on before – in a thickly grown plantation, perhaps, or at the bottom of an old gravel-pit if I could find one. I should leave the body there and trust to luck it wouldn't be found till time and weather had made it unrecognisable.'

'Quite good in theory,' Mitchell admitted, 'only in practice you wouldn't, because you would be afraid of being seen by someone; for I think that to a murderer all the world is made of watching eyes. You would feel it was trusting luck a bit too far, and luck's a tricky horse to ride when your neck depends upon it. Remember that chap Rouse, who staged a very ingenious murder in the heart of the country in the small hours of the morning when he could reasonably assume no one was likely to be about – and then was seen by two young fellows who were walking home after a dance?'

'Yes, sir,' agreed Bobby; 'only you've got to get the body away somehow. You can't leave it in the house where you know the police are likely to make a search as soon as the neighbours report no one's been seen about recently – or could you if you hid it well?' he added suddenly, pausing in the act of following Mitchell into the waiting car.

'Well, could you and, if so, where would you hide it?' Mitchell asked. 'Jump in,' he added, as Bobby still hung hesitating on the footboard.

'If there is really any body there,' Bobby said slowly as he obeyed and Mitchell started off. 'It can't be buried in the garden, for that's so overgrown it's certain no one's been in it for years. There are the cellars, of course –'

'Cellars have been examined; Ferris took that in hand,' Mitchell said. 'It's quite certain they haven't been disturbed any more than the garden. We can rule out cellars and garden. They're the usual places chosen, and the worst of that is, once they've been drawn blank there's apt to be a tendency to be less careful about the rest of the house.'

'The water tank?' Bobby suggested.

'Ferris ran the water off and looked there,' Mitchell said. 'Nothing except spiders and a dead mouse or two. He went over all the rest of the house, too, even the attics, though the dust made it plain no one had been up in them for long enough.'

'Then I don't quite see ...' said Bobby, and relapsed into silence.

They were back near Tudor Lodge now. Mitchell stopped the car, and he and Bobby completed the journey on foot so as to attract as little attention as possible. Indeed, they escaped even the all-seeing eye of Mrs Rice, who, recently released from her remunerative exile in the country, was now visiting Oxford Street, getting rid there of most of her *Sunday Photo's* cheque. To obtain admittance, Mitchell and Bobby went round to the side door, and Mitchell, before putting in the lock the key with which he had provided himself, remarked to Bobby:

'We've had the lock examined by an expert and he found distinct traces of wax. That looks as though someone had been taking an impression to make a new key, so as to be able to gain entry. None of the shops round here have any record of such an order, so it can hardly have been Miss Barton getting a new key made because she had lost the old. So who was it?'

He did not wait for an answer, but opened the door, and they both went in and along the passage into the dim and shadowy hall.

'Nowhere down here that hasn't been closely examined,'

Mitchell said. 'Carpets undisturbed, walls untouched, every cupboard or box or receptacle looked into. As for the attics, no one's been up in them for years.'

He led the way up the stairs, and on the landing paused a moment, then went into the large front room where furniture and floor alike had been so chopped about and torn up in the endeavour to obtain fuel. Bobby was beginning to understand now what was in Mitchell's mind, and he went across at once to the great yawning gap in the flooring where several boards had been torn away, and afterwards, as chips around showed, chopped for firewood. He turned and looked at Mitchell, who nodded silently. Bobby knelt down by the gap and thrust his hand under the flooring. He drew it back at once.

'There's something there,' he almost whispered.

'Your hand is covered with lime – with garden lime,' Mitchell said.

'So it is,' Bobby said, looking at it.

'Tear up another board,' directed Mitchell.

Bobby obeyed, Mitchell helping. A cloud of white lime arose and set them coughing, and there became visible an end of material that Bobby reached down to and touched.

'It is satin,' he said; 'all rotten and yellow now, but it's satin. Wedding-dresses are made of satin,' he said.

He groped beneath the board again, and something else came away in his hand. He withdrew it, looking at it doubtfully. Mitchell said:

'That was a wreath once, I think – a wreath of orange blossom. Pull up another board.'

They did so, and pulled up with it a long strip of lace, faded and yellow.

'The wedding veil,' Mitchell said slowly. 'God, she must have had on her old wedding finery; she must have had it on still when they pushed her under here.'

Bobby reached into the space now revealed between flooring and the ceiling of the room below, and as gently and reverently as he could drew forth the poor, frail, worn-out body that had been so callously thrust there out of the way. It was so small, so slight, so shrunken, it might, as it lay there in faded wedding garb, have well been that of a little child.

Mitchell bent over the body and looked at it long and earnestly.

'What a life! What a death!' he muttered. 'Whatever she did all those years back – do you know, I've an idea she would have liked to think she had on that wedding rig-out of hers when it ended, even though the end was what it was.'

'Yes, sir,' agreed Bobby, 'but I· think many of us will be keener in finding out who did this than we were on tracking her when we thought that was our job. Looks as if she had been strangled,' he added.

Mitchell nodded.

'Those marks on the throat show that,' he agreed.

'Well, that's murder all right,' declared Bobby.

'Murder long ago and now murder to-day,' Mitchell mused. 'Things work themselves out at the end, I think.'

'I was thinking,' Bobby said, half to himself, 'all the time we were combing England for her, she was lying here – lying here, too, while we walked over her head when we searched the house. She must have been here when we found that other in the Saratoga trunk. I suppose that explains why everything was so carefully swept up between the two rooms. The murderer was taking care none of the lime should be left lying about to give a hint of what had happened. That explains the shoe, too. It must have fallen from her foot when the body was carried in here. It explains the pearl we found, too. The necklace string must have broken somehow.'

'Probably when whoever it was took her by the throat,' Mitchell said. 'Quite possibly murder wasn't intended at first. It wouldn't take much to kill a frail old woman, once you had her by the throat, and the first intention may quite well have been merely to grab the necklace. I daresay that looked fairly safe. She couldn't have offered any resistance, and her story might quite easily have been put down as a mere crazy delusion on the part of a cracked old woman.

No one would have thought it very likely she went about the house wearing a pearl necklace worth ten or twelve thousand. I wonder if those bruises on the throat will reveal any finger-marks?'

'There's one point worth remembering,' Bobby remarked. 'Everyone I saw in the house was wearing gloves. Was that merely an accident? Of course, Con Conway wasn't, but then I suppose he might have come back again.'

'The lime must have come from Humphreys',' continued Mitchell. 'He'll have to explain that. But suppose he says it was in the shop when he left it? Nothing to show the contrary. It was in the stock-book apparently but not entered as sold. He'll have to be questioned, though. Did he know about the necklace? He may have. Is that where the money comes from he seems to have got hold of somehow recently? But would he have been able to get rid of the necklace so quickly? Would he have had any idea how to set to work to get anything for it? Con Conway could have managed that part all right; no criminal in all the country with more experience in that way. He would know where to go in London; he wouldn't even have to go abroad. If it looks bad against Humphreys, where the lime came from, it looks worse against Con. Even this new stunt of his about running straight may simply mean that he's lying low till he thinks things look safe. There's still the snag that neither Con nor Humphreys seem the murderer type, but perhaps that doesn't amount to much and there's always the chance that murder wasn't intended. It would have taken so little to kill the poor old soul, and Con certainly, and Humphreys very likely, knew about the necklace, and since it happened both of them have tried to disappear. It can't very well be both are guilty, but it may easily be one. Or there's Mr Yelton. We know he knew about the necklace; he has been seen near the house; his firm has not been doing well; he was hard pressed for money, and just recently his firm has suddenly paid off a big overdraft. If it wasn't for Con and little Humphreys I should almost think that good enough to proceed to arrest on. Then there's the Yelton girl herself. It's possible she thought those pearls wasted in the possession of a half-lunatic old woman; that she tried to get hold of them by coaxing or wheedling, and that when that didn't work she tried to snatch. If the old woman resisted and there was a bit of a scuffle, and in her excitement the girl pulled too hard – there's always the point that with a feeble, worn-out, half-starved old woman anything might so easily kill her. If that's what happened, that would explain her extreme agitation when you saw her at the door. Then afterwards, when she read about the discovery of the body in the trunk she may have known nothing of before, she would see that was a good explanation to offer if she were traced and questioned. Blessed if I don't think there's quite a good case against her, too. And then there's the Aske young man. He knew all about the necklace, and he's the last person to have been seen at Tudor Lodge. Also he's an inventor, and an inventor needing money to develop his ideas is hardly responsible – lots of them would murder half the population of the country for means to carry on. He says she offered him the necklace, and we know he was in possession of a key; but is it true she gave him one, or did he get one made from the wax impression that somebody certainly took from the lock, and did he only secure the old key in place of this new one made after he had been in the house? What do you think, Owen?'

'Well, sir, the way you put it,' Bobby answered slowly, 'I think we could get a conviction against any one of them if it wasn't for the others. I'm inclined to think myself, sir, it must be someone else altogether, someone who has covered up his tracks so well we haven't got sight of them as yet.'

'It may be,' agreed Mitchell, 'it's that way; but so far as we know no one has been seen near the house except those five, barring postmen and hawkers and so on, and they could hardly know anything about the necklace. Of course, there's that in Humphreys' favour – nothing to prove he knew about the pearls, though he may have done.'

'There are two points that are rather specially bothering

me, sir.' Bobby remarked, 'One is I can't help feeling there's some kind of family likeness between Mr Yelton and someone I've seen some time. But he doesn't seem to have any relations at all, and certainly there's no resemblance between him and Miss Yelton. And there's the old question why Humphreys made such a point of boasting about sales of things for the garden. We know now that was all lies, as his own books show a loss. But if he had any idea what the lime was wanted for, wouldn't he have kept quiet instead of talking so much about what he was selling for gardens?'

'Sometimes the more you talk about a thing, the more you talk suspicion away from it,' Mitchell observed. 'Look at the way that hole in the flooring the poor old lady made herself, and that none of us ever thought of looking into, was staring us in the face all the time.'

'Yes, sir, I know,' Bobby admitted; 'but no one was actually looking for a dead body. We had no actual grounds for believing she had been murdered and her body hidden here. It was only a general search on general lines, not specially for a dead body.'

'All the more reason it should have been found,' declared Mitchell. 'Anyone can find what he's looking for; the point is to find what you don't know's there. Though it was only lime being missing, and my remembering the sweeping that had gone on just in this spot, that made me think of it. There's always a reason for everything, Owen, if only you can spot it.'

'I suppose there is,' agreed Bobby a little ruefully, and repeated, 'if only you can spot it.'

'Plain now the reason in this case was so that no lime should be left lying about,' Mitchell went on, 'just as it's plain, too, she's been murdered for the sake of the pearl necklace, though unless we can get more information I still don't see how we are going to identify the thing. Even if we found it in the pocket of one of the suspects, I daresay Treasury counsel would still want proof of identity. You had better cut along, Owen, and report while I wait here. I'll have another look round while you're away. Oh, and first thing, before you do anything else, ring up Major Griggs and ask him to hold Humphreys for us or the little blighter will be vanishing again.'

But when Bobby carried out these instructions, back came the prompt reply that it was too late. Humphreys had already disappeared. His wife was still at the cottage, where they had taken a room, but she protested entire ignorance. There was evidence that Humphreys had slipped out by the back door, and that he had mounted a bus travelling to the nearest town. But there all trace if him had been lost for the present.

'Conscious guilt or simple panic,' Bobby mused, as he hung up the receiver. 'Anyhow, I don't suppose it'll very be difficult to find him again.'

Chapter 24

MR YELTON'S COLLAPSE

BUT this proved altogether too optimistic, and the days passed by without news of Humphreys. He had slipped into the busy, crowded world as a drop of water into the sea, and it seemed to be going to prove as difficult to find and identify him as one drop in the ocean from another.

In other directions the usual routine was being carried out. The news of the fresh discovery in Tudor Lodge roused, again, the public interest to fever, indeed almost to cup-final pitch. There was some difference of opinion as to whether the police deserved great credit for having made the discovery, or severe censure for not having made it before. The little group of people known to have been in touch with Tudor Lodge were all interviewed again, officially and non-officially, and nothing more of any importance or interest was obtained from any of them. Mrs. Rice's hopes of a further profitable if secluded holiday, diversified by visits from charming young newspaper men, were nullified by the conviction of sub-editors that she had been 'sucked dry' – as they put it in their brutal way – and the story was already beginning to subside again from front to inner page when Mitchell sent for Bobby.

'There are two fresh points established now, that may prove important,' he said. 'The first is that a number of valuable pearls have been put on the market recently. No one seems to be quite sure where they've come from, but together they would make up just such a necklace as Miss Barton is reported to have possessed. Such evidence as we've been able to collect suggests that the first sales were made in Holland and Belgium, and by an Englishman, at about the time Mr Yelton paid off his firm's overdraft that the bank was pressing him about. But we can't get any reliable description of the Englishman, and it seems certain Mr Yelton has not been out of the country recently. We did get so far as to ask him where the money came from he paid the bank. He was very indignant, but finally said it was the result of successful speculation in Reichmarks, though he protested he neither would nor could give details, as some of his associates abroad might have offended against their own country's regulations. That may be true or not, but it's a plausible story in itself, and a plausible excuse for refusing us further information.'

'I suppose, sir,' Bobby asked thoughtfully, 'that means we may take it as established that Miss Barton's necklace was really of great value, and that it's a fact it was stolen and then got rid of on the Continent?'

'The first sale may have been in London, for all we know at present,' Mitchell pointed out. 'I don't see much hope of our ever being able to indentify the pearls, or recover them. The other point is more likely to be useful. The examination of Miss Barton's body makes it clear death was caused by strangulation. All her organs were quite sound and healthy

– spare living makes sound bodies, apparently. So probably she wasn't quite as feeble as her shrunken, shrivelled appearance made her seem. There are bruises on the body that make it likely she put up some sort of resistance, and the marks on the throat suggest that her murderer wore gloves. The important thing about that is that under the fingernails are tiny scrapings of leather. The laboratory report says they are coarse in texture, have been treated with a yellow dye, and probably come from a new, almost unworn, pair of gloves.'

Bobby was listening intently. Tiny scrapings from the murderer's gloves! Was it possible such microscopic fragments would prove a link in the chain of evidence to bring him to justice? Too much to hope for, it seemed to Bobby, for how were those faint scrapings to be linked up with any special gloves, or those gloves with the wearer? But Mitchell was going on speaking.

'The suggestion is, of course,' he was saying, 'that there was some sort of struggle, and that Miss Barton clutched at her murderer's hands when he had her by the throat, and so scratched these fragments of leather off the gloves he was wearing in order to avoid leaving any finger-prints. You know, of course, we've never found a single finger-print in the whole of Tudor Lodge to help us?'

'No, sir,' Bobby answered, his mind still full of the strange, the terrible significance of those scrapings of leather, and of a great wonder at the thought that the very precaution the murderer had taken to avoid discovery might prove his undoing.

'Aske is described by Mrs Rice as wearing tan-coloured gloves that time she saw him in Tudor Lodge,' Mitchell said.

'Yes, sir, I remember that,' Bobby answered quietly.

'That may mean everything or nothing,' Mitchell continued, in a brisker voice. 'Unluckily too much time has been lost for us to be very hopeful. Even if the gloves are still in existence – and a prudent murderer probably destroyed them long ago – any marks and scratches made on them will have worn off by now. Then, too, there are tens of thousands of pairs of tan-leather gloves in existence.'

'It may give us a line to follow,' Bobby said musingly.

'What I want you to do,' Mitchell continued, 'is first to visit Mr Yelton. Talk to him quite frankly about the gloves. See if he has anything to say and if he appears interested, and report your impression to me. Then call on Aske. Don't talk to him quite so frankly, but try to get him to tell you if he has any similar gloves, and if he has bought any recently.'

'Very good, sir,' Bobby said. 'There's no news of Humphreys yet?'

Mitchell shook his head.

'Anything to suggest?' he asked.

'I was just thinking,' Bobby suggested diffidently, 'that he is such a nervous, scared little man, it might be possible to try to bluff him into coming forward himself, if we got the *Morning Intelligence* and the *Daily Announcer* and one or two of the other big papers to put in a statement that Humphreys, wanted in connection with the Tudor Lodge mystery, has been practically traced.'

'Practically,' murmured Mitchell, 'is a useful word.'

'Yes, sir, that's what I thought,' agreed Bobby. 'And then the paragraph might go on that an arrest is momentarily expected – anything may be expected – and that the extremely grave suspicions directed towards him are largely caused by his failure to report to the police; though there is still the possibility that Mr Humphreys is unaware of the wish of the police to interview him, so that if he did come forward, even now, much of the suspicion attaching to his name would be at once done away with.'

Mitchell smiled grimly.

' "... said the spider to the fly," ' he quoted. 'Well, carry on. Call in Fleet Street, in your way to Yelton, and see if they'll do that for us. Tell each of them that, if it does result in Humphreys coming forward, they'll each of them be able to say it was all through them. Report as soon as possible.'

'Very good, sir,' said Bobby, and withdrew.

He had no difficulty in arranging for the publication of the proposed paragraph, and then went on to the offices of Messrs. Yelton & Markham, where, when he was shown into Mr Yelton's private room, he received a shock, for indeed, he would hardly have thought it possible anyone could have altered so much in so short a time. For Mr Yelton's former appearance of physical vigour and well-being had entirely changed. He seemed to have turned, in the brief space since Bobby had seen him last, into an old man. He looked shrunken and bowed; his cheeks had fallen in; his hands trembled; his formerly dull and placid but clear enough eyes had grown heavy and bloodshot – there were lines beneath them that suggested sleepless nights; and that he watched Bobby's entry with an apprehension that was almost panic was fully evident. So surprised was Bobby at the other's changed appearance that he stood quite still, staring at him, and Mr Yelton burst out angrily:

'What are you gaping at? With all this worry it's a wonder I haven't been driven into my grave, with newspaper men chasing me about, and people pointing at me in the street, and one thing and another, till I can't even play a round in peace – enough to send you out of your mind,' he cried, and, indeed, he spoke a little wildly, as though the nervous strain he was under was almost too much for him.

'I am afraid anyone whose name is associated with a sensational murder, or double murder, in fact, always has a lot to put up with,' Bobby said, gently enough, but watching keenly.

'I don't know why my name was ever mentioned,' Yelton complained, though a little more quickly. 'I've never had anything to do with it. I know nothing about it from beginning to end.'

'It could hardly have been avoided, could it?' Bobby pointed out. 'I take it you're the only known relative of the man whose body we found at Tudor Lodge?'

Mr Yelton, who had risen to his feet when Bobby entered, sat down again. He seemed to be about to say something, but changed his mind. Bobby asked quickly:

'There are no other relatives, are there?'

'Well, you've checked that already at Somerset House, haven't you?' Yelton grumbled.

He seemed to be controlling himself better now, and he lighted a cigarette with a hand that was fairly steady. Bobby made no reply to his remark, though he knew that, in point of fact, careful enquiries had been made, without success, to see if any relations could be traced. Apparently Mr Yelton had told the exact truth in that respect; and, watching him now, Bobby wondered if it was only the worry naturally resulting from his connection with so sensational a case that had caused so strange and so dramatic a change in his appearance. But a good many people of the Yelton type find such notoriety quite agreeable, and there had been no trace of nervousness or strain observable during Bobby's previous visit, though already, even then, there had been police interviews, newspaper men calling, the summons to give evidence at the inquest, and a good many other signs of the public interest the case has aroused. Bobby had reason to believe, too, that a cheque had been offered, and accepted, for an *Announcer* interview, in which Mr Yelton had chatted about the case in general, and his unfortunate uncle in particular, without showing himself unduly distressed by the attendant notoriety. Why, then, this abrupt change in his demeanour?

Could it be the result of conscious guilt? Bobby wondered. But, then, if he were guilty, he must have been conscious of his guilt during all the time when he had seemed comparatively untroubled. And, if it came from fear of further discoveries, why had that fear, which must have been present before, have become operative only now? Or was there some other cause for this apparently recent nervous breakdown?

At any rate there was the chance that, as sometimes happens to people in a highly excitable, nervous condition, Mr Yelton might now be inclined to be communicative. An urge to talk is often felt, in such a condition, as a means of relieving it. But in this hope Bobby was disappointed. His tentative efforts to win Mr Yelton's confidence were quite

unavailing, his exhortations to frankness remained un-
heeded. Mr Yelton would say no more than he had said already – declared that he knew, in fact, no more – insisted,
with a certain vehement sincerity, that he had never even
set foot in Tudor Lodge, or in all his life spoken to, or even
seen, Miss Barton.

Bobby found himself more than half believing this was the
truth, and yet could not help feeling that something more
than the notoriety inseparable from any connection with so
sensational a case was weighing on his mind to cause so great
a change, so sudden a collapse, in a man of a type by no
means sensitive or highly strung.

Somewhat abruptly he began to question Yelton about
gloves. The other appeared merely puzzled, or perhaps even
a trifle relieved, at the change of subject; it was fairly obvious,
at any rate, that the subject had no significance for him. He
possessed, he declared, no tan or yellow gloves, nor any
leather gloves that he could think of. He had gloves in
reindeer, in suède, in ordinary kid, but not in leather, he
thought. He seldom wore the things, he explained, except in
very cold weather, and then there was a pair of fur-lined
that he put on. Impossible, he explained, to hold your club
to advantage if you were wearing gloves.

In fact he grew more like his former self as he answered
Bobby's questions about gloves. He even managed to produce a kind of chuckle that had grown a rarity with him of
late as he remarked that the only person he could think of,
at the moment, whom he had ever noticed wearing yellow
gloves was Mr Jennings, their head clerk, the round little
elderly man of the uncertain aspirates, and the adopted
hoity-toity manner, whom Bobby had noticed before.

But Bobby did not think that suggested itself as a very
promising line of enquiry, and he left the offices of the firm
with a strong conviction in his mind that either Mr Yelton
was, in fact, guilty, or else that he possessed some information – or that some suspicion possessed him – wherefrom he
went in secret terror.

Bobby set himself to think out what that could be.

Could there be some hidden connection between him and Humphreys? But of that no trace whatever had come to light.

Or could it be that he had reason to suspect his own daughter – that it was Dorothy who was guilty? A difficult, even a repugnant thought, and yet one that would fully account for her father's nervous collapse.

Suppose she had seen in the pearl necklace a means of rescuing her father from ruin? Suppose she had taken that dreadful course in a last effort to save him? Suppose that were the source of the payment he had recently been able to make to clear his overdraft at the bank? Possibly he had taken the money without knowing its origin, and only after using it might he have begun to suspect where it came from.

If so, so terrible a thought working in his mind might well account for the change, both mental and physical, now apparent in him.

Chapter 25

SCRIMMAGE

IT was to the flat occupied by Mr Yelton and his daughter that Bobby now proceeded. That he should see for himself whether the daughter showed any sign of the nervous strain and agitation the father had so clearly betrayed seemed to him important, but when he knocked at the door of the flat he at first got no answer and yet heard sounds from within to show the flat was occupied. He knocked again – again – a loud, authoritative knock. This time the door was flung open almost immediately by an excited, flushed-looking Dorothy, who evidently recognised him at once.

'Oh, it's you,' she cried, with an old mixture of relief and apprehension, and, not stopping to ask him his business, dashed back across the box-like hall into the tiny sitting-room.

Bobby followed quickly, without waiting to be asked, for it was evident enough that something unusual was happening, and in the sitting-room he found presented an interesting tableau of young Mr Aske with clenched fists, blazing eyes, and a face white with passion, standing over the prostrate figure of another man, whose face was covered with blood streaming from an extremely swollen nose, while above it one eye was rapidly becoming eclipsed in a rainbow blaze of many colours and a swiftly rising Mount Everest kind of a bump.

'That'll teach you,' said Aske, without specifying what teaching was supposed to be implicit in the scene.

The prostrate man began somewhat unsteadily and hesitatingly to get to his feet.

'What's all this?' demanded Bobby.

Aske bestowed on Bobby a glare that seemed to indicate entire willingness to continue towards him the teaching already offered to the gentleman unsteadily and doubtfully rising from the floor.

Dorothy, drawing a long breath in preparation, let herself go in a swift and indeed torrential explanation of just exactly what she really thought of Mr Alfred Aske. It was long; it was emphatic; it was detailed; it concluded with a passionate peroration expressing a fervent hope that never again would those orbits cross each other wherein moved respectively herself and Mr Aske; and pitiable indeed was it to watch how the triumphant swagger of the proud male who has just knocked his rival down – glorious gesture throughout the ages – became changed to that of the naughty little boy caught stealing jam by his nurse and well aware that now it's across the knee and the slipper for him.

'And just look,' added Dorothy, with fierce finality, 'just look at the mess on the carpet.'   -

'I'll get you a new one,' muttered Aske.

· 'When we require you to refurnish the flat for us, Mr

Aske,' declared Dorothy with great dignity, 'we will inform you of the fact.'

By now the formerly prostrate gentleman was on his feet again. His nose was still bleeding; his eye was still swelling; there was, indeed, not much sign that either process was ever likely to stop again. With a handkerchief already little more than a sodden mass, he was trying to mop up the so freely flowing gore, and Bobby led him into the bathroom and there administered first aid on the most approved principle of the ambulance classes it had been part of his duty to attend in the early days of his service. He said to the sufferer:

'I am a police officer. If you wish to take proceedings, I am available as a witness.'

'No question of proceedings,' mumbled the other through Bobby's handkerchief he had now borrowed and was rapidly reducing to the same sodden condition as his own. 'Pure accident ... boxing lesson ... own fault entirely ... misunderstanding ... nothing more.'

'I see,' said Bobby, and went back into the sitting-room, where Dorothy was abusing her victory – for no woman is ever magnanimous in triumph – by rubbing the salt of silent scorn into the wounds already inflicted by the lash of her indignant tongue.

'May I ask what this is all about?' Bobby said.

'Mr Aske,' said Dorothy loftily, 'has been behaving like ... like ... like ...' But there she gave it up, obviously quite unable to think of anything in the whole created universe to which it was even possible to think of comparing Mr Aske's conduct.

'Who is the other gentleman?' asked Bobby, as gurgling sounds from the bathroom became more and more apparent.

'Mr Markham, father's partner,' Dorothy explained, a little colour coming back into her cheeks that had before been pale with anger or fright or both.

'And if he says anything of the sort again, I'll lam him another,' interposed Aske.

'Oh, oh,' gasped Dorothy, quite bewildered by this sudden effort at self-assertion on the part of one who had appeared so thoroughly and deservedly crushed, brow-beaten, and sub-dued. One could almost see her thinking that this insolent uprising must be suitably dealt with. 'I think you had better go, if you don't mind, Mr Aske,' she said very firmly. 'I hope you will please understand that after your disgraceful behaviour to-day I never wish to see you again.'

It was a knock-down blow as cruel as effective. Mr Aske metaphorically sprawled. Bobby felt quite sorry for him, and also a little contemptuous, for indeed his own day was not yet. Aske – how little he cared for Bobby's presence! – drooped, wilted, wailed:

'Oh, I say, Dorothy, I say ...'

For all answer, Dorothy looked extremely determined and resolute; indeed, one could only wonder that so small a face could find room for the expression of so much determination and resolve. Thoughtfully and kindly Bobby collected for the dazed youth his hat from one corner, his gloves from another. He said:

'Your gloves, Mr Aske. Do you always get them from Barselod's?'

'I never go to Barselod's; I get my things from the Stores generally,' Aske answered, with all the meekness imaginable, for in fact the spirit had gone out of him.

Bobby was turning the gloves over in his hands. They were tan; they were leather; they showed faint scratches here and there, but only such as normal wear might cause. He said:

'As you know, I am a police officer, and, since proceedings in court may follow all this, I must ask you to tell me what has happened.'

But that neither of them seemed in any way anxious to do. There had been a quarrel. Bobby observed that he had al-ready managed to deduce that fact for himself. Markham was a bounder and a cad. That was Mr Aske's contribution to the desired explanation. Mr Aske had behaved like a brute. That was Dorothy's contribution. Mr Markham, emerging from the bathroom with a fresh handkerchief – one belonging to his assailant that Bobby, having exhausted his own, had commandeered – held firmly to a still uncertain nose and an eye swelling as visibly as ever did widow under the influence of successive cups of tea, repeated that it was all due to a misunderstanding, an accident.

'Next time,' observed Mr Aske moodily, 'the misunderstanding will be worse,' He added to Bobby the palpable lie: 'We had a row about politics – Russia and Fascism and all that, you know.'

'Exactly,' confirmed Mr Markham. 'Next time I shall be better prepared with more effective arguments,' he added viciously.

'I think you had better both go at once, please,' interposed Dorothy.

Mr Markham moved towards the door.

'I hope you will think over what I was saying,' he said to Dorothy. 'It wasn't exaggerated in any way whatever.' To Aske he said: 'I don't intend to take legal proceedings, but you needn't think that this ends it. It doesn't.'

He vanished. Aske looked piteously at Dorothy. She looked relentlessly at the door. Mr Aske crept towards it, very, very slowly. Dorothy remained the picture of Nemesis in the most severe mood possible. Aske opened the door a crack – hardly enough to let a mouse pass through. Dorothy drew herself together.

'You need not call again, Mr Aske,' she announced.

'Oh, I say,' wailed the unhappy youth. He vanished through the door as though those fatal words had fairly flung him through it. The next moment it opened again and Aske's head reappeared. 'Wish I had lammed him twice as hard, and next time I will, too,' he announced, and with that vanished once more.

'Well, I never!' gasped Dorothy, breathless again.

Then she looked at Bobby, evidently inviting him to follow the other two. But that he had no intention of doing, though this somewhat tumultuous scene on which he had stumbled had not exactly helped him in his purpose of discovering whether Dorothy showed any signs of nervous excitement and strain as her father had disclosed.

'I've called again,' he exclaimed, 'to see if you can't help us on one or two more points about Tudor Lodge. You've no idea how important even the smallest detail may turn out.'

'Oh, but I've told you everything over and over again,' she protested.

'There are just one or two points,' he insisted. He added with intention: 'Nothing you can say now can hurt Miss Barton.'

'No, I know,' she answered. 'But it's all so sad and dreadful to think of her living like that, and dying like that.'

'You know we think it was her pearl necklace she was murdered for?' he asked.

She made a little gesture of assent. She seemed fairly composed, however, except for the after-effects of the scene they had just gone through, and Bobby thought to himself that either she was entirely innocent or else that she possessed an extraordinary power of self-control. But, then, women often do possess that power. Changing the subject a little, Bobby said:

'I am afraid I called at rather an unlucky moment – or perhaps at a lucky one.'

'Mr Markham was rude and Mr Aske was very silly,' she answered briefly. 'That's all.'

He tried to get her to be more explicit, though without at first much success. But it was easy to see that the two men were rivals; and it appeared that Markham had been pressing his suit for some time, though until recently Dorothy had hardly been inclined to take him or it very seriously. To her he had always simply been her father's partner, but apparently Markham himself had, until Aske's arrival on the scene, entertained stronger hopes than Dorothy had ever realised.

'Of course, I always had to be nice to him,' she explained. 'He was dad's partner.'

But now it appeared that what had disturbed her so much was that this afternoon, calling on the pretext of leaving a message for her father, Markham had begun to use towards her a mixture of threats and of claims upon her gratitude.

'I don't care,' she burst out, 'if he has saved father and the firm and me, too, from bankruptcy. I'm not going to marry him for that. I can earn my own living, can't I?'

'Of course,' agreed Bobby, even though he knew well that earning a living in the chaotic, lunatic-directed world of to-day is not always an easy task; 'but if Mr Markham is a partner, he saved himself when he saved the firm, didn't he?'

'It was about some money he got on the Continent,' Dorothy explained. 'Father told me. It was some speculation of his own. I suppose he could have kept the money. I don't know. He put it all in the business. He said there were all sorts of silly laws, and if he had been found out he might have been hanged for it. Father says there are new regulations about money and speculating in the exchanges and that sort of thing, and that in some countries you might be shot if you were caught doing it.'

'I didn't know it was a capital offence anywhere,' Bobby observed.

'Mr Markham said what he had done he wasn't a bit ashamed of or sorry for. He said it was only stopping silly waste – a sort of madness – but he risked his life, because, if he had been caught, that's what would have happened. And he wanted to make out I owed him father's life, because he would probably have committed suicide if the business had failed, and I said I didn't know anything about that but I wasn't going to marry him. And he got so excited I ran to the door to get away from him, and he followed me, and then, when I opened it, Mr Aske was there, and they quarrelled, and Mr Markham said something and Mr Aske – oh, he was angry; he just hit out, and Mr Markham went down such a flop, and I was glad. Of course,' she added primly, 'I wasn't going to encourage Mr Aske to behave like that.'

Bobby reflected that it rather looked as if Aske were less far from pardon than at the moment he probably feared. It was also fairly plain that the dressing-down he had received had been in part merely Dorothy giving vent to her excitement, just as now, once started, she was finding it a relief to talk.

'I shan't dare say a word to father,' she said.

'I called partly to make some enquiries about him,' Bobby observed. 'I thought he looked very ill.'

Dorothy, who had been moving about the room putting back in position the disarranged furniture, and who hitherto had been talking fairly freely, paused and straightened herself. Her expression changed. It became alert and watchful and a little uneasy.

'He is very worried,' she said. 'It is making him ill ... the business, I mean,' she added quickly, as if afraid Bobby might think she attributed his worry to some other cause.

He tried to persuade her to answer him more freely, insisting that every shred of information she could give, however apparently irrelevant, might yet prove important. But she only repeated what she had said before – that she had already told everything she knew – and Bobby had to retire, a little disappointed, with no fresh information, except that the claims Markham had put forward, though no doubt exaggerated, since speculation in the exchanges, even if a sufficiently serious offence in many countries, is nowhere punishable with death, yet appeared to corroborate Mr Yelton's story of the source of the money used to pay off the bank overdraft.

'Unless they made up the yarn together,' Bobby mused; 'and that would imply Markham as an accomplice, which doesn't seem likely. Still, it does point to him as a possible new candidate for suspicion, though there is nothing to suggest he knew anything about Tudor Lodge, or had ever heard of the existence of the pearl necklace.'

He mentioned this idea to Mitchell on his return to the Yard, but Mitchell shook his head.

'I think we may take it as fairly certain that neither Mr Yelton nor Miss Yelton mentioned the necklace to anyone else,' he said. 'If Markham knew about it, he must have known from some other source, and I don't at present see what that could be. But you can put in a bit of work on Askes' gloves, though it doesn't sound a very promising line.

Bobby called therefore at the Stores, and, when he had explained his errand, was allowed to examine Aske's account. There, plainly entered, almost immediately after the date Aske had given as that of his first encounter with Miss Barton, was an item recording the purchase of a pair of yellow leather gardening gloves. A little excited, Bobby reported the fact to Mitchell by phone. Mitchell answered:

'Interesting. The laboratory report specially mentions that the scrapings are very coarse in texture and probably came from gardening gloves.'

Chapter 26

HUMPHREYS FOUND

FOR a time the centre of the investigation moved to the Continent; though, in Glasgow, Con Conway, placidly showing the Glaswegians how to buy and sell at a profit apples and bananas and such other of the kindly fruits of the earth as he could pick up cheap, was kept under the patient surveillance of a puzzled police; though the search for the missing Humphreys was still pursued in their very dreams by zealous detectives all over the country; though even Mr Yelton, apparently all intent upon justifying a handicap threatened by a new and meddlesome committee, was by no means exempt from observation; though an unfounded rumour that young Mr Aske had been seen in Hatton Garden, emerging from the office of a famous specialist in pearls, caused considerable perturbation at Scotland Yard; though, in fact, every other line of enquiry was still diligently pursued. But it was on the Continent that the most strenuous efforts were made, only to collapse into complete failure as it became evident that the seller of the pearls had covered up his tracks so effectively that there was little hope of ever discovering his identity, or even of obtaining a description of him.

Everything had been done through intermediaries. But a good price had always been obtained. There had been no hurried thrusting of the pearls on any available purchaser. They had been offered to firms of good standing, a fair though not excessive price had been asked, the need for secrecy had been satisfactorily explained on the ground that the pearls were the property of a lady of social standing who was obliged, by financial stress, to dispose of the gift of an old friend, but wished to keep the transaction hidden both from the friend in question, and from her husband.

The story had been plausible enough to win an acceptance not sharpened to unnecessary criticism by any strong objection to the comfortable, if not excessive, profit the transaction promised. Moreover, verisimilitude had been added to it by the name, given in great confidence, of the lady in question, together with a note signed by her on note-paper headed by her address. It was a convincing detail that removed all misgivings, though Mitchell's discreet enquiry showed that letter and note-paper were barefaced forgery, and the use of the lady's name entirely unauthorised. She had sold no pearls; she had, in fact, no pearls to sell – she only wished she had, she said pathetically, in answer to the afore-mentioned discreet enquiries, as she swept a few more unpaid bills from her buhl writing-table into the waste-paper basket.

'No doubt Miss Barton's pearls; that much is clear enough,' pronounced Mitchell, 'but I don't see any chance of proving it. Probably no one alive has ever had more than a glimpse of the necklace Miss Yelton and Con Conway got, and, now the pearls composing it have been scattered, identification is more hopeless than ever. And I don't see much chance, either, of identifying the Englishman who sold them. If it's Humphreys, he has more brains than we've credited him with. Of course he may have had the whole thing worked out and prepared beforehand. If it's Conway, I should have expected him to go to work in a different way – but, then, perhaps he did. All this may mean the necklace was got rid of in England to some receiver, and it's the receiver who disposed of it abroad. That would mean, even if we trace the pearls to him, we shan't be any further forward when we've no means of establishing identity. Upon my soul, it's almost a wonder they didn't send the thing for sale to Christie's.'

'I think it must have been sold in London, in the first place,' Bobby agreed. 'None of our suspects seem to have been abroad recently – except, of course, that Yelton and Markham have been carrying out these exchange speculations they talk about. I suppose that means they must have been in touch with the Continent somehow.'

'So I thought it just as well to get Bournemouth to check up Markham's having been in a nursing-home there at the times mentioned,' Mitchell remarked. 'That seems O.K. The report says he was admitted and left on the dates given, that he had a letter from his firm practically every morning, and always sent off a reply the same day, in time to reach London by the last post – which, of course, would be first delivery next morning for the office. Besides, there's nothing to show Markham was ever near Tudor Lodge, or had ever heard of Miss Barton or her possible possession of jewellery. The only thing about him is he has suddenly got hold of some money. But he has used it for the firm, apparently obtained it on the firm's account, and the explanation of exchange speculation is plausible. In any case he is duly entered in the Bournemouth nursing-home as arriving two weeks before your encounter with Con Conway, and as having had a slight operation on the same day, I think, as your meeting with Con.'

'I gathered from what they told me at the office,' Bobby said, 'that he really ran the business from Bournemouth all the time he was there. I don't think Yelton's much more than a figure-head, and I think he knows it, so he finds compensation in his golf.'

'I wonder if it's possible he finds compensation in other ways, like picking up pearl necklaces that are doing no good to anyone,' Mitchell mused. 'It's a possible motive. He knows he is considered no good at the office, where Markham has taken over almost the whole direction of the business, and vanity might urge him to re-establish himself by suddenly providing fresh capital. A bit far-fetched, perhaps, but then the whole affair's far-fetched, Lord knows, and that pearl necklace in the possession of a feeble old half-crazed woman living all alone was simply asking to be stolen. To some people it wouldn't seem like theft, merely saving it from being wasted and putting it to good uses.'

'Well, sir, for my part,' declared Bobby, 'I'm beginning to think it's no one we know anything about.'

'You mean we have been barking up a whole series of wrong trees?' Mitchell asked. 'Possible. But we can't very well start investigations without something to go on – no use pursuing a ghost. I've even had the postmen on the Brush Hill round questioned. None of them seems to have known anything, or to have had any idea that Miss Barton was anything but an eccentric old woman living alone in extreme poverty, or ever to have noticed anyone near the house. In fact, apparently, no one ever did, except occasional bill distributors, and, of course, Humphreys and his errand-boys and assistant who delivered the old lady's standing order twice a week or so. Humphreys we can't trace, he's vanished very successfully for the time, though we may get word of him at any moment, and Mrs Humphreys is being closely watched. The last two or three errand-boys he employed have been questioned, but it's fairly clear they don't know anything. There's still the last assistant he had – the man the note in the books says was sacked for pilfering from the till. He is about the only person even remotely connected with the case we haven't questioned. Difficult to trace, too, when all we have to go on is a vague personal description, the knowledge that his name is Jones, and as likely as not that's an assumed name, and finally he hasn't come forward in answer to our appeals, and isn't very likely to, when he knows there may be a charge of theft advanced against him. I think you saw him once when he was coming away from the house after leaving an order there?'

'Yes, sir,' said Bobby.

'You would know him again?'

'Oh, yes, sir, at once,' Bobby answered with confidence.

'Even if he had shaved his moustache – I think I remember you said he had one?'

'Yes, sir,' answered Bobby, still more confidently. 'If I think I may have to recognise anyone again, I generally try to make a sketch of them with a moustache, and then another without a moustache. You get used to the kind of difference a moustache makes, and, of course, a false moustache is about the commonest dodge there is.'

'Then that knocks on the head a sort of idea that was running in my mind,' Mitchell remarked. 'You've never found out why you thought you had seen someone once with some kind of family resemblance to Mr Yelton?'

'No, sir,' answered Bobby, a little ruefully. 'I'm beginning to think, now, that perhaps I had seen Mr Yelton himself some time before, and noticed him and then forgotten him again. There's one point, sir,' he added, 'that I've been thinking about recently, and that may have been overlooked. When I met Jones, if that's his name, he had a pair of yellow gardening gloves in his basket he told me had been ordered by another customer he was taking them to.'

'We had better have another look at Humphreys' books,' observed Mitchell, 'and see if we can trace that customer. Is it possible Jones is someone who had heard of Miss Barton in connection with the "Mad Millionaire" story and took the job with Humphreys in order to get a chance to have a look at Tudor Lodge without rousing any suspicion?'

'Yes, sir,' said Bobby doubtfully. 'Only, if Jones was really a crook after a big thing like this pearl necklace, would he be likely to let himself be caught at the till? Would he have condescended to such a petty theft for one thing?'

'You mean,' asked Mitchell, a little amused, 'you could trust a big-job man not to put his fingers for coppers in a till just as you could trust a bishop not to – professional honour in both cases?'

'Well, yes, sir, that's what I meant,' agreed Bobby. 'Besides, if it was like that, Humphreys' behaviour still wants explaining – why he's shut down his shop and disappeared, I mean, and where the money came from that he certainly got somewhere. You know, sir,' he added abruptly, 'I can't imagine a little man like Humphreys, after years of suburban respectability as a small shopkeeper, suddenly mixing himself up with theft and murder. It's ... it's not –'

'Not psychological,' suggested Mitchell. 'But psychology's not an exact science yet; and then, anyhow, what they call a complex will aways explain anything, especially if you add a repression. Do you know, I think it might be a good idea if you were to see Aske again and get him to try to remember if Miss Barton ever said anything, when she was talking to him, about Humphreys or his assistant. If it's true, as Aske says, that she offered to give him the necklace, it's just on the cards something had happened to make her uneasy about keeping the thing and she wanted to get rid of it. You can just put that to him and see if it seems to suggest anything. In a case like this, one must follow up every line, however faint. You did make a report about the gardening gloves he bought at the Stores, didn't you?'

'Yes, sir,' Bobby answered. 'They are there, at the house, and in use, but there wouldn't be any possibility of identifying scratches now. I don't know if chemical analysis could prove identity with the scrapings found under Miss Barton's nails.'

'It could, and it has,' Mitchell answered quietly. 'A pair of identical gloves, taken from the same manufacturer's stock, has been tested. But there's always the difficulty that thousands of pairs of the same make have been sold both to the Stores and elsewhere, and there's no way of pinning down those scrapings to any one pair. It's a link, but only in a chain not complete yet by a long way. But you can visit Aske –'

The house phone on Mitchell's desk rang. He answered it, and then looked across at Bobby.

'Got Humphreys at last,' he said. 'Nailed him landing at the docks. They are bringing him along in a taxi.'

Chapter 27

REVELATION

In the interval before Humphreys' arrival, Mitchell turned placidly to other work, whereof a C.I.D. superintendent has always a plethora on hand. But Bobby, with fewer responsibilities pressing on his mind, prowled restlessly from one corridor to another, from one room to the next, until more or less politely requested to remove himself with speed elsewhere, since other people had work to do, if he hadn't. It is scarcely an exaggeration to say that the whole Yard was grateful when presently he was summoned back to Mitchell's room.

'Humphreys will be here in a minute or two,' Mitchell told him. 'He's been cruising, apparently. I've been in touch with the ship he was on; got the captain on the phone. He's been quite in the fashion.'

'Not a bad stunt for anyone who wants to keep out of the way,' Bobby commented.

'No,' agreed Mitchell, 'not now it's so popular. Wonder the big shipping companies didn't tumble to the idea before, though; they ought to have taken a hint from the old *Skylark* on Brighton beach years ago. Seems it's a small coasting steamer he joined at Bristol the same day he disappeared, after you had interviewed him. Now cruising's all the rage, every coasting steamer is on the look-out for anyone wanting a cheap trip, and, if it isn't a passenger boat, then they just sign you on as purser or captain's clerk or something of that sort. Luckily one of our men spotted him as soon as they put in at the docks this morning.'

'You know, sir,' Bobby observed thoughtfully, 'I'm not so jolly sure now Humphreys isn't a good deal deeper than we've been giving him credit for.'

'Can't run a small grocer's shop in London all your life without learning a lot,' declared Mitchell, 'especially about human nature. Being a small shopkeeper in a London suburb means a wide experience of life; it isn't like being one of those swell, high-up business birds who are just like children, and innocent as babes outside their own offices and their own jobs.'

The door opened, and Humphreys appeared in the charge of Inspector Ferris, to whom he had been first taken on his arrival. He looked bronzed and well after his sea voyage, but was evidently in a mood of sullen apprehension. To Mitchell's pleasant greeting he replied by an attempt at bluster – rather like a Pekingese snapping a challenge at a stately bloodhound, Bobby thought, as he watched the little grocer trying to browbeat Mitchell.

'What right have you got to bring me here?' he demanded truculently. 'That's what I want to know. Where's your warrant? Ever hear of Hocus Corpus?'

'I have indeed,' agreed Mitchell solemnly. 'We often tell

each other here that Hocus is the safeguard of every British citizen.'

'Very well, then,' said Humphreys, 'that's all right, and if I choose to walk out of that door, who's going to stop me?'

'Provided you don't try, the question won't arise,' Mitchell pointed out cheerfully. 'And now, as you've asked us if we've ever heard of Hocus, as we have, let me ask if you've ever heard of what is meant by being an accessary after or before the event?'

'I don't know what you mean,' grumbled Humphreys, with a sort of sulky uneasiness. 'I'm respectable, I am, and always have been, and there isn't anything I've done that isn't.'

'You've given us a good deal of trouble to find you,' Mitchell reminded him. 'It was almost as if you had gone into hiding.'

'Not me,' declared Humphreys stoutly. 'I sold my business. Anything wrong about that? Me and the missus went off for a holiday before looking round for another. Then you come interfering, as shouldn't ought to be allowed with respectable people, and so the missus said: "Go for a cruise, like what the *Announcer* prints the pictures of." So I did, and why shouldn't I? And then I'm fetched along here, and what I want to know is, for why?'

'Because we want to ask you a few questions. We think you might be able to give us certain information,' Mitchell explained.

'If you mean about Tudor Lodge and the old girl there, well, I can't,' retorted Humphreys. 'I never saw her hardly. I don't know nothing,' he declared, with a really magnificent gesture.

'There are just one or two points you can help us on, I think,' Mitchell persisted. 'For example, why did you tell people you were making a big profit on your new garden line, when you weren't?'

Humphreys looked at the Superintendent with something like contempt.

'What do you expect a business man to say when he's trying to make a sale?' demanded the little grocer with withering scorn. 'How bad he's doing and how rotten everything is? If you had a likely buyer in view, with lots of cash, wouldn't you blow about how well you was doing? Cry stinking fish, I suppose, you would – I don't think.'

'You did make a sale finally?'

'Of course I did. If the business was still mine, wouldn't I be looking after it instead of having a holiday cruising?'

'The person you sold to doesn't seem in a hurry to take possession,' observed Mitchell. 'The shutters are still up. Can you tell us his name?'

'Don't know it.'

'A little unusual that, surely?' suggested Mitchell.

'I didn't want to know his name,' retorted Humphreys. 'All I cared about was if he was willing to pay my price, and if he had the cash. It's a party what won a big prize in the last Irish sweepstakes,' he went on. 'Thousands. Lummy, the luck some have! If I buy a ticket, I never get nothing – not a thing. But this party did, and so he was looking out for a good sound paying business he could put his money in and keep it safe from friends and relatives what was doing their best to suck him dry.'

'How did you get in touch with him?' Mitchell asked.

Humphreys put on his most obstinate expression.

'That's my business,' he said. 'Nothing to do with anyone else. The deal's not completed yet, and I don't want it messed up with any of your interfering.'

'Oh, we shan't interfere,' Mitchell assured him.

'What else are you doing now?' Humphreys retorted.

Mitchell hesitated, then decided to try another line.

'You had an assistant, a man named Jones,' he said. 'We are anxious to interview Mr Jones. Can you tell us anything about him?'

'What for? Why should I?'

'Because we think it possible he may have had something to do with the murder of Miss Barton.'

Humphreys first stared and then burst into laughter the others found a little disconcerting, because it sounded so genuine.

'I did think sometimes that's what you had got in your heads,' he said, 'only it seemed so silly. Well, if that's all, I don't mind telling you Jones wasn't his real name, and what his real name is I don't know and don't want to know; nothing to do with me nor you neither. Just about three or four months ago he started coming into my shop and looking around, and buying one thing or another – a tin of sardines or a quarter of cheese or such-like. Then one day he got talking, and he says: "Want to sell?" and I said: "Want to buy?" I said, smart like. "Want to buy?" I said. "Wouldn't be paid to be found dead in a hole like this," he said; and I said: "Clear out, then," quick like, I said, quick and hasty like, never being one to put up with cheek and impudence, not from no one,' repeated Mr Humphreys with emphasis, looking slowly round the while, as if daring any of his listeners to take up the challenge. 'Because,' he explained firmly, 'cheek and impudence I never could stand, so I said: "Well, then, clear out," I said, just like that. So he said: "Might find you a purchaser at a good figure if you'll do the right thing along of me afterwards," he said. I said: "What's a good figure?" I said, and he said: 'How about two thou?"'

'Big offer,' commented Mitchell. 'What did you say?'

'Said prompt and quick like,' answered Humphreys, 'that if he got that figure he could have half, not taking him very serious like and speaking, so to speak, at random. Though, mind you, the business is a good business, and worth more than many what's sold for two thou or even more, only with times being bad, and all this unemployment and such-like, you can't always get what a thing's really worth. So I said, generous like and not caring to bargain: "Get me two thou and take half," I said, and he said: "Done," he said, just like that. "Done," he said. "Put it in writing," he said. Well, no harm in that as I could see, so I done it and he took a stamp out of his pocket – a sixpenny stamp he must have brought along all ready – and stuck it on and said: "This is my act and deed," so I knew it was all regular and binding. Then he helped me put the shutters up, which was a thing he didn't have no notion how to do, but I showed him, and we got a jug from the King's Head and talked it over friendly like, and he explained how he had cousins what had won big in the Irish sweepstakes so their life was a burden to them ever since along of all their friends and relatives trying to touch 'em, and they was thinking of buying a good, sound, high-class business they could put their money in and be sure of a comfortable, easy living ever after, while being able to tell friends and others their money was all invested and none left to give away.'

'And you thought your shop –' began Mitchell, and paused. 'Well, go on,' he said.

'Why not?' demanded Humphreys defiantly. 'Wasn't mine as good as anyone's?'

'Go on,' repeated Mitchell.

'Well, what he said was, how about me taking him on as an assistant so he could tell his cousins from his own experience just what a little gold-mine the business was – same as it could be,' added Mr Humphreys, still more defiantly, 'if only worked up according with capital, such as the same I've never had. Only he told me I must start a garden line, because this cousin of his was a bit dotty about gardens, and it always cost him such a lot trying to grow sweet peas where he lived down Islington way he felt certain sure seedsmen and such-like fair wallowed in profits, and he would jump at the idea of working up a big line hisself in garden stuff.'

'Do you really mean,' Mitchell asked now, 'that you seriously believed a yarn like that?'

'I believed it all right when the cash came along,' retorted Humphreys, 'same as you would have done – cash being cash, ain't it?'

He waited a moment to see if anyone wished to challenge this proposition, but, finding it seemed to meet with general and grave acceptance, he went on:

'I'm not denying I had my doubts at first, for the lies the most respectable will tell when wanting credit soon takes away all faith in human nature. I defy,' declared Mr Humphreys earnestly, 'the most trusting to work a year behind a counter in Brush Hill and then believe a word on oath, even if it's a churchwarden says it. But two hundred quid, money down, that's different – all done up in bundles of twenty-five each – that I do believe. Wouldn't you?'

'Anyhow, I always believe that money is money,' agreed Mitchell.

'Just what I say,' declared Humphreys, quite pleased; 'almost my very own words, and though the money come later on, I didn't see then why I shouldn't give him a trial. I reckoned I could watch him if he was up to any game – lummy, when you've had to do with errand-boys all your natural there isn't much of what games they can be up to that you don't know backwards by heart. But this chap Jones turned out a good worker and very willing, though knowing nothing, but done his best, that I will say, and got on pleasant like with all the customers, though he never seemed to get the knack of weighing right, so there was nothing left of twenty pounds of butter when he had weighed out eighty quarters. Always ready to deliver, too, which, along of my feet from standing on 'em so much, I never care about. Got on well together, we did, and he wrote to his cousin, and said what a fine business it was and to come along and see for himself, which he did according.'

'Did you see him?' Mitchell asked quickly.

'No. Jones said: "Hadn't you better keep out of the way?" So I said :"Perhaps may be so," I said, and I done it. No sense in going out of your way to have questions asked, and there was Jones to answer all as well as me and better. So afterwards he told me his cousin was nibbling but he didn't know if he would spring the two thou. "How about seventeen fifty?" he said and, I said "Hum," just like that I said "Hum," not wishing to jump like at it, and he said "How about his having anything he could get over one thou?" and so I said "O.K." to that, I said.'

'No wonder,' observed Mitchell. 'Very much "O.K.", Mr Humphreys. You must have known perfectly well your business wasn't worth anything like even a thousand pounds.'

'A thing's worth just what it will sell for,' retorted Humphreys.

'There is such a thing as misrepresentation and conceal-ment of facts,' Mitchell pointed out sternly.

'Nothing doing,' retorted Humphreys, his perky self-assurance undiminished. 'No misrepresentation or conceal-ment either. For why? Because there wasn't nothing repre-sented by me one way or another. There was the business, there was the books, all open as the day. All I said was: "That's my price," I said. Of course, I laid it on a bit about what I was making out of the new garden line, but that was only straight-forward, legitimitate business talk – adver-tising, as you might say, same as a big firm, if it finds it's do-ing bad, gets in new capital by claiming it's never done so well before. Advertising ain't truth, is it?' demanded Mr Humphreys defiantly. 'And that's all I was doing – just advertising.'

'But you thought it prudent to get out of the way all the same,' observed Mitchell.

'Didn't want trouble. Why should I? I wanted a holiday, not a lot more trouble, don't I tell you?' Humphreys demanded.

'Any trouble being a possible action for fraud,' commen-ted Mitchell.

'There wasn't none,' insisted Humphreys. 'Immediate possession required, so we bunged off and not at all for nothing else.'

'Do you say you don't know the name of whoever you sold to?'

'No, and never wanted to – not me,' answered Humphreys. 'All I wanted was to know was their money good. It was.'

'Has the rest of it been paid?'

'No. Due Friday next, before noon.'

'You expect to receive it then?'

'Of course I do. Why not?'

'Who from?'

Humphreys shrugged his shoulders.

'I shan't ask so long as I get it,' he answered.

'Suppose the payment's not made?'

'Then it's all off. I've got all the papers yet. What I've sold is an option, if you see what I mean. If the deal don't go through, we go back to the shop with two hundred clear profit and start fresh.'

'I see,' said Mitchell slowly. 'You are safe either way. What is Jones's real name?'

'Told you already, I don't know.'

Nor could further questioning shake him. He persisted that all he had done was to name a price for his business and all he had worried about was safeguarding himself on the money issue. He had his £200. If the deal was completed, all well and good – from his point of view. He admitted it would have been a satisfactory sale, but pointed out quite truly that he was fully entitled to ask any figure he chose – £10,000 or £20,000 for that matter. If the deal finally fell through, he had at any rate his £200. Even Mitchell's acid comment that the whole transaction looked uncommonly like a conspiracy to defraud left him quite unmoved. There was no conspiracy or misrepresentation that he knew anything about or felt in any way responsible for. All he could be induced to admit was that he realised there might be some subsequent dissatisfaction on the part of the purchaser.

'If you must know,' he confessed finally, 'that's why I didn't tell nobody where I was going. I didn't want a lot of argufying and such-like. So I thought it best to keep out of the way, and so I should have done only for your meddling and interfering.'

'I put it to you,' Mitchell said abruptly, 'that all this story told you by the man Jones was merely part of a scheme for getting familiar with Tudor Lodge and with Miss Barton's habits.'

But Humphreys only looked as stubborn as ever.

'How should I know?' he demanded. 'What he said was reasonable, and there wasn't any cause for me to look behind. What he was after was getting a good fat commission selling a sound business what only wants working up to be a little gold-mine with capital behind – and capital there would have been all right – thousands – all won in the Irish sweep. I never won anything,' he repeated resentfully, and evidently felt that the flagrant injustice of others winning prizes that never came to him rendered both right and proper any manoeuvre likely to remedy that injustice by transferring at any rate part of the prize-money from the winner's pocket to his own. 'Nothing wrong about selling a business for what it'll fetch, is there? Nothing wrong about getting or paying a commission on a sale, is there?'

'Did Jones never say anything about Miss Barton, or ask any questions that you thought peculiar at the time?' Mitchell enquired next.

Humphreys fenced with this question a little. Finally he admitted that Jones' interest in Miss Barton, and some questions he had asked about her mode of living, had for a moment made him faintly suspicious. But only for a little, and only while Bobby was questioning him on the occasion of their first meeting, almost as if with reference to the enquiries Jones had been making. But he insisted that it was natural enough for anyone, first hearing of Miss Barton's eccentric way of life, to show curiosity concerning it, and he insisted, too, that after his first show of curiosity Jones had never displayed the faintest interest in Tudor Lodge or its eccentric inmate. In fact, declared Humphreys, that passing uneasiness and suspicion had so entirely left his mind that he had simply never thought of it again, and never would have but for this cross-examination he was now being subjected to, and that, for his part, he considered pure waste of time.

'Take it from me,' he declared, 'nothing to do with Jones –

all Jones was after was his commission. Quite right, too. Saw a chance to do a deal, and you,' said Mr Humphreys reproachfully, 'you worry me and him about murders we hadn't nothing to do with – speaking for certain for me and next door to it for him.'

From this position it proved impossible to move him, and it really seemed he had no information to give about the mysterious Jones, either as to identity or as to how he could be traced. As completely as though he had disintegrated into thin air did Jones seem to have vanished, and finally Humphreys had to be allowed to depart, with a stern warning not to try to disappear again.

'Do you think his story is true, sir?' Bobby ventured to ask Mitchell after the departure of the little grocer.

'As far as it goes, yes,' Mitchell answered. 'It explains why he vanished in the way he did, for, of course, he knew perfectly well there was likely to be trouble over the sale, if it was ever actually made. A business like his is a swindle at anything like fifteen hundred or two thousand or whatever the figure was supposed to be. If his story's true, he must have known perfectly well he was taking part in a swindle, only the temptation was too much for him – I expect he had never even dreamed of such a sum. A thousand pounds is a thousand temptations, and it's as much as most of us can do to resist one. All the same, it looks as if he may have given us the true explanation, and that Jones was out, not to murder Miss Barton and steal her pearls, but merely to swindle his prize-winning cousin. We've got to trace Jones, but it's going to be difficult. Even if Humphreys' story is true, it's quite likely he's bolted with his share of the swag – or with all of it, for that matter. The two hundred to Humphreys may have been just to keep him quiet for the time, and if Jones has gone into hiding he has had plenty of time to cover his tracks. We must do our best to check up on Humphreys' story, and meantime you had better visit Aske and see if you can get anything fresh out of him, though our chief job for the moment must be tracing the elusive Jones.'

On this errand, therefore, Bobby departed, though indeed it seemed to him that the hope of tracing any individual of whom so little was known as was known of 'Jones', was slender enough. On his way to visit Aske it was this problem which chiefly occupied his mind, but he saw no way of approaching it with much hope of success.

It was fairly late by now, and Aske had returned from his work at the factory where he was engaged. He did not seem specially pleased to see Bobby again, and, indeed, said something to the effect that Scotland Yard's version of the celebrated 'third degree' seemed the very effective one of a perpetual, non-stop interview.

'I've already told you fellows everything I know at least ten times over,' he protested wearily.

So Bobby said how sorry he was, and dropped a tactful hint that on the occasion of their last encounter – or, rather, immediately after it – Miss Yelton had seemed much less unforgiving and stern and implacable when Mr Aske had departed than she had done while he was still there. So then the young man brightened up considerably, only at once to grow gloomy again.

'I wrote,' he said in melancholy tones. 'The letter came back – unopened.'

'Served you right,' pronounced Bobby.

'Why?' demanded Aske, bristling.

'For writing instead of going yourself,' explained Bobby.

'Oh,' said Aske, thinking it over.

Confidential relations thus established, Bobby broached the subject that had brought him. But Aske knew nothing about Humphreys or his assistant, and did not think Miss Barton during their conversation had made the least reference to either of them. But it was evident that his thoughts were elsewhere.

'Of course, I know I made a fool of myself and lost my temper,' he confessed confidentially, 'and I suppose it isn't quite the thing to slug a fellow in a lady's drawing-room, but, all the same, the blackguard deserved it, and a lot more as well.'

'Meaning Mr Markham?'

'Yes, the bastard!' Aske said, and then paused and half smiled. 'I was only being vulgar and abusive,' he said, 'but it is the fact that that's what he is – a bastard.'

'Oh, is he?' said Bobby, not much interested. 'Not his fault, I suppose.'

'No,' agreed Aske, 'but I asked some fellows I know in the City about him. It seems he's the illegitimate son of one of the Yeltons who was mixed up in some rather specially dirty business with the sister or daughter of one of the staff. Got money out of her, too, and there would have been a prosecution and a first-class scandal, only the Yelton family managed to hush it up by promising to provide for the kid's education and to give him a job in the office later, with a view to his becoming a partner.'

'Do you mean,' stammered Bobby, 'you mean ... that's true ... you're sure ... ?'

'True all right,' Aske answered, a little surprised at the other's apparent excitement. 'Why? Markham is really Mr Yelton's first cousin – there's a strong family resemblance if you see them together.'

'My God, I never thought of that,' Bobby cried, and fairly ran for it – out of the room, out of the house, down the road to the station as fast as he could tear, leaving Aske in a state of some doubt as to whether drink, lunacy, or mere eccentricity accounted for Bobby's behaviour.

Chapter 28

CONCLUSION

In spite of all his haste, Bobby found when he got back to headquarters that Mitchell had departed homewards. Few enterprises are more perilous than for a junior to pursue with business or official problems a senior to the privacy of his home and leisure; and Mitchell, wrenched from that happy trinity of pipe, book, and wireless that preserves us all from the risk of too intense a concentration on any one of the three, was by no means inclined, at first, to accord Bobby a boisterous welcome.

But he grew thoughtful and placated as he listened to the story told him.

'What about the Bournemouth nursing-home alibi, though?' he asked. 'There seems evidence that Markham was actually there. Weren't you told at the office that he was still settling business questions for them from Bournemouth? Didn't they write to him nearly every day, and get a reply back from him by return of post – wasn't that what they said? And, if he was in a nursing-home at Bournemouth, he couldn't very well be masquerading as Humphrey's assistant.'

'I've been thinking about that, sir,' Bobby answered. 'I don't think it would be difficult to manage if he got someone to impersonate him at the nursing-home. Any office letters his substitute there received, he would send on at once to Markham at Brush Hill, writing the address in pencil. Markham would get the letter at Brush Hill by the last post; he could easily steam it open, write his own reply, re-seal the envelope, erase the pencil address and write the firm's address, and then make a journey to the office to drop it in the letter-box. It would be there next morning with the other letters, with the correct Bournemouth postmark, and no one would be likely to notice the envelope had been tampered with. Why should they?'

'It could have been managed like that,' Mitchell agreed, 'and, if Markham is really a son of James Yelton, he might easily have known about Miss Barton's jewellery. Quite likely he had been taught that only the hope of getting hold of it prevented his father from marrying his mother. He may even have believed that Miss Barton used her jewellery to get hold of his father, so that the whole thing may have

seemed to him a kind of justifiable revenge. I don't suppose
he suspected the truth about the murder, though, or probably he would have given information; but it's quite likely
he had been brought up to regard her as the reason why he
was illegitimate, and her jewellery as the cause of his mother
having been let down. And then, when he found the firm in
low water and being pressed by the bank to clear their overdraft, then he began to remember Miss Barton's jewellery
and plan to get hold of it. That's your theory?'

' Yes, sir,' answered Bobby. 'I think there was something
else, though, that was pushing him on as well. I think there's
no doubt he wanted very badly to marry Miss Yelton. Only,
she wasn't attracted, and his idea was that if he saved the
firm and her father from ruin, then he would have established a sort of claim on her.'

'She didn't see it that way?'

Bobby smiled – a superior, world-weary smile, a rather
pitying smile.

'Aske had got in first,' he explained. 'They're in love with
each other, all right.' He smiled again, tolerantly, amusedly,
the smile of one who for himself was far above such amiable
weakness, and Mitchell, noticing it, felt for the moment a
little uneasy, remembering, as he did, that those who think
they stand fast should take the most heed. But Bobby went
on: 'You can see that from the silly way they look at each
other, though I imagine Miss Yelton would most likely have
turned Markham down in any case. I don't suppose she
would ever have married Markham – not to save all creation,
let alone her father's firm. That sort of thing is a bit out
of date – Victorian. We don't go in for those self-sacrificing
stunts to-day.'

'Probably Markham didn't see it as self-sacrifice,' observed Mitchell.

'No,' agreed Bobby, though a little doubtfully. 'Besides,
it's pretty clear she and Aske will be fixing it up before long.
She's been giving him blue blazes the way she would never
dare unless she knew she had him nailed for good, and he's

taken it lying down and asking for more – as he never would unless he was nailed for good.'

'Know all about it, don't you?' grunted Mitchell. 'You wait a bit, my lad, your turn'll come all right enough.' He added thoughtfully: 'Can we be sure of identification? Counsel will make a lot of your having seen him twice and not recognised him either time.'

'Well, sir, the first time I saw him I only had a glimpse of his back as he was leaving his office,' Bobby pointed out, 'and the second time his face was pretty badly knocked about. He had a swollen eye as big as your fist, and his face covered with blood from his nose, and his handkerchief up to it all the time to stop the bleeding. But the moment Aske told me he was a blood relative of Mr Yelton's, and of the family resemblance between them, I knew at once why Mr Yelton had always reminded me of someone I had seen before. It's not so much any one feature – the shape of the nose is quite different, though it's big enough with both of them, and their eyes are of a different colour too. And there's a big difference in height as well. Markham is over six foot, and Mr Yelton is hardly average height. But they both have the same way of walking and of holding themselves, and the same expression – and an odd way of looking down at you. Mr Yelton manages to do that, somehow, to people who are much taller than himself. It's difficult to describe, but it's quite catching – even the little fat head clerk manages something of the same sort.'

Mitchell thought for a moment.

'Better see about establishing identity,' he said. 'Someone from the nursing-home on the negative side, and someone who could swear to him as Jones, Humphreys' assistant. I don't think we had better trust Humphreys – he hasn't the guts to be a murderer, but he's a lying little twister, and he would let us down like a shot if he wanted to. Probably he would want to, too; most likely his only idea now is to wriggle out of all connection with it, for fear of being hauled in as an accomplice.'

'I don't think there's any real question of that, is there, sir?' Bobby asked.

'Oh, no,' Mitchell agreed. 'He certainly knew nothing about the Tudor Lodge business. Though he wasn't so much an accomplice as a principal in trying to sell his wretched little shop for about ten times what it was worth – but there's nothing in that for us, as the whole story was bunk. It served its purpose, though, in shutting his mouth and making him want to keep out of the way of any questioning that might have put us on Markham's track. He wasn't going to come forward and talk at the risk of spoiling such a magnificent sale as Jones-Markham promised him, the little rat.'

'I expect he would be quite capable of swearing he didn't know Markham again,' Bobby agreed. 'He's badly scared of being brought in on the murder. There's Mrs Rice.'

Mitchell smiled faintly.

'An observant lady,' he said. 'Yes, get Mrs Rice, and I'll see about someone from Bournemouth. The case is fairly complete as it is, but no case can be too strong.'

So it came about that, next day, at the bookstall of the tube station near the offices of Messrs. Yelton & Markham, two ladies waited as the evening rush hour approached. They were evidently expecting someone with whom they had rendezvous, for they watched carefully the endless crowd streaming in on the way from work to home and leisure, and, at a little distance, Bobby waited in the background, while Inspector Ferris read, with attention, the sporting news in the evening paper, and occasionally offered a comment to the ticket collector at the gate.

All at once Mrs Rice turned towards Bobby. She indicated a tall man who had just hurried in.

'Yes,' she said.

The nurse from Bournemouth, by her side, shook her head.

'No,' she said.

Two soft, half-whispered common words that doomed a living man to the gallows.

Bobby stepped forward and signed to Inspector Ferris.

'He's shaved his moustache, but it's Jones all right that worked for Mr Humphreys and took my order somewhere else, so we had no Sunday dinner,' Mrs Rice said.

The Bournemouth nurse said:

'That's not the gentleman who was with us – nothing like him.'

The man at the gate was apparently making some difficulty about letting the tall new-comer through. The tall man said something angry and impatient. Ferris touched him on the shoulder.

'Mr Markham, I think, sir,' he said. 'Also known by the name of Jones, when acting as shop-assistant to Mr Humphreys, a grocer at Brush Hill. I am an officer of police, and I must ask you to come with me to Cannon Row –'

He had not time to finish the sentence, for Markham jumped back, and made as if to run in a last wild effort at escape. But Bobby was standing just behind, and put out an arm to stop him. The scuffle was so brief it hardly attracted any attention, it might have been caused, not by the despair of a man's last effort for his life, but by a dropped umbrella or a stray dog under someone's feet.

'That's no good, Mr Markham,' said Ferris quietly. 'Better come along without making trouble. We've a car waiting.'

Markham said no word, but walked from the station, by the side of Ferris, to the waiting car, and therein entered like a dead man entering a hearse.

THE END

31172994R00125

Made in the USA
Middletown, DE
21 April 2016